OUR MOTHER IN THE LAKE

ABE MOSS

GRIM HEART PUBLISHING

NOVELS BY ABE MOSS

THE WRITHING

BATHWATER BLUES

BY THE LIGHT OF HIS LANTERN

LITTLE EMMETT

UNDER THE WICKED MOON

GILLS

A GHOST ARRIVES

RUBY HOLLOWAY READS AFTER DARK

THE DREAD VOID SERIES

INTO THE DREAD VOID (BOOK 1)

AMID THE SINKING DARK (BOOK 2)

BEYOND THE PHANTOM GLOW (BOOK 3)

ON THE BITTER HORIZON (BOOK 4)

THROUGH THE WITCH LIGHTS (BOOK 5)

ACROSS THE HAUNTED STARS (BOOK6)

FROM THE GODLESS ABYSS (BOOK 7)

UNTIL THE DREADED END (BOOK 8)

PROLOGUE
THE BASEMENT

The basement was dark as a cave, muggy as a crowded locker room, and stank of old, cloying death—the scent of something expired long ago, seeping from the porous rock like the remnant of a bad dream.

It had been hours since the door opened last. Long enough that the man at the bottom of the stairs watched the light around its frame fade from bright afternoon to dull evening to gloomy dusk to pitch black night. Long enough that his shoulder had turned numb, and his neck formed a kink where it was bent. Long enough that the drugs in his system had begun wearing off, so that his vocal cords trembled back to life and he could actually hear himself again—if only to moan in the dark. Still, he couldn't navigate his binds. The twine around his wrists and ankles bit until his flesh was raw. His limbs were so heavy, anyway, that even if he freed himself, it was unlikely he could carry himself up the rickety stairs. Not even on hands and knees.

And then, in the very late hours of night—or the earliest hours of morning—the door unlocked. It opened. A figure stood at the head of the stairs, a shadow peering down. It stayed there for a prolonged time, watching, saying nothing. The man at the bottom of the stairs breathed a little harder, heart beating a little faster.

Then the figure descended. One slow step at a time. One groaning stair at a time. On the final stair the figure stopped, still watching, and in the basement's cavernous silence they sighed heavily through their nostrils, as though dissatisfied.

"Oh, Cameron..." The figure took one further step down, bare feet settling onto the damp, rocky ground. "It's truly unfortunate things worked out this way..."

The man on the floor tried to move, tried to so much as squirm, but remained motionless where he lay. As if he were already a corpse. He moved his tongue in his mouth, dry as a dirty, neglected kitchen sponge, and could barely utter an audible word.

"...*please,*" he gasped.

His captor crouched beside him. The basement was dark enough that proximity did nothing to reveal their features.

"*Please,*" he repeated. His voice rasped, tickling the back of his dry throat. "*Don't...*"

His captor blew air from their nostrils again, this time with the brevity of humor. Amusement.

"But you should consider yourself lucky, Cameron. You're better off down here, with me." The figure raised its head, peering up at the basement's dark ceiling, pondering for a moment. "Much better off than the others..."

His captor lowered their dark gaze, observing Cameron

2

with eyes Cameron couldn't see, but seemed able to study him just fine in the absolute darkness. The figure bent forward slightly, and pushed Cameron so that he rolled off his numbed shoulder and onto his back. Then the figure crouched over him, took the neck of his shirt in both hands, and tore it apart with ease, revealing Cameron's bare chest underneath, heart thumping violently against his ribs.

His captor placed a hand on his chest, as if to feel his beating heart, and said, "What awaits the others is so much worse."

There once was a sapling, green and brand new, who dreamed of being big, like the forest he knew.

"Like my brothers and sisters, and my mom and dad, too!"

A family of giants, all bigger than he – his mother the biggest, most beautiful tree:

"Someday you'll grow big," she said. "You'll be just like me."

— ANNE MAISEL, *THE LITTLE SAPLING*

PART ONE

THE SAPLINGS

I

THE LETTER

T he rain was coming down in bitter, billowing sheets, and as was normally the case on terribly ugly days like these, twenty-five-year-old Drew Prescott found herself reminded of terribly ugly things.

Standing beneath the awning of the building's entryway —a department store, she believed—watching the tow-truck driver secure her *reliably unreliable* piece of shit to his winch in the glossy downpour, Drew became momentarily lost in those thoughts. Those memories. *Ugly things* which always seemed to transpire when the weather was foul, at least as she remembered them through the accordioned timeline of her memory.

Like how it had rained the day she broke both wrists at lacrosse practice. Or how it had rained the day she lost her first graphic design job out of college—terminated for tardiness, in regards to showing up to work and delivering after deadlines both.

Or like the day her father had died. A day she remembered most vividly of all—the blood as much as the rain. A truly ugly day, that...

"Hello?"

Drew was so focused on the rainwater in the gutter—yes, it was *definitely* the gushing rainwater which arrested her so —that she hardly noticed her car was fully rigged to the tow truck, and that the driver now waited beside her with narrowed eyes, his dark eyelashes catching beads of moisture even beneath the hood of his jacket. He had to shout over the storm, the rain drumming on the awning overhead, the traffic splashing through the street, and Drew startled to the abrupt sound of his voice.

"I'm sorry?"

"I said, are you riding with me to the shop?"

"Oh! Sorry. No, thank you. If you'll just leave my keys with the front desk, I already called ahead."

The driver nodded curtly and without another word hunched his shoulders and hurried back to his truck with quick, sweeping steps through the puddled rain. Drew remained where she was, sheltered for now.

Even with a perfectly good interruption—a distraction handed to her on a silver platter—she allowed her twisted mind to return in an instant, for the blood and the *ugly* things to rush up like they'd never been washed away to begin with. Because they hadn't.

Blood never washes away.

Luckily her phone began to chirp and shake in her jacket pocket. She pulled it loose, checked the illuminated screen, cursed under her breath—"...*fucking kidding me...*"—and swiped her thumb to ignore the call. As soon as she did, she was notified that her missed calls totaled nine. She stuffed her phone back into her pocket, pulled her jacket up over her head, and began jogging home, clueless as to what ugly things awaited her there.

Her nineteen-year-old brother was sitting outside her apartment entrance, on the ground in the damp shadows of the entry alcove like some Dickensian orphan, his brown hoodie pulled over his head, a mess of thick black hair weeding out from around his forehead like a splintered horn. Drew flared with several emotions at the sight of him: surprise, annoyance, a bit of dread, and underneath it all, an unflinching affection. She climbed the few cement steps to the front doors, which were slightly recessed into the building, providing Isaac his woeful shelter. He glanced up, wide-eyed and pleading before he even knew who she was.

"What are you doing? Why are you sitting out here?"

"I called twice and you didn't answer your phone," he said, and picked himself up off the ground.

Wrinkling her brow, Drew pulled her phone out again.

"Did you walk home?" he asked. "You're soaked."

Drew answered monotonously as she scrolled through her missed calls, confirming that Isaac's two were lost between the other seven. "My car is fucked…"

"Oh," Isaac said. "Again?"

Drew stuffed her phone back into her pocket. "Yeah, again. Why are you here?"

Isaac chewed the inside of his cheek anxiously. Both of

his hands were stuffed into the front pocket of his hoodie across his belly, where he was clearly holding onto something.

"I have something I need to show you..."

"Okay. What is it?"

Isaac scowled. "Well, not out here, obviously."

Drew pulled her apartment badge out from her pocket, and as she held it to the entry security pad, a voice called out from behind: *"Drew!"* The security pad's red light flashed green with a beep. Drew pulled the door open. Then the voice called out again, this time loudly enough that her name registered. *"Drew!"*

She stopped, holding the door. Over her shoulder she saw him, splashing his way across the street with an umbrella opened over his head. *Quentin.* He stopped at the bottom of the steps, peering up with his mouth slightly open, breathing hard, his eyes sad and confused like a hurt puppy's. With his one free hand, he lifted his palm toward the sky in a shrug, to express the disbelief his eyes already conveyed so well.

"What the hell's going on?" he said.

Drew regarded the darkly handsome man at the bottom of her apartment steps with an open mouth of her own, speechless. She looked once at Isaac, as if to confirm painfully that yes, her brother was going to witness this.

"I'm sorry," she answered.

"I've called you, like... I don't know how many times!" He climbed one step, two, closing the distance so that he wouldn't have to shout so loudly over the rain and traffic. "Why aren't you answering your phone?"

"I can't talk right now," Drew answered simply. She followed with another nervous flick of the eyes to her brother who regarded her like an alien. When she looked to Quentin again, the confusion had only deepened, his eyes now narrowed nearly shut. "I'm sorry, I just can't do this right now..."

"Then when?" Quentin asked, shaking his head. His lips pulled back from his teeth, lifting his face to see her at the top of the steps as the rain splattered his front.

Drew motioned for her brother to step into the building already, as her feet puppeted her in that direction of their own free will. She changed hands on the door, standing in its opening, as Quentin appeared more and more betrayed with each new raindrop on his face, with each additional shuffle of Drew's feet across the entry's threshold.

"Drew!" he said, not believing his eyes. "I want to talk about this! Let's talk about this!"

Drew rattled her head pitifully. "I can't. I'm sorry. I just can't. Not right now. I'm sorry, Quentin."

And with that she took a final step behind the door, both feet on the rug inside as the indoor security beeped to signal that the door was shut and locked once more. Quentin remained, watching from the steps like a mirage in the downpour. Drew turned her back on him at last—out of sight, out of mind—and started hastily through the dim, smallish lobby toward the elevators on the other side.

"What the hell was that about?" Isaac asked, following quickly to keep up. "I thought you guys were... you know, getting serious."

"No," Drew said. She punched her finger against the elevator call button. "And it's none of your business. Don't ask me about it anymore. Please."

She breathed a sigh of relief as the elevator doors opened. They moved inside. She pressed another button. Fourth floor. The doors closed them in and the elevator started up. Another sigh, this time to collect herself.

"So, what is it you wanted to show me?" Drew watched her brother from the corner of her eye, his hands still stuffed into his hoodie's pocket. "What did you bring?"

Isaac seemed to hesitate. No reply, though his hard, sharp knuckles bulged against the inside of the pocket as he seemed to grip whatever he hid there. He pulled it out without a word. A battered envelope. For just an instant, he held it with one hand, pinched between his thumb and index, and Drew noticed the terrible manner in which the envelope quivered in his grasp. It wasn't just his hands. She turned to see him fully then, his silence drawing her concern, and found him trembling head to foot.

"Are you okay?"

Now it was Isaac who sucked in a deep breath of air. The elevator arrived at Drew's floor. The doors jerked open. They lingered inside anyhow, the envelope in Isaac's hands beginning to feel heavy in Drew's despite not even holding the damn thing.

"Let's wait until we're in your apartment," Isaac said finally, and proceeded into the hallway, leading the way to Drew's door. Now it was she who followed hurriedly behind him, her curiosity mounting.

I'd hoped Quentin was the ugly thing coming my way, she thought, staring vaguely at the back of her brother's head until they arrived at her apartment door. She unlocked the door and let them in. She flipped the light switch by the door, which only illuminated the floor lamp in the corner—no ceiling fixtures here. Her apartment was a cozy one-bedroom affair, very sparsely decorated for a young woman's dwelling, or at least she'd been told as much by a handful of men who believed that meant something.

Isaac finally pulled his hood from off his head as he paced distractedly across his sister's living space, revealing his shapely jet-black hair underneath. He turned in a circle, eyes glued to the envelope in his hands. Drew was about to ask him once again what it was, when her phone began to ring. She checked, saw it was another call from Quentin, and ignored it.

"You should sit down," Isaac said, his eyes *still not leaving* the envelope he held.

"You're being weird," Drew said, putting her phone away. "Maybe *you* should sit down."

Oddly enough, Isaac took his sister's advice. He sat on her sofa, hunched forward over the envelope. Drew remained standing for a moment, simply watching him, until he finally lifted his eyes to see her, and motioned for her to sit beside him. She almost laughed at this point, suspicious of a joke even when her brother's face appeared entirely grave. Instead of laughing, she peeled off her jacket and hung it by the door, then joined her brother on the sofa.

"Okay," she said with a huff, plopping down. "What is this mysterious envelope?"

Isaac opened his mouth to reply and then didn't. A guilty expression came over him suddenly, as he turned and handed the envelope to Drew without explanation. She'd never seen her brother so coy. She took the envelope from him. She held it, and suddenly her heart was hammering for no reason at all. The envelope wasn't as dry as it should have been. Maybe the rain, maybe Isaac's nervous sweat. This wasn't a joke, she decided, and for the life of her she couldn't begin to guess what Isaac might have received in the mail to make him so... unlike himself.

"Well, what is it?" she asked.

"Open it."

Drew raised her eyebrows exasperatedly. She flipped the envelope's flap, and pulled out three sheets of college ruled paper. The single lamp in the corner provided just enough light to make out the penciled handwriting as Drew unfolded the letter, separated the three pages, and read the first line at the top of the first page:

Dear Drew and Isaac,

She stopped reading there. Her heart wasn't merely hammering now—it was using her ribs as chisels, threatening to press them right through her chest. Unable to continue reading blindly, unable to endure the inevitable, she turned the second page of the letter over, spying its end on the other side where the writer had signed their name:

I love you both, and I hope to see you soon,
Julianne

"What is this..." Drew asked aloud, turning the letter back. She regarded her brother, whose dark eyes were round as jawbreakers in his skull, dry with fear. Fear of what, though, she wondered? "Isaac..."

"What does it look like?" he said. He held his hands in his lap, fingers twisting fitfully around each other.

"Is this real?"

"Yeah," he said. "It came in the mail, if that's what you mean."

Drew set down the letter for a moment, dreading to read it further. She picked up its envelope instead, which she studied and confirmed that it was blank. No writings of any kind.

"How did this come in the mail? There's nothing, no address, it's blank."

"I don't know. It was just... in my mail."

"When? When did you get this?"

"Uh, yesterday? Or no... two days ago."

"Two days ago? And you're only telling me now?"

Isaac shrugged helplessly. "I didn't know what to do with it. I didn't know if you'd even want to see it..."

"Of course I'd want to see it."

"I didn't know how you'd take it, I mean. I just... I don't know. You still haven't even read it."

Because I don't want to, Drew thought. Her heart was still going like mad, an animal come to life inside her. She took up the letter again, holding it in both hands. Now she was trembling, the paper vibrating in her grip.

Dear Drew and Isaac,

And again she paused. She blinked her eyes, which had

spontaneously started leaking, and willed them to stop this very instant. She breathed through her mouth as she continued, as her nose had suddenly turned runny with the tears she forbade from springing to her eyes.

Dear Drew and Isaac,

I honestly have no idea how to start this. How on earth do you start a letter like this? I suppose the most obvious thing to say would be I'm sorry. I'm sorry for what this letter might do to you. Almost as sorry as I am for needing to write it in the first place. I'm sure this will come as a shock to you both. I could fill an entire journal with apologies and it wouldn't be enough. I'm sorry for the last thirteen years—

Drew paused to wipe each of her eyes, which were blurred with moisture. Isaac fidgeted like a nervous wreck beside her, clearly anticipating what her reaction might be. She took a deep breath, then held it uncomfortably as she resumed reading:

I'm not writing you this letter to ask for forgiveness. I don't deserve it and I would never expect it. I'm writing because after all this time I think it's only fair. You deserve to know what happened, and where I've been. I won't lie, I'm *writing this for selfish reasons, too. I want to see you again. I'd rather tell you everything in person. About where I am now. And where I'm going...*

Drew startled as Isaac stood from the sofa, scratching the back of his neck as he crossed the living room toward the bathroom, muttering as he went. Probably he felt the tension building, coagulating the space between them with each written line she read until he couldn't sit still any longer and so excused himself. Drew watched him go until the bathroom door was closed, the light on the other side casting his shadow along the bottom of the door. Then she brought her feet up on the sofa, sitting cross-legged with the letter in her lap. The rain was still coming down dark and heavy outside, plinking off the living room window. She took another breath as she found her place:

I'd rather not say too much here, and save the details for when we might see each other face to face, if you'll permit it. But I'm also aware you might be skeptical. I tried to think of some way I might convince you that it's really me, and all I could come up with were memories. Once again, I'm sorry, but it's the best I could do.

Isaac, my sensitive boy. Do you remember the book I used to read to you? I swear you asked me to read it every night for a year straight. Nothing else would do. I forget the name, but it was about a little tree, growing from a sprout, with dreams of growing big and strong like all the members of its family, which if I remember right was the whole forest. You were so taken with that book, it didn't matter that we'd already read it a hundred times. You were captivated each time like it was the first.

And Drew, my lovely daughter. Do you remember the road trip we took just the two of us, driving the Florida Keys? You'd just turned eleven, already becoming a young woman, and I thought it the perfect way to celebrate. I have this image of you stuck in my mind that I'll never forget: in the passenger seat, the window rolled down, the ocean air making an absolute mess of your hair... dirty blonde just like your father's...

Drew's bated breath hitched in her throat. The beautiful imagery the letter conjured was made ugly in an instant, and she shuddered with the thought, her lungs quivering as much as the letter in her hands. She glanced to the bathroom, where Isaac was taking his time. She swallowed it down, the memory, and continued reading with her guard a bit higher than before.

... I think of that weekend just about every day. You and me. It's a precious memory of mine.

I hope these are enough to prove myself. I don't have much else. I don't have much time, either. It's too much to explain in a letter (trust me) but I'll be gone by the end of June. If you receive this when I've been promised you will, you should have about a week to decide.

I hope you both understand when I ask that you not tell your father about this, or go to the police. Of course I'd understand if you did. But in order to protect myself, and the people I'm with, I've arranged an intermediary to handle transport, and instructions at the end of this letter for how you might reach them. I'm sorry for the short notice. I know I'm asking a lot, and it's uncomfortable and bizarre. I wish it could be done differently. I wish I could explain more in this letter, but I can't. This is the only option we have at the moment. I'll understand if you can't make it. Or if you don't want to make it. But in any case, I'll be waiting...

I love you both, and I hope to see you soon,
Julianne

On the third page, isolated from the rest, were the instructions the letter mentioned earlier. Drew skimmed these vaguely, before she set the pages down and stared at the bathroom door, her mind empty. Thoughtless. There *were*

ABE MOSS

thoughts, but they flitted about like dead leaves in the wind, hard to follow. Then the bathroom door opened, as if Isaac could sense she'd finally finished. He saw her, with the pages loose in her lap, and he stood awkwardly in the doorway, trying to gauge her vacant expression.

"Did you read it?" he asked, to which Drew nodded, a bit comatose. "All of it?"

"I read it," she said simply. She lowered her gaze to the letter, and felt that she'd already forgotten most of it.

"And?"

"I don't know. I really don't know what to think..."

"You think it's really her?"

Isaac's voice was more than hopeful. He believed, Drew could tell, and he wanted desperately for her to believe as well. His decision was already made. She heard it in his voice. Not only that, but she knew her brother. His decision was made the moment he finished reading the letter himself, two days ago. That was the reason for his reluctance in sharing it with her, Drew knew. Because he feared that she'd burst his bubble.

Did she believe it was truly their mother? The woman who vanished from their lives thirteen years ago without a trace? Without warning? Without so much as a goodbye? The woman Drew had believed to be dead for so long— whom she'd *wanted* to be dead for so long, because it was oddly easier that way.

It was the only reason good enough, she thought.

"If it's really her," Drew began, her eyes scratching wildly at the handwritten pages before her, "then that means she's

22

been alive all this time. She's been out there somewhere, living her life while we..."

The emotions returned. A painful lump in the throat.

As she struggled to speak, Isaac returned to the sofa. He sat down, took the letters from her lap, and began to read them again for himself while his sister tried to sort her thoughts, to rake those dirty, *ugly* leaves back into a neat pile so that she might more easily submerge herself in them.

Isaac started to say something but Drew interrupted with, "She doesn't even know about dad."

"Yeah," Isaac said. "I guess it makes sense, though, depending on where she's been—"

"She doesn't know about dad," Drew repeated, "which means she hasn't checked on us at all in the last thirteen years, not even once."

"I mean... even with the letter, we don't really know what happened, or the circumstances..."

"Our mom left us, not a word of warning, and now she's suddenly decided it's in our best interest to know the truth? When she's about to leave again, from the sounds of it? Is this really about us, or is it all about her?"

"There's literally no way to know until—"

"We *should* take this to the police," Drew interrupted again. She snatched the letter from her brother's hands. "She's a missing person, after all. She wasn't kidnapped, wasn't murdered, didn't fall off a cliff. She's been alive this whole time..."

"We're not going to the police," Isaac said. He took the letter back. Drew didn't try very hard to hold onto it.

"We should."

"We're not," he said definitively. "That's the last thing I want to do."

"Well, we're not going on this sketch-ass scavenger hunt to find her, either." Isaac regarded his sister like she'd slapped him, to which she said simply, "We're not."

"Speak for yourself…"

"Isaac." Drew took the letter from him once more. She let the pages go with loose fingers, never holding onto them too tightly, as if afraid they might rip apart. Drew shuffled them until she came to the very last, where she skimmed the instructions again. "She wants us to drive to some podunk town… to meet a complete stranger… and climb into his car? Sounds like a great way to get murdered, Isaac. How could she possibly think we'd agree to this? And why is it even necessary? Where is she hiding, exactly?"

"I think the letter is real," Isaac said. "And if it's real, I don't think mom would lead us into danger."

"You know nothing about her," Drew said. She regretted it the moment she said it—the moment her brother visibly winced beside her.

"Neither do you," he retorted.

"I know she abandoned us. I know that much."

"We don't know why she left," Isaac said. He folded his arms stubbornly, sitting slouched with his dark eyes daggered across the room at nothing in particular. "Maybe she had her reasons…"

Drew's blood boiled. Part of her wanted to take her brother by the shoulders and shake him.

"What reason could possibly be good enough?" she asked him, her voice betraying her slipping composure.

"I don't know! Maybe this is our chance to find out."

Isaac met Drew's gaze then, neutralizing her burning coals with his ice-cube stare. Drew scoffed softly, shaking her head. She regarded the pages she held, feeling helpless to convince her brother of the insanity contained in them. For thirteen years she'd believed their mother to be dead. And now...

While she ruminated on this, Isaac took the letter back a final time. He folded the pages up and slipped them into the envelope, which he stuffed back into the pocket of his hoodie. Then he stood from Drew's sofa and said with barely any emotion at all, "I'm going. With or without you."

And that was that.

She was there again. In the passenger seat. The windows down. Salty Atlantic air breezed against her face, while her mother belted out Alanis Morissette from the driver's seat. The ocean sparkled with crystalline sunshine, almost blinding, bright enough that she couldn't admire it for too long or else her head would start to ache. She turned to watch her mother instead, bare shoulders shimmying as she sang. She caught her mother's eye, then caught her infectious grin on her own mouth because why not? Then something in the backseat moved. Bouncing in place. She turned to see what it was, who it was, and discovered that her father had joined them this time, his head lolling back, his blood-stained teeth exposed in his open mouth, the rear windshield jeweled beautifully with brain and bone.

Drew woke just in time to stop the scream in the back of her throat. It rasped there, balled up in a knot that she quickly gulped down. She was terribly hot. Hot and *wet* under the covers. She flung them off, the cool air touching her with a pleasant chill. Her heart was still pounding. She rolled to the other side of the bed, away from the sweat, and lay in a shivering stupor, the skin across her arms and thighs rippling with goosebumps.

First she thought of the dream from which she'd just awoken. Then from there her mind kicked into gear, remembering the letter, her argument with Isaac, how suddenly her whole world seemed precariously balanced on a sky-scraping *what if?* What if the letter was real? What if their mother had really been alive all these years? What if this was truly their last and only chance to see her again?

What if I couldn't care less?

Despite the notion, Drew found her hands curling into fists. She *did* care, there was no denying that. But not for the reasons her brother might. The only reason Drew could fathom wanting to see their mother again at this point would be to shatter her nose, she thought. For shattering their lives and never bothering to come back and help pick up the pieces. This plea to see her children wasn't about them, Drew knew. No, apparently she was leaving again—whatever she'd meant by that in her letter—and sought closure before she did. Her own closure, not theirs.

Thirteen years. Thirteen goddamn years, and it's a vague

letter she sends. Asking us to risk our safety while she sits prettily wherever she is, waiting. Just waiting.

Even in the dark, Drew's sleep-deprived mind saw red. Her balled-up fists tightened, knuckles clenching, fingernails biting into her palms, becoming hot all over again despite the covers being tossed aside, as the sweat sizzled off her back like steam. Her fists ached for something. Release. A target.

To the shadows, she whispered, *"Fuck your closure."*

2

THE RENDEZVOUS

T wo days at the shop and four-hundred dollars later, Drew's reliably unreliable was ready to go. She paid at the front desk, received her keys, and pushed outside into the humid, sunshiny parking lot where her car waited amongst a row of other Georgia-plated misfits.

Halfway there, a familiar voice called her name from the lot's entrance, someone crossing the sidewalk toward her.

Jesus, not again.

It was Quentin. Drew's stomach blossomed with acid at the sight of him hurrying toward her, looking like he'd come straight from the golf course in his khaki shorts and green polo. He was panting, car keys dangling from his hand as he'd jumped straight out of his BMW at the curb. The look on his face was one of desperation, his brow knitted with fear, his grimacing mouth struggling to find purchase on the words tripping off his tongue.

"What did I do?" he said. "Just tell me what I did."

Her mind momentarily blanked. As he came near, she put up her hands, urging him to keep his distance.

"Was it something I said? Did I... did I..."

As he racked his brain for some explanation not even Drew could provide, she voiced the first thought that came to mind, which was "What the hell are you doing here, Quentin? Are you following me?"

His previously anguished expression lifted in momentary confusion—or rather, a deer-in-headlights gaze. His mouth fell agape but no words followed. Not for a second, at least. Then he seemed to find his bearings again, his eyes darkening with impatience, a bewildered rattle of the head.

"Why are you ghosting me?" he asked, ignoring her question altogether as she'd ignored his. "I thought things were going well between us?"

"I'm not ghosting you, Quentin..."

"You're not? Then what do you call it? How many times have you ignored my—"

"I'm just not interested anymore, all right?" Drew blurted. That sour pit in her belly ignited with aggression. "I'm done. That's all. I'm done."

"I don't believe you," Quentin said, even when his face was pinched with hurt. "Something must have happened. Tell me what I did wrong. There has to be *something*. Things were going great, and then all of the sudden..." He let out an irritated sigh. "I like you, Drew. I *really* like you. I don't get why you're doing this."

"Because I don't feel it," she said bluntly. "Simple as that. I'm sorry."

"I'm supposed to believe that? After four months, and you couldn't tell me face to face? No, I don't believe you..."

"Believe what you want."

Drew started for her car again, her key fob gripped so tightly she could crumple its plastic under her thumb with ease. Instead she lightly pressed the button there, watched her car's lights illuminate to signal the doors were unlocked. Behind her, Quentin's footsteps followed quickly across the pavement, his khaki shorts swishing together along the way until Drew felt her hackles prickling.

"Leave me alone!" she exclaimed, whirling on him.

He stopped in his tracks. "Are you seriously doing this?"

"Yes. We're through. We're done. End of story. I don't want to see you again. I don't want to hear from you again. You can stop blowing up my phone, because I'm not answering. This is it."

Quentin was stunned. He turned his face slightly, watching Drew warily from the corner of his eye.

"You're something else. You know that?"

To this, Drew forced a smile.

"That's right. Now you're getting it. Consider this a bullet dodged."

She climbed into her car. She fired it up. She pulled out from the row of vehicles on either side of her, doing her best not to look straight at the shadow waiting in her blind spot as she maneuvered safely around it. As she pulled out into the street, she chanced a final glance into her rearview and saw him there, watching her leave, and all at once she burst into tears.

With her bag packed and thrown into the backseat, Drew waited outside Isaac's dormitory, drumming her fingers on the steering wheel, eyeing the clock as the minutes ticked by, as well as her phone nestled in the center console for any new calls or texts. Surprisingly after their previous encounter, Quentin finally relented. Drew tried not to think about him too much. But in those moments that she tried, her mind simply wandered toward other unsavory things which she evaded only by returning her attention to the former, until her brain was stuck in a pinball game of half-formed thoughts...

Then the passenger door opened and her every muscle tensed with surprise, having not noticed Isaac's emergence. He swung himself into the car, dropped his backpack onto the floor between his feet, and pulled his door shut with a sigh of relief.

"Sorry it took me a minute," he said. "I didn't want to forget anything."

"Put on your seatbelt," Drew told him sternly, as she checked her mirror and proceeded to ease out into the road, their journey officially begun.

It was more than a two-hour drive from Atlanta to Murphy, North Carolina. A drive during which Drew had planned to let Isaac do most of the talking, intent on keeping her thoughts to herself, as they'd only rile her brother. Naturally

31

they each had their own reasons for entertaining this trip—for indulging their mother's insane request—and Isaac wouldn't like Drew's one bit, she already knew. When asked what changed her mind, she'd simply told him "There's no way I'm letting you go by yourself," which was most of the truth, at least.

"You haven't told grandma or grandpa about this?" she asked shortly after they departed. "Right?"

Isaac answered as if it should have been obvious, "No."

"What about your therapist?"

"No," he said again, as if that should have been even more obvious. "Why, did you tell yours?"

"I don't go anymore, so no."

With her eyes on the road, she peripherally glimpsed her brother watching her closely. His mere *shape* was enough to interpret his thoughts then. His judgements.

"Maybe you should," he said. "Scratch that. You definitely should..."

"I've already spent most of my life in a therapist's office. I think I'm good for a while."

"Hate to think where you'd be if you hadn't."

To this, Drew almost replied *'and I wonder where we'd be if not for the woman we're about to see'* but she kept her lips pressed tightly instead.

Crossing state lines left them about fifteen minutes until arrival, according to Drew's GPS. And as soon as they passed the 'Welcome to North Carolina' sign, Drew's burbling stomach notified her once more that none of this was okay. Not the letter, not the invitation, not their willingness to oblige. There was still a chance this was some weird trap, she thought. She hadn't dropped her guard. She imagined their mother murdered, her deranged killer reaching out with what little knowledge they possessed about Drew and Isaac in order to lure them in. A trip to Florida, a children's story book... and here their asses were, buckled in for the ride. Gullible clowns. Drew knew this to be far-fetched, but her mind was a morbid one, and liked to theorize the worst at all times.

She kept such thoughts to herself.

She also sympathized with Isaac, even if she didn't agree with him. She sympathized with his desire to investigate, to see this through even against his better judgement. She knew he had his reasons. He wasn't stupid. Not *usually*. They'd spoken very little about their mother over the years, truth be told. They spoke very little about most things that mattered, actually. That's what the therapy was for, Drew told herself.

"What if we see her," she asked, ten minutes until their destination, "and she's nothing like you hope?"

Isaac stared at the lush greenery along the highway, saying nothing for a time.

"I'm not expecting anything," he said.

Drew was twelve when their mother left. Isaac was only six. Whatever memories he had, they were few, and more than likely pleasant ones. Drew had many more than he did, of course.

And it wasn't all bedtime stories.

"That's it. There."

Isaac pointed toward the corner store in question. There was a single car parked near the side of the building, most likely belonging to the attendant inside. Drew parked near the other side of the building, at the edge of the modest parking lot. As soon as they were parked, she shut off the engine and regarded her brother beside her, who twisted eagerly in his seat, searching for their mother's intermediary —a person whom their mother gave no description within her letter.

"If at any point we feel something's wrong," Drew said, "then the whole thing's off. Okay?"

"Yeah," Isaac said, barely listening as he craned his neck to search the surrounding street.

Drew took shallow breaths, reminding herself on occasion that a deeper one would help settle her nerves. She glanced into all her mirrors, turning likewise to peer at the surrounding street and the bodiless establishments on the other side, as well as the rolling, leafy-green horizon rising above everything in all directions. It was a pretty little town, she thought. More traffic coming through than she'd expected, which was something of an odd comfort.

"I gotta pee," Isaac said at last, unbuckling himself. As soon as he said it, Drew agreed it was a good idea.

They headed inside the convenience store. The door gave a quaint jingle as they entered. The attendant behind the front desk—an older gentleman, his bald scalp covered in sun spots—gave a wordless but friendly nod to acknowledge their arrival. They quickly found the bathroom—a single one, which meant taking turns. Drew told her brother to go ahead. She perused the snack aisle nearby while she waited. Every now and then, she glanced to the front counter and found the attendant watching her. Not with suspicion, but curiosity.

"Where you from?" he called to her.

Drew forced a smile, then reluctantly moved closer and said, "Atlanta."

"Your first time in Murphy?" he asked, to which Drew nodded. "You come to see the Ten Commandments?"

God no, Drew thought, and shook her head in reply.

"We get a lot of religious folks stopping by to see the Ten Commandments..."

Drew wasn't sure what he meant by that, and felt not even a modicum of interest in pursuing the topic. Then it occurred to her that it might not be such a bad idea to let someone know—even a complete stranger—what they were up to, in the event that they should go missing.

"We're actually waiting for somebody," she told him. "Someone's supposed to pick us up here, I mean..."

The attendant lifted his head slowly in what Drew thought would be the start of an understanding nod, but then he held his chin raised, looking down his nose at her with the first sign of skepticism in his eyes.

"I see," he said. "Friends?"

Drew hesitated. There was no way to be honest without raising eyebrows. But maybe she *should* raise eyebrows, she thought. She and Isaac would stick out a little more in this man's memory if she gave him something to think peculiar.

The whole truth would be too much, of course. It was a rabbit hole of explanation. So instead she settled on something vague. Because oftentimes, obscurity in and of itself was enough to raise eyebrows.

"Sort of," she said. "Something like that, I guess."

Drew held the old man's gaze as he seemed to wait for more, but she left it at that. At which point the man finally lowered his chin, lowered it further and further, until he was looking at Drew with his eyes upturned in a somewhat grim fashion.

"You be careful, now," he said. His clear eyes narrowed slightly, just for a second, as if focusing the lens of his vision upon her. "Lots of strange folks in these small parts, I'm sure you know. And these days they don't just keep to themselves like they used to..."

It was then Isaac emerged from the bathroom hallway. Drew offered the attendant an appreciative smile, saying nothing in reply.

"I'll be waiting in the car," Isaac said, as she passed him on her way to the bathroom.

The bathroom was dingy but as clean as anyone could hope for. Drew made quick use of it. When she was finished, she hurried back through the store, and felt a pang of guilt for not buying anything as the attendant gave her yet another friendly nod. This time, however, although his mouth smiled, his eyes retained some hidden disquietude as Drew returned his expression with a half-smile, half-grimace of her own.

Good, she thought. He would remember her face.

Stepping outside into the smothering humidity, Drew

glanced frantically about the parking lot for any new arrivals. Spotting nobody, she peered along both intersecting streets, the traffic coming and going in little handfuls, and quickly made her way back to their car, parked in the building's shade. She climbed behind the wheel, but left her door open for the air, just as Isaac had left his.

She was just about to ask Isaac if he'd seen anyone yet when he suddenly said, "I want to show you something, but I don't want you to be mad."

Drew frowned. Not a great way to preface something.

"Okay. What is it?"

Isaac hoisted his backpack up from between his feet and into his lap. He unzipped it, dug around inside, checked over either shoulder guiltily as if someone might be watching them, and then paused with his eyes upon whatever it was, considering. Drew sparked with irritation.

"Well?"

Rather than pull it out, Isaac tipped his bag toward Drew so that she could see inside. What she saw sent her stomach flipping end over end like a football. Buried between the clothes he'd packed, sitting dangerously like a coiled snake, there lay a gun. A pistol. Drew inhaled sharply at the sight of it.

"Where the hell did you get that?"

"My roommate loaned it to me," Isaac said, tilting his bag back toward himself. He eyed the gun inside with a nervously bitten lip. "Just in case. Are you mad?"

"No," Drew answered without pause. "Do you even know how to shoot it?"

"Sure. It's not complicated."

"Is it loaded right now?"

"It wouldn't do us any good if it wasn't..."

Drew wasn't sure if the gun made her feel safer or more afraid—the possibility that they might need it seemed a bad omen all on its own. Then Isaac reached into the bag again, digging around for something else, and produced another object in his hand, which he offered to Drew on his flattened palm. A switchblade. Drew flicked her eyes between the knife and her brother with mounting dread.

"You came prepared."

"I'm surprised you didn't."

"Is that for me?" she asked, as her brother held it out closer. An offering.

"Take it. Just in case."

Just in case. In this context, Drew couldn't help hating that particular arrangement of words. She took the switchblade from her brother. She turned it around in her hand, studying it, then pressed the button on its side and watched the blade spring out in the fraction of a blink. She folded it back up with a satisfying *click*.

"Is this your roommate's, too?"

"No, it's mine. You should keep it in your pocket."

"Just in case," Drew said.

"Just in case," Isaac repeated.

She did as her little brother suggested, and slipped the switchblade into her righthand pocket.

We're only staying a day. One night. That's it.

Isaac zipped his pack up and placed it back on the floor between his feet. Drew's stomach was alive with little insect feet, skittering about like they'd enjoyed this morning's coffee.

"Aren't you a little worried?" she asked her brother. "That we might need these things?"

Isaac shrugged. "I don't know. Not really. I've gone on Grindr dates sketchier than this."

"Okay, that doesn't make me feel any better..."

"Drew and Isaac?"

They both flinched in their seats. Drew audibly gasped, recoiling from the voice beside her, from the figure bent at her door, leaning in to get a good look at them both. A middle-aged man with dark, shoulder-length hair hanging about his face, and a thick but shapely trimmed beard to match. As soon as Drew turned to see him, pulling back with her heart in her throat, she caught a whiff of something she thought she recognized as beard oil. An ex of hers had used something similar. A pleasant, nutty, vanilla scent.

"That you?" he said, his emerald-green eyes showing a distinct lack of amusement at their jumpiness.

"Yes," Isaac blurted.

To Isaac's answer, the man offered a smile which didn't even attempt to reach his eyes.

"Good," he said. "I'm ready when you are."

He turned his head to his vehicle parked behind them, whose arrival Drew hadn't even noticed. She'd been too absorbed in Isaac's hidden arsenal. It was an ordinary, smaller-sized pickup truck. Dark gray and spotted with plenty of dirt, as well as a bit of chipped paint and rust around the wheel wells. Drew had to really crane her neck to see it, reluctant to step out beside the man.

"Why can't we just follow you?" she asked, already knowing the answer but feeling troublesome enough to ask anyway.

"Not many people know about the place we're going. And we'd like to keep it that way. Oh. And before I forget..." He reached into his back pocket and produced a folded up sheet of paper. He handed it to Drew, who unfolded it from the comfort of her seat and discovered it was another letter from their mother. "Your mom thought maybe you'd want that once you met me. Apparently I'm not... personable."

Drew read the letter over quickly—a meaningless reassurance, mostly, that they could trust this man, who apparently went by the name of Kent. Drew wasn't sure how the letter helped anything. If the first letter was a farce, the second did nothing to lessen suspicion.

"So your name's Kent, huh?" she said, as she handed the letter over to Isaac who took it eagerly like someone starving for scraps. "The intermediary."

"That's right," he said, a strange note of pride in his otherwise deadpan tone. "I'm something of a middle-man for our commune. That truck of mine is the only vehicle that enters and leaves."

The errand boy, Drew thought.

"Commune? What kind of commune?" she asked, her interest piqued.

"Just a community of likeminded individuals," Kent said. Even monotonous as he was, it was clear by the subtle shift in his stance that Drew's probe made him uncomfortable. He'd come to pick them up, not answer questions. "So are you coming, then? Or should I—"

"We're coming," Isaac answered, apparently finished with the letter. He grabbed his backpack, swiveled out of his seat, and shut the door behind him in one fluid motion, his feet already moving on the pavement before the door slammed shut.

Meanwhile Drew climbed out like her ankles were shackled together, dragging an iron ball behind them. She opened the back door and grabbed her bag from behind her seat, then proceeded to lock the car.

"Will this be okay for the night, do you think?" she asked Kent, regarding her car.

Kent grinned, and this time it reached his eyes, branding them with handsome crows feet—his genuine amusement somehow more off-putting than his previously phony variety.

"A night?" he said. "Sure. Best not to leave anything valuable in it, though. Just to be safe."

Drew stood uneasily, watching Kent as he returned to his truck. Isaac was already there, arriving at the passenger door with his hands around the straps of his backpack like a kid eager for his first day of school.

This is fucked.

She'd known it from the start. She should have gone to their grandparents—their guardians after the death of their father—and told them everything. Of course she'd already thought of this countless times. Lost sleep over it, in fact. If she'd done this, Isaac would have gone haywire. He would have denied all of it, kept the letter hidden somewhere. He'd have gone on his own. For whatever reason, this was more important to him than anything. All Drew could hope to do was keep him safe.

"You coming or not?" Kent called, the driver's door open, his hand resting on its frame.

Drew glanced toward the convenience store, and was mildly surprised to see the attendant in the window, watching them with that same look on his brow—vigilant, unbelieving. He met Drew's gaze and she flashed a hollow smile. Then she started after the others at last, dragging her ball and chains as quickly as her sneakers would take them.

Keep him safe or die trying.

3

THE COMMUNE

"So this commune," Drew said, five minutes after departing the corner store, "you said something about likeminded individuals? Likeminded how?"

Kent drove slouched in his seat, one hand on the steering wheel, his body turned ever so slightly away from them, away from Isaac beside him in the middle. Body language which didn't get much clearer than that. Uncomfortable. Imposed upon. This truck was an object of pride for him, in one way or another. Perhaps just the ownership alone, considering it was a shared commune he came from, apparently.

"Just a group of people who value a common life philosophy," he said.

"And what's that?"

Kent's mouth and lips worked as if he chewed on the end of something—a toothpick that wasn't there.

"Living and providing for one another," he said, "in the heart of nature, the way humanity was meant to thrive. No social media. No internet at all. Away from these big cities, overcrowded and overstimulating. Too many ingredients in the pot, too many emotions... *commingling*. It's all bound to boil over eventually..." He shrugged hastily, as if it all should be obvious, hardly worth explaining to the two of them. "It's where mental illness starts to fester, in my opinion..."

Drew and Isaac exchanged glances. Isaac smirked a little, finding it funny. Drew struggled to see the humor, frankly. Her mind had been thinking one thing since Kent mentioned a commune. Another semi-morbid notion— mostly an issue of word association, really, but one she couldn't avoid.

Which was: *we're about to meet a real-life cult.*

About twenty minutes out of Murphy, following some winding roads into the hills and around the various river bends, Kent pulled the truck off the side of the road and parked them in the wild grass and underbrush.

It was Isaac who voiced, "Why are we stopping?" and it felt somewhat a relief for Drew, hearing the alarm in his words, confirmation that his guard wasn't entirely down.

"Pop that open," Kent told Drew, pointing to the glovebox above her knees.

She did as he said. Inside were various papers—registration and the like—as well as a couple lighters, a pack of smokes, a little flashlight, and some dark, grimy-looking handkerchiefs. Of course, it was the handkerchiefs Kent indicated next.

"I'm gonna need you both to blindfold yourselves from here on out. Until we arrive, anyway."

"Wait, what?" Drew's hands remained glued to her lap, unwilling to touch anything she saw in the glovebox. "Are you serious?"

"I'm serious," Kent said, his voice as serious as it'd ever been.

"We really need blindfolds?" Isaac asked.

"Really," Kent answered drably.

Isaac laughed then—a short noise in the back of his throat. A coping mechanism.

"Are you gonna murder us out here, or..."

Kent smiled again, his eyes creasing with authentic humor. He took a deep breath, looked into his rearview mirror, pulled his hair behind his ear with a swift, casual motion of his hand, and then sighed like someone who had predicted an argument and was rather bored to be proven right.

"If I was a killer, don't you think this would all be a little much? I'd have better luck just finding victims at rest stops."

"That makes us feel so much better," Drew said.

Isaac reached across his sister and took one of the blindfolds out. Drew observed him as he placed the handkerchief around his face and attempted to tie it behind his head.

This is so stupid. I'm so stupid. This is crazy. Completely, utterly crazy...

Her instincts were screaming, her entire body electrified with pure *get-out-of-here* energy, and yet she found herself reaching for her brother, reaching for his fumbling fingers against the back of his head, taking the handkerchief from him and helping to tie it nice and neat. Then she took the other from the glovebox and did the same around her own face. The handkerchief smelled of motor oil and dust. Once she had it knotted behind her head, she opened her eyes and was sufficiently blinded, only a meager light seeping through the fabric. Then not only did she *feel* stupid, she knew she looked it, too.

"There," Kent said, and reached across the both of them to shut the glovebox. "Not so bad, right?"

Neither of them replied. As Kent pulled them back onto the road—as Drew became increasingly aware of every bump and turn that sent her jostling or leaning in her seat—she found herself all the more grateful for the gun Isaac had packed into his bag, as well as the knife tucked securely in her pocket.

After so long, the journey only became bumpier. Twistier. Even with their eyes covered by Kent's oil-change rags, it was clear they'd left the main roads and were now following roads less traveled. *Much* less traveled. Deep into the woods, up into the hills, the truck rattled and groaned as they maneuvered through dips and divots, the terrain less than welcoming. Isaac made sad attempts at conversation, attempts Kent was clearly not interested in reciprocating.

"Do you know our mom? Do you know her well, I mean?"

"Julianne?" Kent said, considering. "Yeah, I know her."

Isaac said nothing for a moment. "What can you say about her?"

"She's a... nice enough lady..." Kent's tone foreshadowed a definite *'but.'* He managed to avoid the word, at least. "A bit shortsighted, inviting the two of you out here. It's even more shortsighted that we're allowing it, but at the end of the day, it's not my decision."

"Whose decision is it?" Drew chimed in, hoping for a name, hoping for another piece to the puzzle.

"You'll meet everyone soon enough," Kent answered.

At that, the insects crawling through Drew's stomach swelled into full-blown butterflies.

Eventually the path smoothed out, became more deliberate. Then Kent slowed the truck, little by little, until they came to a complete stop.

"You can take off your blindfolds now."

Drew listened as Isaac scrambled for his. She reached for her own, worked her nimble fingers at the knot she'd left purposefully loose. When she pulled it down, the light hit her in the worst possible way. Shimmering, square in the face. Bright as reflected platinum. It shimmered because it sat atop the gentle surface of the lake before them, the reflected afternoon sun beaming directly through Kent's windshield into their eyes. There was hardly a moment to shield herself from it before a dull ache formed in the pit of her skull. Drew dropped her gaze to her lap, blinking.

"Jesus…" she muttered.

After a moment, she looked up carefully, avoiding the sun's reflection as best she could, and surveyed their surroundings.

They were parked beside a modest cabin, constructed at the edge of a small lake—an oblong, bean-shaped body probably about 2 square miles in surface area, surrounded by nothing but forest and a further sprinkling of other cabins around its edge, which Drew could only make out vaguely through the reflected sunlight.

When Isaac finally got his blindfold off, he visibly winced likewise.

"How many people live out here?" Drew asked, noticing with each passing moment another cabin she hadn't before, truly *encompassing* the lake.

"Currently," Kent said, thinking, "about twenty-four, I believe. With sixteen cabins total. We encourage sharing spaces, which means we have a few empty at the moment. You'll have a space to yourselves."

Drew appreciated that she didn't need to ask—that Kent probably knew exactly the kinds of concerns they came with.

"Which one's our mom staying in?" Isaac asked, shielding his eyes with his hand as he studied the place.

"She's on the other side of the lake," Kent said. "I'll take you both there shortly. But first…" He opened his door and climbed out with a weary groan, then stood peering in at them with eyes that said *'you planning on getting out anytime soon?'* But what he said with his mouth was, "First there's someone else you need to meet."

The decider, Drew thought, and felt a nervous pang in her gut. She grabbed her bag from the floor and climbed out of the passenger side. Her legs rejoiced as she set her feet on the dirt, unfolded for the first time in more than an hour or so.

"You're welcome to leave your bags with me," Kent said. "I can drop them off at whichever cabin's available."

Drew held Isaac's gaze as he slid himself out from the truck onto solid ground, each of them wary of the idea.

"I think we'll just hold onto our bags ourselves, if that's all right," Drew answered.

Kent shrugged. "Suit yourself."

He slammed his door shut and started toward the nearest cabin beside them. These were traditional log cabins. Nothing too fancy about them. Single level, one or two windows in the front, nothing painted, nothing decorated. Not outside, at least. Kent cast one glance over his shoulder to ensure they were following in his footsteps. Drew glanced once again to the blinding lake, taking special note that it was entirely void of people. Not a single swimmer in sight. Near its far side, she spotted a single large dock which also held no one at the moment. She squinted in the blazing sun's reflection, searching the lake shore all around the perimeter that she could see, and for now couldn't spot a single living form. Then she glanced the other way, toward the dirt road they'd arrived on, which went snaking into the woods down a steady, gentle slope behind them out of sight.

Only now did she truly realize just how *trapped* they were. At the mercy of strangers, their mother included...

If she even exists.

Suddenly Drew's fantasies of laying into their mother seemed ill-advised. It would prove awkward at best, dangerous at worst. Should things go poorly, what recourse did they have?

Please Mister Kent, we're ready to go home now...

Kent now stood near the front door of the cabin beside them, waiting once more for Drew and Drew alone. Isaac was already there, holding onto the straps of his backpack with white knuckles and wide-eyes, hardly hiding his own anxiety. Drew had to remind herself to pick up her feet as her sneakers scuffed the dirt.

"The founder has asked that I introduce you first, before taking you around the lake," Kent said.

"The founder?" Isaac asked.

Every cult has its leader, Drew thought, her prior assumption beginning to take a more tangible form.

Before Kent could knock on the cabin door, it opened. Another man appeared in the doorway—bright faced, bright eyed, tall and lean as a basketball player, she thought. Like Kent, the man in the doorway had longer hair, only his was red and pulled back into a tight bun. And rather than a full beard, he maintained a clean goatee, red as the hair on his head and finely trimmed to a tapered point off his chin. He wore a basic, black t-shirt and black sweat pants. Drew wasn't wholly sure what it was about the man—*the goatee, it's definitely the goatee*—but she felt an immense distrust from the moment she laid eyes on him. Perhaps it was the manner in which he smiled, showing all his pearly whites, perfectly aligned, perfectly square like she'd only ever seen in tooth-paste ads.

"You must be Julianne's," he said, beaming. Drew felt incapable of returning his warm greeting, and was disconcerted to see Isaac having a much easier time of it. "Isaac? And Drew?"

Drew tried to smile, but knew it looked nothing like one. The man hardly paid much attention to her, anyway. A fleeting look, before focusing all his attention on Isaac, whose gaze he held much longer. This was a salesman at work, she thought in an instant. Targeting the more likely buyer.

"My name is Blaine Kipling. I just go by Blaine. Is it all right if I speak to you both inside for a moment?"

He stood aside and gestured toward the innards of his cabin. Isaac didn't even look at Drew before heading inside. That *get-out-of-here* energy was reaching new heights, causing her limbs to ache with a need to *move*, to *run*, with nowhere to go. She followed behind Isaac, first moving past Kent who stared solemnly down at his feet, more than likely eager to be rid of them. Then she moved past Blaine in the doorway, an entire head and a half taller than she was. Their eyes met, hers peering up, his peering down. Piercing blue, as bright and unreadable as the surface of a cold lake. Then they were inside, and the door shut behind them.

"You're both welcome to take a seat, if you'd like."

The cabin was cozy and rather plain, and yet seemed more put together than Drew's own apartment, as far as *intent* went. Blaine had taken careful consideration into making this his home, while also making a clear effort to remain simple.

Humble. It was mostly one, open room. A living space with a round wooden table and four chairs surrounding it, placed upon a large, pale green rug on the floor. Nothing adorned the perimeter. There were two windows on either side of the front door, plus one larger window at the back, where Drew was startled to see someone standing beside it, watching them. A man, hands clasped reverently behind his back, watching Drew with seemingly no expression at all. She was reminded of the Royal Guard, standing still as statues, relentlessly immobile. The man by the window would have made a poor fit for the Royal Guard, however, with his patchy blond facial hair and his wild, blonder mullet. His eyes remained on Drew and Drew only, watching as she moved toward the table and chairs in the middle of the room. Increasingly uncomfortable, she looked away, taking in the rest of the empty cabin with nervous, sweeping glances.

There were two other doors within the cabin, besides the entrance. One which must have led to a bedroom, as it led to the one large corner of the cabin's interior that wasn't open to the rest. The second door was across the cabin near the rear window, where the blond man stood in between, silent as a sentry. That door led into just a small pocket in the corner, likely a storage closet.

Isaac took a seat at the table. Drew joined him, sitting directly across.

"Would either of you like some tea?" Blaine asked, and moved toward his wood-burning stove which was currently alight, a kettle sitting on top.

"I think we're good," Drew answered quickly, for both herself and her brother. He didn't argue.

"We mostly just want to see our mom," Isaac said rather bluntly.

"Julianne," Blaine said, almost reminiscently. He folded his arms, then paced slowly toward them from the stove. "She's been a very welcome addition to our community here the last year or so…"

Last year or so, Drew thought, adding this to the puzzle. She'd expected this to be the place their mother had vanished to all this time, not just the last year. *Or so…*

"Where is she now?" Drew asked, impatient.

"Most likely at her cabin," Blaine said, his eyes moving from Isaac to Drew, then back to Isaac. "I wanted to meet you both first. Partly as a precaution, to make sure you're both who you say you are."

"We're very suspicious, we know," Drew said.

Blaine smiled from the corner of his mouth, watching her with a slyness that suggested he hadn't expected her to be clever.

"I've known you both less than a minute, and yet I can already see you're undoubtedly Julianne's children." He lowered his gaze, thinking on something else. A slight exhalation. "And… I also wanted to go over some quick ground rules before setting you loose around the commune."

"Ground rules?" Drew said.

"Correct. This is a sacred place, you see. The people here, including myself, respect the land a great deal, and the natural resources it provides. Above all, we respect the lake."

That dull ache which had sparked in Drew's skull now throbbed suddenly, reminding her of its niggling existence.

"There is no swimming in the lake. No bathing in the

lake. No fishing in the lake. The lake is off limits except for special circumstances."

"What kind of special circumstances?" Isaac asked.

"Are you all right?" Blaine asked, ignoring Isaac as he noticed Drew cringing like she was.

"Yeah," she said. "Just a headache, is all."

"Would you like something for it? I think we have some ibuprofen in the main cabin."

Drew shook her head stubbornly. "No, thank you. I'll be okay."

More than anything, she didn't want to ingest anything these people gave her. No tea, no pills, not anything. Not now. Not yet. Not until it was confirmed this place was *real,* that their mother was *real,* that she and Isaac weren't about to be chopped up and served at this weekend's barbecue.

She glanced once to the rear window, to check on the silent man standing dutifully beside it, and found him still watching her intently, expressionlessly, like a painting on the wall whose eyes followed yours like an optical illusion. She was almost about to ask aloud *'Do I owe you money or something?'* but was interrupted before she could utter a word.

"Well, if you change your mind," Blaine said, "Kent can show you where we keep our first-aid supplies." Then he clapped his hands together abruptly, smiling once more with the spirit of a scout leader on a camping trip. "Anyway, that's it for ground rules! We might be out in the wilderness, but the wilderness is our home and we prefer to treat it as such. Simple as that. Capeesh?"

Did this guy really just say capeesh? she thought.

To her horror, Isaac replied for them both: "Capeesh."

Blaine did something then that made Drew wince with secondhand embarrassment—a curtsy, or some kind of bowing motion, his arms opening gracefully to each of them in their seats—and with theatrical enthusiasm he exclaimed, "Welcome to Our Mother's Lake!"

4

THE REUNION

Following their meeting with commune leader Blaine Kipling, Drew and Isaac were promptly handed back into the supervision of Kent, who waited leaned against the side of his truck while the sun continued sinking toward the horizon across the lake behind him. He straightened as they exited the cabin, his face stony as ever.

"Ready for the tour?" he asked.

Drew looked over her shoulder, searching for Blaine who had already closed himself back inside his cabin, along with his unusually mute, mullet-rocking companion. Isaac traipsed toward Kent innocent as always, and replied "Ready when you are."

Drew kept silent as they made their way around the lake's shore, trying to listen to Kent as her mind consistently wandered. She couldn't help peering across the lake's still surface, toward each of the nondescript cabins dotting its circumference. One of them belonged to their mother. Which one would it be?

They passed a handful of cabins along the way, and finally Drew got a glimpse of some other residents. They were all dressed similarly, in their plain t-shirts and sweats, all various colors but clearly all the same style. Drew imagined Kent running his weekly errands into town, buying bulk packs of shirts and sweats from Walmart or wherever was cheapest. The other residents gave them cursory glances as they passed, none friendly, until Kent waved and forced them to do the same, at which point their scrutinizing gazes barely softened.

We are not wanted here, Drew thought.

One cabin they passed was alive with music. *Live* music, emitted through the open windows. A man played his acoustic guitar inside, belting out what was obviously a self-written ballad. Drew only needed to hear a slice of it to know he'd probably already tried his hand in Nashville and failed miserably. Apparently Blaine's cult was the next logical step down.

"While I do make trips into town for supplies, we do a lot of our own gardening here at the lake."

Kent pointed to several raised garden beds, currently home to many leafy green *things.* Drew recognized tomato plants, absolutely spilling with half-ripe tomatoes, as well as several varieties of squash.

Then a strange noise caught Drew's attention and she found herself looking a bit farther ahead.

"We've got a couple chicken coops as well," Kent said, indicating the noise she'd heard. "One here, and another on the other side of the lake. Just for eggs, mostly, unless one dies."

"Winters here must suck," Isaac said.

"Not too bad," Kent said. "It never gets as cold as you'd think."

The chickens clucked as they passed, some a little agitated as their voices croaked long and loud. Drew imagined that even *they* were wary of the newcomers, giving her and Isaac nasty chicken side-eyes as Kent paraded them past.

"How long have you been here?" she asked Kent.

"Longer than anyone but Blaine," he answered vaguely. "Which is why I've always been more than just a regular resident. Blaine trusts me to handle the supply runs, like I said. More of a right hand, you could say."

Again he spoke with a tone of pride, which told Drew that Kent considered himself superior due to his 'extra responsibilities,' as well as being the only resident in denim jeans. A teacher's pet, if she ever met one...

It was a good twenty-five-minute walk around the lake before Kent finally directed them toward one cabin in particular. Drew peered back across the lake to see just how far they'd come, making out Kent's truck small and distant on the other side. All at once her heart began chugging fitfully against her sternum, drumming through her whole body until her legs became jelly-like with the vibrations, and her breaths became shallow and difficult.

There was a woman outside who was *not* their mother. Young, around Drew's age, doing stretches on a mat which she'd rolled out for herself on the rocky dirt just outside the cabin's entrance.

"Sherry, have you seen Julianne?" Kent asked as they approached.

Sherry was currently mid-lunge as she looked to Kent, and then noticed Drew and Isaac standing cluelessly behind him. Her face lit up, not exactly *cheerful* but intrigued. She stood from her lunge, hands on her hips, a glowing sweat from head to toe.

"She's inside writing, I think," she answered.

"Wait out here," Kent said.

He knocked on the door before gently opening it ajar, peering inside. Drew's heart was positively pounding now. No amount of deep breaths would relieve the anxiety cinching her airways. Kent stepped inside and closed the door behind him. The other woman, Sherry, offered them a smile as they waited.

"You must be her kids," she said, stepping off her mat and approaching them. "Isaac, yeah? And... don't tell me..."

"Drew."

"Yes!" Sherry said excitedly, her voice rising to a bird-like pitch. "That's right! Like Drew Barrymore."

Drew hadn't expected to dislike anyone more than Mr. Goatee, but right out of the gate Sherry made a strong case for herself. Not that Drew had anything against Drew Barrymore, but it was a tired comparison by this point in her life. She gave no reaction to Sherry's comment except for an empty stare. Sherry chose to focus instead on Isaac.

"I've heard a lot about you. Both of you. Your mom talks about you all the time..."

"Nothing about the last thirteen years, though, I'm guessing," Drew said.

Sherry's sun-kissed skin seemed to blanch even in the warm glow of the falling sun. Her throat flexed as she swallowed, hard—choking down any remaining assumptions she had about the new arrivals. Drew stole a glance at her brother, just enough to notice his disapproving grimace directed her way. If he was disappointed by *that,* Drew thought, he would soon wither and die hearing the rest of what she'd come to say.

And then the cabin door opened.

The three of them—Drew, Isaac, and even Sherry—physically tensed as Kent emerged. Behind him, another followed. A petite figure appeared in the doorway, through the doorway, into the softening evening light.

Out of nowhere, Drew felt rather dizzy. Like the ground was slowly pulling out from under her feet.

She'd told herself it would be for nothing, coming all this way. She'd told herself it would be the death of them. And yet of course some part of her had believed it might be true. She hadn't come *just* for Isaac, after all. Some part of her wanted it to be real. And it was. And nothing could have prepared her for it. All of her fantasies, the practiced dialogues, the imagined scenarios she'd played through over and over in her mind's eye in order to mentally brace herself were for naught. The scathing monologue she'd prepared for this moment went out of her just like the wind in her sails, the air in her lungs. Breathless. Speechless. Her legs nearly buckled. Beside her, Isaac was already falling apart. A shameless mess. He choked on his sadness, except it wasn't really sadness. It was a slick, sobbing boulder in one's throat, the same that appeared in Drew's now, without her even noticing until she heard it in her brother's voice.

"Mom," he said. And that was it.

The woman before them crumbled likewise. She was beautiful, Drew thought, in the moment before it happened —when she'd first stepped out, her dewy face pulled in two directions, brows raised high with wide-eyed disbelief, her pink mouth falling open in the other direction with involuntary awe—but at the sight of them, and at the *sound* of them, she could hardly hold herself together. As Isaac shuffled toward her pitifully, sagging at the shoulders, head drooping under the weight of all the emotions which had sprung into it, Julianne Prescott opened her arms to him, crying and smiling simultaneously so that her teeth showed glistening. She threw her arms around her son, lifting her chin high to place her head over his shoulder, she was so small. Much smaller than Drew remembered. A tiny, black-haired pixie of a thing. Together like they were, it was clear Isaac was her son. Drew was another story, but she'd always known that. She was more her father's daughter, with his eyes, his hair.

While they embraced, Drew couldn't move at all. She stood rooted, sneakers in the dirt, that boulder-sized lump still aching in her throat, barely able to squeeze a single breath around it. With her head raised over Isaac's shoulder, Julianne opened her eyes and peered past him, straight at her petrified daughter, and suddenly Drew couldn't manage it. Her eyes darted helplessly, finding Sherry beside them, who wiped tears from her own eyes as if she were part of this in any meaningful way. A sudden annoyance sparked in Drew, and with that one simple emotion, she was reminded of the others she'd come prepared for. The hurt. The anger. The resentment.

What do you know, Sherry? Why should you cry? What do you know about any of this, or anything at all for that matter?

Of course, this wasn't about Sherry. Drew's mind was simply tailspinning.

She returned her attention to the woman in Isaac's arms. Julianne's eyes were closed again, her soft lips mouthing words only Isaac could hear, and the lump in Drew's throat mysteriously shifted, *lifted,* smoke-like. She set it loose with a shuddering breath. Meanwhile her resentment hardened, taking the form of a jagged rake in her mind, which dredged up so many other old things. Ugly things. Memories, mostly. Things which had happened throughout her life, her adolescent years especially, things she really could have used some proper guidance for, and not from her aging, ultra-conservative, ultra-religious grandmother. Things she'd learned too late. Things she struggled to learn even still. Like trusting the little voice that tells you something's wrong. Something isn't right. Like learning how to say no and *mean* it, and believe it, and not to let anyone convince you otherwise. Or in the aftermath of such shortcomings, simply having someone to turn to, to confide in, to talk you through it because they'd *been there too.* She regarded her mother now, pulling away from Isaac gingerly, her skin aglow, radiant, looking as healthy as anyone could hope to be in this life, and she recalled all of these things one after another in quick succession like bubbles bursting on the surface of a boiling pot, her resentment solidifying more and more until it sank to the bottom and became scorched there.

Julianne was looking at her again. With one arm around Isaac, she held out the other, an invitation which was lost on Drew at the moment. Lost in translation. Tears had sprung to Drew's eyes again, but these were different. She blinked them away, spilling down her face, and in the clarity that followed she caught her mother saying something more to her brother. Something which looked like, *'I think your sister is...'* and the rest was lost as Drew's vision filled with tears again.

"Drew," Isaac said, loudly to try and break the spell she was clearly under.

It was then Drew found her own trembling voice, and she said, "Where have you been?"

Her voice was a little smothered. Strangled. She blinked more tears away. Her mother looked sympathetically between her and her brother, before letting Isaac go entirely. She moved toward Drew, a few languid steps, her wet face trying to smile for Drew's sake.

"I know you probably have a lot to say to me right now..."

"Where have you been?" Drew repeated, and somehow her voice was only becoming *more* strained. Was the lump returning? She was finding it difficult to breathe again...

Julianne grimaced knowingly, expecting this. "I've been lots of places," she said. "I can tell you all about it, if you want. If you'll let me." She looked Drew up and down, from head to toe to head again, and her pained expression warmed with admiration. "My God, you're so grown..."

She moved closer. Another couple of steps, and suddenly Drew's legs remembered themselves. They wished to retreat. To take a step back for every step her mother took forward. The lump *had* returned, as well as a couple hot coals behind her eyes, and it became a great effort to see through the blurring waterworks.

"You left us." Drew's cheeks were streaming now. Her mouth contorted against her will as she tried to speak. "You just left us..."

"I know." Julianne stepped closer. "I know..."

"You just left us..."

"I know..."

Drew took another step back, sneakers barely supporting her wobbly knees. Julianne took another three steps toward her, closing the distance. Drew let her heavy head fall, wishing to hide herself away as she could no longer control herself, couldn't plug the emotions up. Another step back. And another. Her body was on autopilot as her mind reeled. A short circuit. Her mother came closer all the while, until Drew could hear her shuffling feet. She took one last shaky step back and plunged her sneaker right into the edge of the lake, followed quickly by the other, soaking her feet up to her ankles. With nowhere left to go, her mother caught her at last.

"Come here."

Julianne wrapped Drew up in her arms. Drew turned limp in her embrace. She leaned into her mother's petite figure like a wilting flower. The fight was gone, lost, bled out of her like a great hole had been torn in her resolve. Her mind was caught in an inescapable loop, between hatred and relief, disgust and comfort, and somewhere underneath it all she noticed the bizarre warmth of the lake around her feet, tickling against her ankles. *Hot,* she thought, like a jacuzzi. Was that right? Was that normal? Her mother whispered affirmations in her ear, which her mind consumed greedily without discretion.

"I know. I know. It's okay. Let it out..."

Then another voice joined them. An annoying buzz in their orbit, like a flea that needed to be squashed.

"Oh... um... you guys... Drew... Drew? Your feet, they're... well..." Sherry cleared her throat aggressively. *"Drew, your feet are in the water."*

Drew stripped off her soggy socks, stuffed them into her soaking wet sneakers, and left them by the door outside Julianne's cabin as she and Isaac joined their mother inside. The interior wasn't so different from Blaine's, in that it was rather empty and straightforward. The cabin contained four beds—simple cots, but a bed was a bed, Drew supposed—and a large, rectangular table in the very center of the space. This was where Julianne had been writing before they arrived, as was evidenced by the composition notebook and pencil left there. Julianne collected these and offered Drew and Isaac seats at the table. Isaac was still rubbing his sore eyes as he sat down. Drew sat next to him.

"A lot of us keep journals," Julianne said, taking hers to her cot. "Blaine encourages it, to help clear our minds."

"That's smart," Isaac said, and sniffled for the last time. "My therapist has me do the same, actually."

Drew already dreaded the tone of this conversation. Julianne returned to them and sat directly across the table. Once more Drew was distracted by her mother's healthy glow. Perhaps the fresh mountain air had something to do with it. Or the stress-free luxury of a childless life.

"I didn't expect you to come," Julianne said, at first folding her arms on the table, then cupping her chin in her hand as she admired them both. "I wouldn't have blamed you for not coming. But I'm so grateful you did."

She smiled. Isaac smiled. Drew remained a steely witness to their smiles. She chewed her lip, still recovering from the embarrassment of her reaction by the lake. She wouldn't let it happen again, she decided. Her guard had fallen momentarily—crumbled disastrously—and she'd rebuilt another in its place already, a stronger one. Sturdier.

"I want to know everything," Julianne said, her gaze ping-ponging desperately between them. "Where do you live? What are you doing with yourselves these days?"

"Don't you feel guilty for not knowing?"

Drew couldn't help it. She *could,* in an obvious sense, but mostly she couldn't. Her breath hissed heavily from her nostrils as she leaned back in her chair, heart still beating hard like a drum. She knew how she must have sounded, how she looked. Petulant. Insensitive. She didn't care. Not at the moment. Isaac wanted this to be a lovey-dovey occasion. A heartfelt reunion. But it couldn't be that. It would never be that, Drew thought, for the woman sitting across the table had too much to answer for. She felt her brother's eyes on her again, felt the heat of his judgement. She glanced his way briefly, just enough to see the look on his face which read, *'Really, Drew?'*

"What?" she said. "How did you expect me to be?"

"I'd be angry, too," Julianne said, severing the tension between her children. "You have every right to be angry with me."

"Where did you go?" Drew asked, cutting to the heart of the matter. "When you first left us, where did you disappear to?"

Julianne's gaze became distant as she thought back to that time—a heart-rending cataclysm for Drew and Isaac, and a footnote in their mother's adventurous, momentous diary, no doubt—her mouth parted slightly in anticipation of the specifics should she remember them.

"Well... I was all over the place, really. You could say I was aimless. Wandering."

"Must have felt pretty good, being free of all that baggage."

"No." Julianne shook her head adamantly. "No, that's not what it was. It was never *that*. That's not what you were to me."

"Then why? How could you just leave us like that?" Drew paused, giving her mother an opening to answer, before she continued instead with, "And don't tell me it killed you to do it, because I can see well enough it didn't."

"I have no excuse," Julianne said, pressing her lips into a frown. "It was selfishness, really. Pure selfishness. I was your brother's age when I had you, you know. Younger, actually. I was eighteen. And your father, well... He was old enough to know better, at least. Better than I did..."

At the mention of their father, without warning Drew's stomach somersaulted, followed by a terrible clenching, as something sour reached up into her esophagus like a wave of clawing hands. It settled momentarily—just for another wave to follow, more powerful than the last.

"Again, I'm not making excuses for myself. I mean, reasons aren't necessarily excuses, after all. That's just... how it *was*."

Drew stood abruptly from the table, the feet of her chair squealing, wood against wood, and she dashed madly for the cabin door. Another wave struck her, splashed up to the rear of her throat. She pulled the door open, stumbled outside into the humid evening heat, and promptly retched into the dirt there. Sherry appeared in a confusing instant, beating both Isaac and Julianne who followed to the open cabin door.

"Oh my," Sherry said. "Are you all right? Here, let's—"

"Stay away from me," Drew said, more as a thoughtful warning than a loathsome request, although she felt both. Her stomach was still in turmoil, hot and slithering, and she feared she might heave again any second.

Then Isaac was there, hunching beside her, a hand on her back.

"You okay?"

"No, I'm not okay," she said, and shivered.

Discreetly, leaning closer to Drew than she liked, Isaac whispered, "Please give this a chance, Drew. Please. Just for a day..."

Drew moved away from him. She wandered toward the corner of the cabin, where she decided to lean and catch her breath, trying to settle the upset inside her. She swallowed, tasting the sour bile on the back of her tongue, and cast her gaze across the lake shore, along the row of cabins curving around its length, and the lush tree line behind them. Another deep breath. She hung her head, eyes closed. Behind her, Isaac and their mother murmured conspiratorially amongst themselves, which Drew didn't like one bit.

Breathe. Just breathe.

"Uh oh," came a new voice. "Everything okay?"

Drew opened her eyes to slits, taking in the approaching figure. A tall, thin, sinewy man with a treacherous growth of facial hair around his lips and chin. The Leader. The Quack. The Goatee. She hung her head defeatedly as he came near.

"She's fine," Isaac answered. "She's just…"

As Isaac faltered, having no clue *what* his sister was, Blaine filled in the blanks.

"A lot of excitement and a whole lot of feelings, I'm sure." He stood before her, giving Drew's downcast eyes a wonderful view of his bare, dirt-stained feet. She refused to meet his gaze—to see the false sympathy on his face. "I just came to let you know we've cleared one of our vacant cabins for the two of you. New sheets on the beds."

Drew turned to see Isaac. Their eyes met, and she pierced his with a message that couldn't have been more clear: *I don't know if I can do this.*

"I really hope you'll join us for dinner," Blaine said. And then to Drew, "If your stomach will allow it."

Drew stood straighter, shoulders back, attempting to

collect herself. She regarded Blaine at last, who hadn't taken his eyes off her since his arrival. Glittering, soul-penetrating, aquamarine irises. His gaze contained a knowing humor, as if he were about to wink at any moment.

He said, "We've got a special treat this evening you won't want to miss."

5
THE LAKE

Not feeling up to further conversation with their mother at the moment, Drew—and subsequently Isaac with some reluctance—were escorted to their personal cabin so they could get settled and drop off their things before dinner. The cabin was nearly identical to their mother's. Four cots, with a large table in between where someone had neatly placed two flashlights for their convenience.

Drew chose the bed furthest from the front door, and Isaac chose the bed across from hers. They each placed their backpacks underneath their respective cots. After setting down her bag, Drew found Isaac watching her quietly.

"What?"

"Are you gonna be like this the whole time?" he asked.

"Like what? Upset? I'm honestly surprised you're not."

Isaac struggled to find the words. "I want to get to know her better, Drew. I didn't get as much time with her as a kid as you did. Whether she's a *good* mom or not..."

"She's not."

"Great. Fine. I didn't come here with a vendetta. Like you did, apparently. And who am I to judge? I'm not perfect, either."

Drew let out an exasperated breath. "No, neither of us are, you're right. But maybe we'd be a lot less fucked up if it wasn't for her. Maybe dad... maybe he wouldn't have..."

"You can't blame her for dad."

Drew paced toward the middle of the room, standing next to the big wooden table. "I'm not even sure she'd care if she knew. I wanted to tell her. I still do..."

"Don't," Isaac said. "At least... don't do it like I know you probably want to."

"And how's that?"

"Like an asshole."

"She should know what we went through."

"But it doesn't have to be about punishing her. None of this should be about punishment. It's about *closure*. That's why we came here, Drew. At least, that's why *I* came here..."

To this, Drew pursed her lips, biting the inside corner of her mouth with something she *wanted* to say but thought better of it. Isaac knew her well enough to interpret the expression, however.

"What?"

"I just don't buy into that stuff."

"What stuff?"

"*'Closure,'*" she said, with air quotes and all.

"What do you mean, you don't buy into—"

"It's a myth, Isaac. It's superstition. It can be whatever

you want it to be—anything you can convince yourself it is. And I already *had* it. When I thought mom was dead..."

"Well, she's not. So maybe now's your chance to get *real* closure."

Drew scoffed.

"Okay, if not that, make this about... I don't know... forgiveness? My therapist says it's *the* most powerful healing tool, and I think she's right. I think maybe if you *tried,* even just a little..."

"I'm not obligated to forgive anyone," Drew retorted. "I don't owe anyone forgiveness, least of all her."

"But what exactly does it help? Harboring all this *resentment*?"

Drew thought she might vomit again. Not *for real*, but her brother's rehearsed psychobabble was certainly getting her there. *Harboring,* she thought? *Give me a break...*

"I'm not expecting us to be some fairy-tale family at the end of this," Isaac said. "I didn't come here for that. I just want to know her. I want to understand her. That's it. You can try to understand someone without having to like them, you know."

Drew couldn't help thinking how lucky he was—too young to have felt the full brunt of their mother's abandonment, too young to fully understand the effect it had on their father. He didn't have to see any of *that*. Not like she did. He was spared those visions, those nightmares. *The ugliness.* He didn't truly know what ugly was. *Of course* forgiveness came easier when your memory wasn't stained so dark...

"I have to pee," she said finally with a sigh, and fled the argument altogether.

She stepped out into the warm evening light, before realizing she had no idea *where* people peed around these parts. The lake was a definite no go, despite her petty temptations.

Strolling toward it with her hands on her hips, she surveyed the shore in search of something else, an outhouse maybe, and as she peered from left to right, a passerby caught her attention. A young man coming her way. He looked up as he approached, and his handsome face—*unbearably handsome,* Drew thought—lit up at the sight of her. He waved. She smiled helplessly, aware of what she had to do.

"Excuse me. Can I ask you something?"

His features were dark, his eyes even darker as he studied her with the hint of a smile on his lips.

"You're Julianne's, yeah?" he said. Already privy to their existence, as every single resident of the commune likely was. "It's Drew, isn't it?"

She faltered, her mouth hanging open stupidly.

"Right," she said again.

He stuck out his hand and said, "It's nice to meet you. I'm Robert."

Drew took his hand, his grasp firm, his skin mildly rough, and couldn't help fixating on the flex of his bicep, or the number of visible veins bulging along the length of his forearms. They smiled at one another. One shake, two shakes, three...

"My bladder is about to explode," she blurted.

Robert quirked his jaw slightly, trying not to laugh.

"I take it you're lost," he said, and released her hand.

"I have no idea where you people go to the bathroom."

Now he *did* laugh. For the first time on this trip, Drew felt her own mouth grinning of its own accord.

"Here, I'll show you."

Bless his soul, he started off at a quick pace. Drew hurried behind him. He took her around the side of their cabin, toward the trees behind it. Then Drew slowed as he started *into* the trees.

"Is this your way of telling me that the forest is nature's restroom?"

Over his shoulder, Robert said, "No. We've got outhouses."

Drew's spirits lifted. She hurried to catch up, and noticed the narrow path Robert followed, a solid lane of trodden dirt between the forest's underbrush. She focused on him as he led the way, studying the manner in which his purchased-in-bulk sweats and t-shirt hung somehow perfectly on his slender body. As she studied these things, she was reminded of Quentin back home—another man whom she'd fancied similarly, once upon a time...

Forget it.

She forced all related thoughts aside. She peered beyond Robert, up the path which seemed to only be leading deeper and deeper into the trees, and suddenly felt another pang of wariness.

"Okay, where are we going?"

"Every cabin has its own outhouse," Robert said. "It's a bit of a walk, is all."

A *bit* of a walk. The farther they ventured, the more she became aware of Isaac's switchblade in her pocket.

"Why is it so far out?" she asked, already panting.

"To keep our living space clean," Robert said. He turned his head as he walked, making his profile visible to her as he said, "We consider the lake a sacred place."

Drew struggled not to roll her eyes. That unsavory word came to mind again: *cult*. Like Blaine, like Julianne, like Sherry, Robert was part of it as well, whatever '*it*' was. She was about to ask him what made the lake so sacred when she was instead distracted by something. Off to their right, where the forest rose steeply along a hillside, she spotted an opening near the incline's base, about ten meters or so from the path.

The dark entrance to a cave.

"Bold of you to put an outhouse near a bear's den," she said, half-jokingly.

Robert looked around confused. "Huh? Where?"

He stopped as Drew pointed toward it, through the trees.

"Oh." He peered toward it momentarily, eyes narrowed. "Doubt it's a bear's den. I've never seen one up here."

This was a mild reassurance, as Drew was already dreading having to make this trip in the middle of the night when her bladder would inevitably wake her like clockwork. She remembered the flashlights on the table in their cabin and suddenly realized what they were for: this insane outhouse jaunt.

"I think you're safe," Robert added, smiling, and continued ahead.

It was possibly thirty seconds later that they came to the outhouse in question. A tall, gray, wooden box with a slanted aluminum roof on top. Pretty drab in appearance.

"Well there you have it," Robert said.

"No crescent moon in the door?" Drew said. "What a letdown."

Robert offered her another friendly smile, before smacking his hands against his thighs—the sign of a job well done. "I'll leave you to it. Unless you need me to walk you back... to keep you safe from bears?"

"Funny. I think I'm good. Thank you."

Robert nodded politely and took his leave.

She stepped into the outhouse—as characterless inside as it was outside, sporting a simple wooden bench with a hole cut in the top, with a few rolls of toilet paper stacked in the corner—and briefly glimpsed Robert's figure disappearing into the trees as she shut the door.

She took a seat and relieved herself, listening to the surrounding sounds of nature as she did: branches rustling overhead, the whisper of things dodging about in the nearby underbrush.

It was only when she finished that she discovered the total absence of anything to wash with. No soap, no hand sanitizer.

Gross, she thought, and then murmured, "Whatever..."

She started back along the dirt path, and decided the first thing she'd do when she got back would be to grab the hand sanitizer she'd packed.

Do these people not wash their hands?

Now she was reminded of shaking Robert's hand, and was torn between cringing or giving him a pass for being so good looking.

As she thought about this, she glanced absentmindedly toward the cave again off the beaten path, its dark opening catching her attention from the corner of her eye... and skidded on her heels as she performed a double-take, coming to an abrupt stop.

Within the cave's dark entrance, there appeared the shape of something she hadn't noticed before.

Because it wasn't there before.

It was the shape of *someone*. A vague figure stood just inside, just deep enough to shed its features in the gloom. Blank as a silhouette. Stiff as a rock.

Because it is a rock.

She stood very still, as still as the figure erected in the cave's shadows. She could make it out—the shape of its legs, its arms at its sides, its dangling hands, its shoulders. Her breaths became shallow, watching as something watched her right back.

Something? You mean someone.

"Hello?" she said.

She was tempted to peer down the path, to see if she might spot Robert in the distance, but feared looking away, feared even blinking lest the figure be gone when she did. Could it have been Robert, she wondered? Playing some kind of joke? They weren't on those terms quite yet. And somehow, she sensed a distinct lack of comedic intent in this. She stared long and hard, studying the manner in which it did not change at all. It did not shift, nor fidget. Unmoving.

Because it's not alive. It's nothing. It's literally nothing.

As she continued to stare into the cave's darkness, and the evening light continued to drain rapidly from the orange-blue sky overhead, the forest around her grew blurry and dim, until the cave was nearly all she saw. The shadows of its entrance deepened, pulling in the light of everything else. Soon she *had* to blink, as her vision strained to make heads or tails of light and shadow, or the depths of the trees between the cave and the path she stood on. So she blinked. And she lost it—or rather, suddenly she wasn't sure if she'd ever *had it* to begin with.

What are you doing, crazy pants?

She asked herself this even as she watched for a moment longer, the cave's visible interior suddenly a wash of *nothing*. No shapes. No structure. Just the dark. She blinked some more, as if she might will the details back. Oddly she was already forgetting the shape. She struggled to remember where in that darkness she'd seen it, or if she'd seen it at all. A mirage.

It was enough to make you stop, she thought, resisting the allure of rationalization. Finally she shook her head. Doubtful.

"Whatever," she murmured again, and started back on quicker feet.

When she returned, she found Isaac outside speaking to the handsome Robert. Robert spotted her coming, then Isaac's gaze followed, and in an instant their conversation fell apart.

"I was just telling your brother dinner's probably about ready, if you're both joining," Robert said.

Drew took a moment to gauge her stomach's fortitude. Was she queasy, or was she hungry? Or was she neither?

"How does that work?" she asked. "In a place like this, I mean."

Robert turned and pointed toward a spot around the lake, where Drew only now noticed a construct that wasn't another identical cabin, but appeared to be some kind of pavilion. A square roof over a large arrangement of tables, where several figures now moved about, already getting started, apparently.

"We eat together most nights, taking turns in the kitchen. Usually soups and stews. You get used to it after a while. Look forward to it, even..."

"All from the stuff you guys grow in the garden?" Drew asked.

Robert shrugged sheepishly. "More or less. Kent buys things from town to make up the difference. You guys ready to head over?"

The clouds in the sky were positively *burning* now, the sun in its final death throes as it vanished below the jagged tree line on the horizon. As their little valley of lake and forest steeped in shadow, Drew made out the yellow heat of oil lamps hanging about the pavilion, as well as many of the cabins around the lake. Even at a distance, the voices of those gathered under the pavilion could be heard, their laughter and chatter.

Drew and Isaac were apparently the last arrivals. Robert led them toward the line at the pavilion's edge, where stew was being doled out from a big pot into ceramic bowls. They joined the end of the line. Drew and Isaac were the only bodies not clad in the same t-shirts and sweatpants and gym shorts as everyone else. Drew glanced nervously from face to face, catching the watchful eyes of those around them. Not every look was friendly, or even apathetic, and once more Drew was reminded: *we are not wanted here.*

"There you are!"

Their mother appeared, her sun-tanned face beaming with a tinge of apprehension as she looked from Isaac to Drew, trying to measure her daughter's disposition.

"I've saved you spots over there," she said, and pointed to one of the outer tables across the pavilion, where her unattended bowl of stew awaited her return. Taking a step back in its direction, she said, "Come sit with me when you've gotten your food."

As they reached the serving table, Drew and Isaac took bowls from the dwindling stack, the same cracked ceramic as all the others. Standing before the woman serving stew from the pot, Drew held her bowl out meekly. Ladle in hand, the woman held Drew's gaze with no avoidance whatsoever, or any attempt to hide her disdain, for that matter. Her dark eyes were black holes, swallowing up the galaxy of freckles which covered the upper half of her face and forehead.

"Jesus, Caroline," Robert said, catching this wordless exchange with his own eyes. "I hope the stew is warmer than your mood."

Without turning her head, Caroline's eyes flashed at Robert for an instant, followed by a dramatic eye-roll as she finally extended the ladle over Drew's bowl and dumped it in. Drew withdrew her bowl with just the one ladleful, content with the small amount, and not to be standing in line freezing to death under Caroline's scrutiny any longer. She moved out of the way, then waited for Isaac before they both skirted around the pavilion toward the table where their mother was seated.

"How's your stomach?" Julianne asked as Drew took her seat.

"Better." She looked once over her shoulder toward the serving table again, where she met Caroline's hawk-eyed stare, still watching with the intensity of a calculating assassin. With a sigh, Drew said, "Real friendly community you've got here..."

"Oh? Why do you say that?"

"She's joking," Isaac answered, like he had any idea.

Julianne watched Drew anyway.

"Okay. Well. I don't know how we're feeling," she said. "Did we want to pick up where we left off?"

After a moment's consideration—curious if her body might betray her again with a belly full of stew—Drew answered, "No, that's all right. We can talk about something else. Anything else..."

"You should start," Isaac told their mother, squirming in his seat. "Tell us about... *everything*. You said you've been all over the place? I want stories."

Julianne laughed timidly, surprised by his eager interest. In a way it was good that Isaac and Drew were on opposite ends of that spectrum—Isaac desperate to learn everything he could, Drew desperate to *burn* everything she could. Her desire not to disappoint her brother too severely kept her in check. For now, at least. So as Julianne began delivering a timeline of her life post-motherhood, Drew merely pushed her stew around in her bowl and listened.

"Well, hmm... Let's see. I guess I'll start at the beginning. When I first left..."

Abandoned us, Drew mentally corrected.

"...I found myself on a bus to nowhere. No plan, really. It was probably the scariest thing I'd ever done in my life..."

Drew would later reflect on how bizarre it was, that after all these years of wondering, she struggled to pay attention to their mother's tale. She zoned out completely. She felt miles away—perhaps a symptom of trying so hard to resist negative impulses. Either she blurted out the next resentful thing that came to mind, or tuned their mother out entirely and remained quiet for Isaac's sake. He wanted to listen, so *let him listen,* she thought.

She felt the others' eyes upon her back. Strangers with bitter impulses of their own. As their mother dived into her exciting history, Drew stole casual glances around them, and more than once looked into the eyes of those watching. They diverted their gazes as soon as she noticed, their mouths mumbling as they spoke amongst themselves.

She peered beyond the pavilion, toward the darkening forest, and noticed the fleeting glints of fireflies at the forest's edge—bright, lemon-yellow bodies swelling and fading, swelling and fading. Numerous and glimmering.

"...where I met the kindest couple of men you could ever hope to meet. These two men were... *together,* you know. It was the first time I'd ever met... you know, *gay men,* before..."

Their mother laughed softly, quite tickled by her own tale, and Drew couldn't help being absorbed back into the conversation for a moment. She looked at Isaac, a fascinated smile glued to his face, and noticed how his eyes twitched ever so slightly as he sensed her watching, refusing to give her the satisfaction of acknowledgment—of acknowledging the irony in this moment. Their mother believed meeting a gay couple was a novel part of her adventure, and yet little did she know...

"They helped me find a job. Just cleaning their offices a couple times a week, was all, but it was something. They paid me under the table in cash, and even helped me find a place of my own for a little while, until I could get back on my feet..."

Drew zoned out again. She allowed her eyes to wander, until she once more met those of another seated nearby. Robert. He was seated with three other men, talking amicably. He smiled warmly, a hint of mischief in those dark eyes of his. Now it was Drew who looked away.

"...and soon after that I joined the volunteer group. It was something to do with political awareness. I can't remember exactly. I never got too invested in the cause. I was more just finding something to take up my time, really. And that was where I met Nicholas. He was... well, unlike any man I'd ever met..."

Even in small doses, Drew felt her pulse quickening. She looked at Isaac, and thought his cheeks must have been terribly sore, holding that phony grin for so long. She regarded their mother without hearing a word, watched as her eyes grew wide with self-interest, as enamored with her own story as her doting son pretended to be.

She peered beyond Julianne, toward the darkening sky, twilight fading into night. She looked to the kerosene lamp hanging nearby, where a myriad of moths were gathered around its light, their dusty wings flickering, bodies drawn in and out, in and out from the lamp's heated glass, attempting courtship with the flame inside...

As she watched this deadly tango, her mother's voice sank its teeth into her again. A word jumped out from all the rest, like a crocodile from the edge of a bayou.

Love.

Somewhere in the midst of describing this man unlike all the other men she'd ever met, this *'Nicholas,'* their mother spoke of love, and it was then Drew couldn't take much more.

"So how'd you end up here?" she asked suddenly, barging her way into her mother's story like a wrecking ball— anything to put a stop to her tale of finding love with a man named Nicholas, who was not their father, who at this point in Julianne's story was probably already dead and she had no idea.

Julianne faltered, her lips still forming the next word she'd been about to speak before Drew's interruption.

"Oh. Well..." Julianne thought about it. "That was just a little over a year ago. I was..." She paused again, lips pursed. "I was down on my luck. I happened to be in Murphy... where you and Isaac were picked up, I think. Isn't that right?"

"Yeah, Murphy," Isaac answered.

"That's where Blaine found me. I was homeless then. Relying on the kindness of strangers..."

Sounds like things didn't work out with dear sweet Nicholas, Drew thought bitterly.

"Found her in Fields of the Wood," Blaine announced, startling Drew as he was suddenly standing right behind her, listening for who knew how long. "That's the religious park there in Murphy. She was standing at the bottom of the Ten Commandments Mountain. I'd never seen someone looking so lost as she did..."

"It was like a sign," Julianne said, grinning now as she admired Blaine in the warm light of the kerosene lamps.

"I could tell your mother wasn't from around here, and I remember asking, 'what brings you to Murphy?' and she answered..."

"'Looking for God, I guess,'" Julianne finished, and together they shared a laugh that threatened to make Drew sick all over again.

"And the rest is history," Blaine said. His icicle eyes held the glow of the lamplight, turning them almost yellow like a cat's eyes. "I don't mean to interrupt. I just wanted to say, when you're all finished, you should come join me on the dock."

And with that, Blaine took his leave.

"What's on the dock?" Isaac asked.

Julianne smirked with just the corner of her mouth, and said, "You'll see."

Blaine was waiting for them, but he wasn't alone. Under the darkening sky, as stars began to twinkle to life over their heads, they made their way from the pavilion toward the large dock, where Drew spotted a second dark figure standing beside Blaine. This figure looked over its shoulder as they approached, clomping across the wooden planks to meet them. It was Kent. He turned back to Blaine and said something more, a secretive whisper, and then proceeded to make his exit, passing them as they came. Drew exchanged a glance with the man. He looked away skittishly, giving Drew the impression he'd been discussing something rather sensitive with Blaine prior to their arrival.

Like I care about your secrets, Drew thought, lying to herself.

Near the end of the dock, Blaine gestured for Drew and Isaac to move ahead of himself, standing nearer to the edge. Drew warily obliged, though suddenly her morbid mind imagined being pushed into the murky water under their feet...

And then what?

She peered down into that murky water. The lake was incredibly still. Not a ripple. The stars were reflected there, growing brighter by the second. She peered farther out, toward the lake's center, and noticed what appeared to be an eerie fog wafting out there over the water's surface.

No, not fog, Drew thought. *It's steam.*

She remembered the warmth of the water earlier, when she'd mistakenly stepped into its shallows. Like a hot bath. She peered around the rest of the lake's perimeter, and noticed a distinct lack of steam anywhere else.

"What are we watching for?" Isaac asked softly, breaking the silence.

"You'll see soon enough," Blaine whispered.

The western horizon bore the faintest remnants of daylight—the deep blue darkness the slightest shade lighter there, diminishing quickly.

Across the lake were a handful of warm spots of light where other residents had lit lanterns outside their cabins. Drew saw their figures moving vaguely as they returned along the shore. She looked once over her shoulder, to see if anyone else was joining them on the dock, but found only her mother and Blaine, who regarded her expectantly, urging her to focus her attention on the lake. She faced forward again, but their eyes remained, like an incredible pressure against her back. For now the lake remained unchanged, and she couldn't begin to predict what it was they waited for...

No. Wait a minute. There's something...

The steam on the water's surface. It was spreading, she realized. She watched as that ghostly vapor expanded from the center of the lake, a gentle white aura rising from the murk. In less than a minute the steam reached them, creeping noiselessly beneath the dock and to the shore. Drew believed she even felt its humid warmth against her in a wave. Like stepping into a sauna...

"What's happening?" Isaac said.

"Watch," Blaine told them.

Drew could feel her pulse through every limb, her every finger. The sensation of rocking on her heels, heart hammering violently in wait. She became even more acutely aware of Julianne and Blaine standing behind them, delighting in their confusion. She stole a glance at Isaac, his eyes pinched, brow set firmly with suspense, until suddenly his gaze widened, lips parted, and Drew turned ahead once more to see for herself.

"There," Julianne said.

Distantly, in the heart of the lake, a bright amber glow

touched the water's surface. It tangled in the steam like fire, a single headlight shining through a morning mist. An unsettling sensation formed in the pit of Drew's stomach at the sight of it. Off balance.

"Do you see it?" Julianne asked.

It was impossible *not* to see, and yet Drew couldn't say what she saw, exactly. Then the light abruptly throbbed, lurching outward in a violent manner, doubling in size. There was something disturbingly *alive* in the movement, in the opening bloom. It paused there, a honeycomb-colored oil spill in the lake's center, the illuminated steam appearing like a phosphorescent platform. But it was only light, as far as Drew could tell...

"It reveals itself at night," Blaine murmured at their backs. "But its energy can be felt at any time. Perhaps you've already felt it..."

Drew didn't know what she was feeling. A ratcheting nervousness for something yet to come—a thread pulled taut, about to snap. A lurking danger. She couldn't pinpoint where her anxiety stemmed. The two strangers standing behind her certainly didn't help. Strangest of all, when she turned to him, she found her brother nearly grinning with glee.

"Incredible," he said. "What is it?"

Leaning in between them, their mother replied, "The spirit of the lake."

"That is our Mother," Blaine added tenderly. "...and we are her children."

PART TWO

THE FOREST

6

THE STALKER

In the near pitch-black of his apartment, Quentin's face hung suspended like a bodiless mask, illuminated in the blue light of his phone as he monitored the GPS device in the trunk of Drew's car.

It'd been stationary for some time now, pinging his phone on occasion with its location some hundred-and-twenty miles away.

A two and a half hour drive, he thought.

He bit the nail of his thumb, staring at the little GPS blip, contemplating his next move.

Was it as he suspected? Was she seeing someone else? Someone in North fucking Carolina? After four months together, she found someone she liked better and decided to shed him like a pathetic snake-skin afterthought?

Because that's what she is. A fucking snake.

He repeated their earlier encounter over and over in his mind. He could hardly think of anything else. Every waking minute, it looped uncontrollably like a compulsive night-mare. He could hear her even now—so snide and dismissive.

"You can stop blowing up my phone, because I'm not answering..."

He clenched his jaw, creating dark hollows in his cheeks in the cold light of his phone. He had to know. He *needed* to know. He wouldn't rest until he did, and that wasn't his fault. It was hers. Toying with him like he meant nothing to her. She was cruel. Sadistic. Practically a sociopath, he thought. Barely human.

He sprang to his feet in the dark, and like a tornado gathering loose debris he gathered up his wallet, his keys, his shoes, and stormed out the door.

He could turn those two and a half hours into two, easy.

He paid closer attention upon arriving in Murphy, following directions off his phone as he navigated the small town in the dead of night. Wherever Drew's car was parked, it was some-where with enough traffic that Quentin's GPS device was pinged regularly on the network by the phones of passersby. As he closed the distance between them, peering up the road toward his destination, it made a lot of sense.

Drew's car was parked in a convenience store parking lot. At this hour, it was the only car present. Quentin parked near the store's entrance. He eyed the vehicle at the edge of the lot, dark and empty, and racked his brain for possibilities on where she might be.

With the 'other man' of course. I don't know...

Why she would leave her car like this to meet someone, Quentin couldn't decide. It also occurred to him that she'd only just picked her car up from the mechanic. Was it possible she'd broken down again? But if that were the case, why hadn't it been towed already? And where could she have gone? Where was she going in the first place? What alternative transportation had she taken?

"You didn't break down here," he murmured aloud, sitting in the shadows of his own vehicle.

After some further contemplation, he entered the convenience store and purchased some water, some peanut butter crackers, and a little container of dental floss. The clerk was just a kid, or looked like one at least. It explained the lack of any other cars in the lot outside, Quentin thought, as he'd probably walked himself to work.

"You know something about that car?" the kid asked, noticing as Quentin stole frequent glances through the front window towards it.

Quentin hesitated. "No. Do you?"

The kid regarded Quentin with a half-lidded, unimpressed stare. Then he shrugged. "My boss told me to keep an eye on it, is all."

Quentin scrunched his lip, trying to appear oblivious. "Interesting…" He looked over his shoulder again, eyeing the car for himself like he wasn't already totally familiar. "What's so special about it?"

The kid simply stared at Quentin, his expression a little too stoic for someone his age, Quentin thought.

"Do you want a bag?" he asked, ignoring the question altogether.

When Quentin answered that he did *not* need a bag, the kid pushed his items across the counter toward him, watching him with those same, empty-yet-penetrating eyes. "Have a good night."

"Yeah," Quentin said, taking his things. "You, too."

In an attempt not to look suspicious, Quentin departed the corner store entirely, and took a short, looping drive around the little town of Murphy before returning, this time parking across the street at one of the neighboring establishments which was now closed for the night. He killed the engine, turned off his lights, and watched.

Every now and then he glimpsed the night attendant passing the windows, restocking shelves or simply strolling between the aisles with his arms stretched over his head, killing time. Eventually another car pulled into the lot, spurring Quentin's interest for a moment until he saw two women climb out. They were in and out in a matter of minutes, then gone. Drew's car continued to sit, abandoned.

When Quentin finished his package of crackers, and brushed the crumbs from his lap, he gulped down half his water bottle, and then proceeded to open his container of dental floss. He watched the sleepy street before him with waning interest. Increasing embarrassment.

Am I a complete moron for sitting here all night watching an empty convenience store parking lot? Am I wasting my time? There's no way to know where she went, where she is...

He was only beginning to floss around his third tooth when another vehicle entered the parking lot.

A rattling pickup truck with an attached tow dolly. It swung in rather hurriedly, pulled along the edge of the parking lot near the street, and parked. A man climbed out. Some long-haired, backwoods hick, Quentin thought. He paused his flossing and watched as the man crossed the shadowy parking lot toward Drew's car. Along the way, the man pulled something from his pocket. A second ring of keys, winking in the scant light. *Drew's keys,* Quentin realized, as the man proceeded to unlock her car and climb behind the wheel.

"What the fuck…"

He leaned forward in his seat, watching closely. Drew's car started up, brake lights flashing. The man pulled her car out from its parking spot and performed a three-point turn, repositioning her vehicle behind his own.

"What the fuck," Quentin repeated.

He watched for several minutes as the stranger rigged Drew's car onto the dolly. Even the store attendant came to watch, standing curiously at the window.

Had her car broken down after all, Quentin wondered? Where was she now? Whoever this man was, he had her keys. His shitty pickup bore no company logo, nothing to suggest he was hired for a tow job.

Eventually the stranger departed with Drew's car in his possession. Quentin started his engine once more and followed.

Careful, he told himself.

He lagged deliberately, hoping to keep enough distance

so as not to draw attention to himself. Slowly, steadily, he followed the two vehicles through town, from one warm pool of streetlight to the next, getting farther and fewer in between, until he soon found himself trailing along dark backroads. The longer this went on, the more confident Quentin became that he wasn't heading toward any auto shop—and the less confident he became that he could comfortably follow without making his intentions obvious.

Shit.

Idling at a three-way stop, with nary a streetlight to illuminate it, Quentin watched as the truck's taillights faded into the distance, into the deep woods outside the town limits. Into the hills beyond...

Maybe she sold the fucking thing, he thought. *Fixed it up and sold it to some guy in the back country who's just gonna strip it for parts in his scrapyard out in the middle of nowhere.*

For all he knew, the road ahead led to the man's private property. Drew was already back in Atlanta. She'd been there all day because the car no longer belonged to her and Quentin was literally driving himself crazy on a fucking goose chase.

He tapped his fingers on the steering wheel.

Or maybe I'm being chicken shit and making excuses.

He turned off his headlights. The three-way stop fell into shadow. He made the turn, onto the lonesome road into the woods, steadily following in the singular direction the stranger with Drew's car had headed. He drove slowly, hunched over the steering wheel, wary of anything that might jump into the road, or of losing track of the road in the darkness as it twisted and climbed into the hills. He peered briefly into the darkness ahead, searching for the truck's lights to appear again. The road seemed to go on and on.

Where the fuck is this taking me?

And then he saw them. Taillights, headlights. They weren't moving. Slowly but surely, as Quentin followed the road closer and closer to the lights in the distance—winking and strobing between the silhouetted pillars of trees—eventually he craned his neck to see them, as the road continued past the place where the truck had apparently pulled off.

"What the hell..."

Quentin slowed. Somehow he'd missed a turnoff. He hadn't a clue where this road was truly headed, but it didn't appear they were headed there anyway. The truck had pulled off into the trees, out into the woods themselves. Quentin rolled a little farther before he parked. He shifted in his seat, casting his daggered eyes through the rear passenger window where he could still make out the truck's headlights cutting blunt swaths of yellow into the forest.

He shut off the engine. He undid his seatbelt and took a deep breath. His mind was racing now, with ideas both rational and irrational. His previous assumptions about Drew's duplicity were out the window, so to speak. Along with the idea that she'd simply sold her vehicle to this man, who appeared to be towing said vehicle *someplace it would never be found again*—

Knuckles rapped hard against Quentin's window and he screamed—felt his entire soul leave his body briefly before snapping back into place like a bungee cord.

"Shit..."

A figure stood in the road. A shadow. It bent slightly,

revealing its face through the glass. Quentin was met with the visage of a man not nearly as backwoods as he'd expected. Dark, shoulder-length hair and a handsomely groomed beard. The man smiled in a friendly manner. Then he motioned with his hand to roll down the window.

Quentin's heart was beating in his throat. There still existed a part of his better judgement that told him to hightail it the hell out of there, but the pressure of politeness won out. He clicked the button on his door, and the window hummed down steadily, letting in the cool, woodsy air.

"Hiya," the stranger said, still smiling warmly—a smile which Quentin only now noticed didn't reach his eyes. "You know, I don't see too many BMWs on these roads. You lost?"

Quentin laughed, feigning embarrassment. It wasn't too difficult, considering he *was* rather embarrassed for being caught. He was also glad for the darkness, or else his face would be revealed for the reddened tomato that it was. He nodded yes, that he was indeed lost, and said—

The fist came in a blur of motion. A soft grunt from the man's lips as his knuckles struck Quentin squarely in the nose. Cartilage crunched. Blood gushed with brutal immediacy, cascading down Quentin's lips. He recoiled. His mind blanked with panic. A rustle of arms and clothes as the man reached through his open window. In a matter of seconds— two, three?—Quentin was wrangled into the man's grasp, a muscular bicep around his throat, jerking him around in his seat and against the door, pulling, tightening, trapping the blood in his pounding skull as he kicked and wriggled like a stupid fish. The stranger didn't stop there. With his arm locked tight around Quentin's throat, he dragged him clean through the open window. Quentin's kicking feet scrambled against the window's edge, until he dropped onto the road. Through all of this, the headlock remained solid, firm. The dark of the woods pulsed darker in his vision. Constricting. The soles of his shoes scuffed the pavement, then scratched, then rubbed gently as the strength went out of him, and the man crouched with his deflating body down to the ground. He tasted the coppery blood in his mouth, still streaming from his broken nose as his vision continued to fade.

Fading, fading...

Gone.

7
THE VOICES

She slept with Isaac's switchblade tucked into her fist, her fist tucked under her pillow. Or rather... she lay awake restlessly with Isaac's switchblade tucked into her fist, her fist tucked under her pillow...

She always slept terribly in such quiet places. Hearing one's own rustling, one's own breathing—let alone the rustling and breathing of another body in the room with you, in the bed opposite yours. Isaac was sleeping just fine, by the sound of it. Drew would have no such luck tonight.

But of course it wasn't just the silence.

There had been so much she'd wanted to say when they'd returned to their cabin. About this place, about Blaine, about their mother, about the lake and its 'strange' phenomenon. The only problem was that she had nothing *good* to say about these things, nothing at all, and she knew Isaac wouldn't want to hear any of it. He was all in. Somehow. It was possibly the most disappointing revelation so far—that her brother was as gullible as the rest of them. As gullible as their mother was, apparently…

He knows better than this. I know he does.

He believed because their mother believed. It was something to bond over. Something to share.

Drew tossed and turned herself into exhaustion, until finally her mind succumbed to something besides paranoia. Then, just as she began drifting off…

Something was scratching. Little claws against the wall behind her head. She opened her eyes in the dark and listened, caught in a momentary confusion. Then it registered, the scratching, and her body tensed, rigid with disgust, with horror, and she bolted upright. She slipped out of bed entirely. She tiptoed hurriedly to the table in the center of the room where they had been provided flashlights. She grabbed one. She returned to her bed, flipped the flashlight's switch, and shined its beam into the messy folds of her blanket. She got down on the ground, aimed the light underneath, toward the place where the wall and floor met, the dust there catching the light in its ancient clumps, where nothing had disturbed it in years, least of all a broom. Least of all a scurrying rat, or whatever it was she'd heard…

Drew rocked back on her knees, resting on her toes, positive she'd heard something scratching beneath her bed. Of course, in the time it took to retrieve the flashlight, whatever it was could have easily scampered into the nearest hiding place. She sighed heavily, the light still pouring out from her hands.

"I hate this place…" she whispered. She eyed her brother's bed across from her own, where his body lay completely still.

If she listened very carefully, his breath emitted in gentle, rhythmic puffs.

Now she was more awake than ever, naturally her bladder announced its need for relief.

Oh great, she thought.

She sat on her bed and put on her shoes. She'd changed into pajama shorts for bed, which would have gone perfectly with the general dress of this place, day or night.

She hesitated at the cabin door, looking once more to her brother sleeping soundly, hidden beneath his blanket, just a tuft of jet-black hair visible above its edge. Then she proceeded outside.

The air was cool but not chilly. She closed the door behind herself, then simply stood for a moment, refreshed by the night air, the scent of the surrounding woods, the sound of the insects. The commune was almost entirely dark, as she drew her gaze around the lake's perimeter, every cabin muted under the starry sky. All except one, which she already recognized as Blaine's. His cabin was alight with a single lantern hanging on the front porch.

Flashlight in hand, she started toward the trees, toward the hidden path there. She aimed her light ahead, dousing the cleared dirt with a warm white beam.

She still thought it rather ridiculous, the distance to their outhouse. Had the *'spirit of the lake'* personally requested they keep their bodily fluids as far from the water as possible?

So the lake gets really warm. Warm enough to create steam in the summer evenings. And a light appears, which no one is allowed to investigate because entering the lake is sacrilege.

It was all too convenient, Drew thought.

Before she could probe these thoughts much deeper, she arrived at the outhouse, a sliver of moonlight along its aluminum roof. She stepped inside, latched the door behind her, and relieved herself as quickly as her full bladder would allow. The forest chirped with insects. She aimed the beam of her flashlight around the outhouse's interior, up into the corners where there existed gaps between the walls and the angled, metal sheet of roofing. Anything and everything could climb inside. Spiders, rats...

Something down in the very hole you're sitting on...

She stood the very moment she finished, pulling her shorts up just as fast. She removed herself with an eager spring in her step, practically bolting onto the dirt path outside, flashlight beam swaying into the trees ahead.

One more day, she thought. Perhaps not even that. Half a day? Could she convince Isaac to leave by tomorrow afternoon?

I couldn't get time off of work, she would tell him. *This weekend was it. Gotta get home...*

This was a lie. She'd already asked for a couple days off, which her boss approved no questions asked. Only she hadn't requested it for the trip, but rather to *recover* from said trip. There was no chance in hell she would be able to return to work Monday morning fully functioning. No chance whatsoever.

"You..."

Moving swiftly along the wooded path, a nearby sound stopped Drew dead in her tracks. She jerked the flashlight toward the trees which threw their huge shadows onto those behind them, creating movement where there was none. She held her breath, shoulders hunched toward her ears, pulse racing. She swept her flashlight beam, catching nothing in its light but leafy underbrush and tree bark and—

No, no, no...

She found herself standing parallel to that dark opening in the base of the nearby slope. The cave. The bear's den. Except there were no bears in the area, according to Robert. None that he'd seen personally, anyway.

And then the sound repeated.

"You."

A chill crept up the backs of Drew's arms, up the back of her neck and scalp. She trained the flashlight on the cave's entrance, where she was sure the voice had called from. Because it *had* called. To her. An unnatural cadence—the echo of a rocky chamber. She pointed her light directly into the cave's darkness but did little to dissolve it. What her flashlight *did* reveal was lonesome. Vacant. No figures waiting in the shadows this time.

"Hello?" she replied. The forest gobbled up her voice. The halo of her flashlight beam wobbled around the cave's entrance, her hand trembling. Keeping it there, she peered farther along the path, searching the darkness ahead for movement. Eavesdroppers, perhaps—spectators of the prank in progress.

"Hello."

She snapped her gaze to the cave again. It was soft, muted, distant, but clear enough to decipher. Someone there. Someone inside, standing out of sight. An attempt to scare her. She thought back to the figure she believed she'd seen earlier in the day, its form indistinct but *there* all the same, until it wasn't. If this *was* a prank, her pranksters were dedicated.

"Do you see us?"

This latest voice was *not* in the cave. It was in the open, spoken someplace between the path and the hillside ahead, in the trees. She flicked the flashlight left and right, searching for it. For a face. Nothing. No one.

"Who's there?" she asked, and *Holy Mother of God* did she hate the sound of her own voice in that moment—her throat gripped tight by the invisible hand of fear. She spoke again, this time practicing a false show of self-assurance. "Come out."

Her words lingered in the air like dust motes, calling attention to the utter lack of noise in the forest otherwise. No insects. No rustling branches or leaves. The kind of silence she loathed. Her own undulating breath and nothing more. And then—

"We see you."

She fled full-sprint back to the cabin. A mindless, autopilot dash through the woods, through the dark, her flashlight in her grip but forgotten, its beam slashing violently from the ground at her feet into the trees with each pump of her arms, her legs, sneakers kicking dirt until she arrived at the cabin at last, the open lake something of a relief —where nothing could hide except for beneath the surface.

She came to a stop near their cabin's front door, sucking air, a hummingbird heart in her chest. "I hate this place..."

She stood for a time, catching her breath. And as she did, something else caught her attention in the distance.

Across the lake, bright lights shone. Headlights, more

specifically, swinging into view from the woods. Kent's truck arrived beside Blaine's cabin. It parked there, its headlights left on, beaming brightly in her direction, bright enough that even at such a distance they made a mess of the surrounding shadows in her vision. She spotted Blaine emerging from his cabin, coming to meet Kent near the rear of the truck, where they both vanished beyond its high beams.

She took one final deep breath for good measure and headed back inside. She closed the door gently behind her.

"Where did you go?" Isaac rasped tiredly, sitting up in his cot.

Her racing heart had settled down. Her fearful thoughts had since relaxed, becoming something else—distrustful, irritated, impatient.

"These people are trying to fuck with me," she said, ignoring Isaac's question altogether.

"Huh? What happened?"

She told him. About her trip to the outhouse, about the voices in the woods. She told him, too, about the figure she believed she'd seen earlier in the day, in the cave. Now that she was back inside, relaying these events to someone else, it didn't seem so implausible after all that someone had followed her out there twice to play their pranks. There were more than twenty members of this community, and a fair amount of them did not want them here.

"Why would they want to scare you?" Isaac asked.

"Did you not see the looks they gave us at dinner? Or all day long, for that matter..."

"Just Caroline, or whatever her name is."

"We're not wanted here," she said plainly, and returned

to her own bed, its springs creaking shrilly as she climbed beneath her covers. She lay her head back onto her pillow, and wiggled around to get comfortable.

"Mom wants us here," Isaac said, his voice quiet and restful across the cabin's darkness.

Drew tried to bite her tongue. But so much of what she'd wanted to say before came burbling up now, like a serious case of acid reflux.

"And why do you think that is? Because I've been wondering all evening and I can't figure it out..."

"Maybe you should use your words and ask her yourself."

Drew lifted her head, peering at her brother's shape under his own covers. She could hardly see him, not his face at least, but she detected the smug, know-it-all tone of his voice perfectly well.

"I think she and Blaine want us to join their little cult," she said. "And I think you're biting hook, line, and sinker."

"It's not a cult," Isaac snapped. The indignation in his voice told Drew everything she needed to know.

"What else do you call a group of people out in the middle of the woods worshiping some kind of lake god?"

"No one said it was a god..."

"So you believe it, then? You think there's some kind of forest spirit living in the lake?"

"I didn't say that, either." Isaac huffed wearily. "All I know is, I saw what I saw. You saw it, too."

"It could've been anything," Drew said. She tried to soften her voice, sensing that her brother was reaching his limit. "Maybe it's some kind of algae we don't know about. Or maybe Blaine rigged up a light fixture under the lake for the sole purpose of fooling rubes like mom into joining his cult...”

“Mom’s not a rube. And it was more than just a light. You saw the fog move across the water like it did. How could Blaine manage that?” He grew quiet. Drew could picture his eyes rolled up in annoyance, lips pressed firmly as he bristled with frustration. “You know... this doesn’t have to be nearly as painful as you’re making it. Why can’t you just give it a chance? You don’t give *anything* a chance...”

“What is that supposed to mean?”

“This is stupid,” Isaac said. He rolled onto his side, showing her nothing but the shadow of his back. “I’m going back to sleep.”

Drew opened her mouth but hesitated. She stared at her brother, knowing perfectly well he was in no state of mind to sleep—not any more than she was, anyway. They would lay awake in mutual vexation for hours to come. The deep silence returned between them, but it was altogether different.

What exactly did he mean, Drew wondered? Give what a chance? These people? This place? Or had he simply meant their mother? She hoped it was only the latter.

Because she had no intention of giving these people anything at all.

8

THE CAPTIVE

He woke once as he was being restrained. Thin but durable twine around his wrists, his ankles, knotted tightly enough to bite. As he came to, lying flat on his stomach in the dirt, listening to the scuffing movement beside him, he began fidgeting. The man promptly straddled him, sitting atop his back, and slipped his arm around Quentin's throat once again. The pressure built up all over again. Head throbbing like a blood bag about to burst.

Then the darkness returned.

Next he woke to the pungent scent of gasoline, intermixed with the distinct scent of his own blood in his nostrils. A cool breeze touched his face. He *tasted* gasoline. Possibly from the dirty rag that was stuffed into his mouth, with another tied around the back of his head to keep him from spitting out the first. The ground wobbled and bumped. He opened his eyes, and the first thing he saw were the tree branches overhead, moving steadily past, a black night sky visible through their crisscrossing web. His hands were bound tightly with twine behind his back. His ankles were bound similarly.

The pickup truck revved slightly as it climbed a steady slope, and Quentin felt gravity's pull upon him, inching toward the truck bed's gate. Then something struck the top of his head and he winced. A sliding gas can—its contents jostling wetly inside. There were two of them. Two gas cans. And something more in the truck bed, resting beside his feet. *Tied* to his feet, actually, with the twine around his ankles. He lifted his head slightly to see it. A chunky cinder block. Probably to keep him from rolling himself out over the edge...

The last thing he remembered was being punched in the nose. Still hurt. His whole face seemed to ache. He still tasted his blood, mildly, against the sharp, heated taste of the gas rag stuffed atop his tongue. He breathed entirely through his nose, which stung going in or out, and whistled slightly as his nasal cavities were halfway plugged with clotted blood.

What the fuck had he gotten himself into?

He imagined the worst. *Deliverance* shit. Maybe he'd find Drew after all, strung up in the woods, barely alive. He should have left it alone. All of it. He should have left *her* alone. Nothing but trouble. Once again he was reminded of her remarks in the mechanic's parking lot.

"Consider this a bullet dodged."

He'd dodged the bullet, sure—and then grabbed the barrel of the gun and put it to his own temple. Of course, he never could have known this would happen. Or *could* happen. But he should have, shouldn't he? It happened all the time, didn't it? They made countless documentaries about it these days. *True Crime.* An entertainment phenomenon.

I just never thought it could happen to me.

Soon the road evened out. The truck rattled less. Part of him wished the journey would never end, that they'd never reach their destination, wherever it was. That'd they'd never reach his *fate.* He didn't want to think about that. He needed to think on something else, anything else, as difficult as it was when his mouth was gagged, his limbs were bound, and the branches above were spelling out his doom with their elegant, skeletal fingers upon the stars...

How the hell do I get out of this?

Just as he began to wonder, the truck began to slow. The trees overhead thinned, fell behind, the night sky showing in full as they arrived in some kind of clearing. The truck came to a stop. Quentin held his gasoline-soaked breath as the driver stepped out. Footsteps in the dirt. He fidgeted painfully where he lay, shoulders aching. The driver appeared, passing along the side of the truck bed. The same bearded man as before, naturally.

"Wakey, wakey..." he joylessly droned.

He unlatched the gate near Quentin's feet, pulled it down. He undid whatever knot tied Quentin to the cinder block. Shoving the cinder block aside, he seized Quentin by his bound ankles and proceeded to drag him ruthlessly across the truck bed, dragged him clean out of it, dropping him onto the hard dirt with a lung-squashing *whoomp*. Quentin wheezed. His sore back cried out dully. His head rang off the hard dirt, stunning him momentarily.

They were parked next to a simple cabin. An oil lamp hung from its porch. The front door opened and another man emerged, whose fiery hair caught sleekly in the glow of the lamplight. He approached them—Quentin and the driver—with his hands tucked into the pockets of his sweatpants, brow furrowed, looking quizzically upon Quentin without the shock or concern Quentin might have hoped for.

"What's this?"

He came to stand over Quentin, silhouetted.

"Followed me out of Murphy," the driver said. "No idea who he is."

Quentin tried to speak, but his tongue wagged uselessly against the soiled cloth in his mouth. The men standing over him seemed to pause, but failed to acknowledge him in any meaningful sense.

"Let's get him inside."

Quentin moaned pathetically as the driver grabbed him beneath each of his arms, pinching at the pits, and hauled him toward the nearby cabin. His bound feet whispered across the dirt. The red-haired man made no attempt to help, but simply paced along behind them, watching Quentin with no expression as he was hastily dragged across the cabin's threshold, across the bare wooden floor inside, and dumped like a sack of potatoes beside the table there. The other man shut the front door behind them.

OUR MOTHER IN THE LAKE

"You haven't spoken to him?" he asked the driver.

"Only to say hello," the driver said. "Thought he was being *real* clever following me with his lights off."

The duo fell silent for a short time, plainly observing him from head to toe, each of their gazes lingering on his own, though Quentin felt nothing in the exchange. No wariness on their part. No caution. They were not afraid of him in the slightest, or what repercussions might come of his kidnapping. Then the red-haired man crouched and, hooking a finger through the cloth tied around his head, pulled it free of his mouth and yanked it under his chin. Then he grasped the second cloth—the one stuffed deep into Quentin's throat —and pulled it free likewise. Quentin gasped with the influx of air into his gasoline-flavored mouth.

"Please," he said, panting. "I don't know what's going on. I just—"

"Why were you following my friend here?"

"I wasn't! I mean... I didn't know who... I didn't know..."

The driver pulled something from his pocket, which Quentin instantly recognized as his confiscated phone. The driver crouched on Quentin's other side. He pushed Quentin, nudging his body to gain access to his hands tied behind his back. Instinctively Quentin folded his fingers into fists.

"Give me your finger or I'll break it," the driver said emotionlessly.

Quentin did as he was told. The man took hold of his index, touched its fleshy pad to his phone's screen. The phone responded with its familiar vibration. Unlocked.

While the driver searched his phone, the other man simply watched Quentin, his crystal blue eyes wandering over his bloodied face pressed to the floor.

"Well, would you look at that," the driver said. He held Quentin's phone so the other man could see it. "How much more trouble are these two gonna bring us?"

The red-haired man took the phone into his own hands, scrolling silently.

"A rather one-sided conversation," he murmured. "Seems our guy's been left out in the cold, so to speak. Nothing to be too concerned about..." He flashed those bright eyes at Quentin again, as the ghost of a smile formed at the corner of his mouth. "Nobody's going to miss a stalker."

"Wait," Quentin said, panicking. "No, that's not it. That's not what I'm doing. I promise you, I have *no idea* what's going on. I don't know who any of you are. I don't know *anything*."

It was as if his voice was muted. Not a single word reached their ears. Not one shred of evidence that they even listened. The red-haired man handed Quentin's phone back to the driver. Then he stood up, crossed the cabin out of sight, and soon returned with something else in his possession. He knelt down again, next to Quentin's head, and Quentin caught only a glimpse of something in his hand—a whiff of something terribly sweet, bordering on rancid—before it was forced straight into Quentin's mouth without warning. With his bare fingers, the man forced a syrupy glob onto the roof of Quentin's mouth, scraped it off against the backs of Quentin's teeth. Quentin choked, gagged, his mouth full of it. Something wet and *thick*. It tasted as sweetly as it smelled, like honey with a hint of something else. Chemical. Medicinal. A bitterness beneath the sugary sweet. A distant cousin to cough syrup. He pressed into it with his tongue, a reflex, and couldn't help but swallow as it oozed down into the hollow of his throat. He sputtered, gasping.

"Take him downstairs."

The driver took hold of Quentin once again, a hand digging into the crook of each armpit. He dragged Quentin deeper into the cabin, toward the door near its rear, what might have been a closet of some kind. Instead a dark descent greeted them there. Stairs. A basement. Carefully, one step at a time, the driver dragged Quentin down into its lightless depths, heels knocking along each wooden plank until finally they struck the bottom. Rough, bumpy rock. The warm, claggy air stank of ripe decay. Quentin was dumped in the heart of the darkness, the only light that which spilled from the open door at the top of the stairs.

"You be good now," the driver told him.

Feet clomped up the wooden steps. The door slammed shut, plunging Quentin into an unknown abyss. He lay still, muscles twitching with exhaustion. The others' footsteps sounded on the floorboards overhead. Their voices were muffled, words unintelligible. Quentin coughed. He still tasted the cloying substance in his mouth, coating the surface of his tongue. What he'd swallowed settled warmly in the pit of his belly like a shot of whiskey, churning and hot.

Then something came over him. A fizzy wave, drizzling down behind his eyes, down the back of his neck, his shoulders. He thought to move, to roll, to wriggle himself across the hard ground in search of something to free his bindings, but his body failed to respond. A severed connection. That warmth in his gut bled far and fast. Comfortable.

In a wounded stupor, he soon found it impossible to even conceptualize escape.

9

THE RIVER

She was stunned to discover she'd fallen asleep.

Birds chirped prettily—and noisily—outside. Morning light shined through the cabin windows, pooling across the floor like orange juice. Her throat was terribly dry. She sat up slightly, and peered toward Isaac's bed across the cabin.

He was already gone.

She wiped the remainder of sleep from her eyes, and then looked about the cabin as if she might find that he'd simply moved to a different bed, which he hadn't. He was simply gone.

He woke up before I did. And he left without me.

There was already a wedge between them. It'd been axed into place since Isaac first brought their mother's letter to her apartment, and she'd done very little to alleviate it. In fact, besides agreeing to come here, she'd unintentionally done almost everything she could to drive that wedge deeper.

"...this doesn't have to be nearly as painful as you're making it..."

Even with a few hours of sleep as a buffer, his words still needled her. She thought he was probably right. She needed to ease up. Be reasonable. Or at least *seem* reasonable, for his sake.

Let's see how long it lasts.

She eyed her clothes on the floor, and her bag which contained a fresh change of clothes inside, and decided to remain as she was. Her baggy shirt and sweat shorts would suffice. She slipped out of bed, put on her sneakers, and headed outside.

The lake's glassy surface mirrored the horizon, where the sun was rising against a smattering of puffy white clouds. The morning air was still cool.

Can't believe you just left me, you dick.

Awkward and alone, she started around the lake. She made her way toward the pavilion where she could see at least five people gathered. Did they eat breakfast together as well? How long ago was that?

"Rise and shine!"

Standing just outside of what Drew presumed was his cabin, blending into its western shade, handsome Robert approached.

"Looking for your brother?" he said.

"How'd you guess?"

Robert pointed not far ahead, toward another cabin which was partially nestled into the woods.

"Last I saw him, he was tending to some of the vegetables with your mom."

"Oh, okay. Thanks..."

"You're creating a bit of a stir," he added, stopping Drew just as she started away. "Probably not too surprising, after some of the looks you were getting last night..."

"Well, if it makes anyone feel any better, you can tell them we won't be staying much longer."

"Oh, they're just being stupid," Robert said. He stuffed his hands into his pockets. He kicked the dirt with the pad of his bare foot. "Probably just jealous that Julianne has family to invite in the first place. Most of us were loners before we ended up here."

"Even you?" Drew said, only a little surprised. "Surely you had plenty of admirers. Probably could have started your very own..." She stopped herself just short of saying the word.

"My very own what?" Robert smiled, and the sunlight turned his dark eyes to a lightly toasted brown. "You were gonna say cult, weren't you?"

"I didn't say it."

"But you wanted to." He laughed, and Drew found herself doing the same. "I was a bit of a loner, yeah. Mostly 'cause I just don't like people. Which is funny, considering I've spent most of my life trying to make music for 'em..."

It was then Drew remembered the music she'd heard before, when she and Isaac had first been led around the lake. Acoustic guitar, and a perfectly lovely voice accompanying its simple tune.

"So that was you I heard yesterday," she said.

"Oh, you heard me playing?"

"I heard *someone* playing, yeah. Was it you?"

Robert shrugged with a coy smile. "Might've been. What'd you think?"

"I thought this place must not be too far from Nashville."

Robert guffawed. The most endearing guffaw Drew had ever heard. For a moment, she nearly forgot she was worried about her brother.

"You got me," Robert said. "I made the rounds there, for sure. Like so many *penniless poets* do, I guess..."

Drew glanced away, toward that cabin tucked into the trees, thinking she should probably cut this flirtation short.

"What did you think of the lake last night, anyway?" Robert asked. "Blaine showed you, didn't he?"

"Oh. Yeah, he did." Drew paused. "It was... interesting."

Robert smiled. "Don't worry, I was skeptical, too. At the start."

"What changed your mind?"

Robert considered, then shrugged. "There's just something about this place, you know? It's hard to describe until you experience it for yourself. Maybe you will, if you stick around."

And just like that, the chemistry between them withered like a sun-scorched flower. Drew suddenly wondered if Robert wasn't perhaps put up to all of this—that he wasn't Blaine's *designated charmer*, sent to recruit impressionable young things with cartoon hearts in their eyes. Unfortunately for them, Drew did not consider herself an impressionable young thing, nor had she ever known the sensation of being swept off her feet.

"I have a life I'm eager to get back to," she answered bluntly.

She allowed her feet to carry her in the direction of Isaac's supposed whereabouts, allowing distance to serve as a natural end to their conversation.

"A job, you mean?" Robert called after her. "Maybe a boyfriend, too?"

Over her shoulder, Drew said politely, "Thanks for the chat, Robert."

At least he told the truth. She found Isaac near the cabin in question. He and their mother were outside, busying about the gardens in the shade. Sherry was also there, Julianne's roommate. She noticed Drew before the others did.

"Good morning!" she called, and waved giddily.

Isaac and Julianne both straightened. Drew took particular notice of Isaac's unenthused reaction. Their mother appeared pleased to see her, albeit not as over-the-top as Sherry.

"Morning," Drew said, coming to stand near the rows of raised plant beds, abundant with leafy vegetables. "What are you guys up to?"

"It's mine and Sherry's day to water," Julianne said. She wiped some sweat from her brow. "Did you have breakfast? There's still food at the pavilion, I'm sure."

"I'm not hungry," Drew lied. She studied the watering pitchers in their possession. "Where do you fill those up? Not the lake, I'm guessing."

"No," Sherry said, very seriously. "No, not the lake. We get water from the river."

"Oh?"

"There's a river that flows adjacent to us, but doesn't connect to the lake," Julianne said. "Not directly, anyway. We get most of our water from there. We boil it for personal use, of course."

"Some of us bathe there," Sherry said, and she lit up again in that eerie way Drew didn't care for.

"You're sure you're not hungry?" Julianne asked. "Are you feeling any better this morning?"

Their mother's concern still felt strange. Drew didn't think she'd ever get used to it, or believe it.

"I'm fine. Promise." She watched her brother as he bent around the tomato plants, pretending to be preoccupied. "How long have you all been up?"

"Couple hours," Julianne said.

"We're early risers here," Sherry added.

That worrisome knot in Drew's stomach tied itself over once again, tighter and pinching. Two hours alone with their mother. Two hours of conversation she wasn't privy to. A sting of jealousy awakened, despite telling herself she wanted no part in this.

"I was thinking," Julianne said, "after I'm done here, I might head to the river for a quick rinse. Would you want to join me, Drew?"

Isaac glanced their way very briefly, not meeting her eyes, and his avoidant body language told Drew everything. They'd talked about her in her absence. Of course they had.

"Without Isaac?" she said.

Isaac shrugged indifferently, then gave her a lopsided smirk. "Not really in the mood to bathe with my sister. Think I'll stay here."

This was planned, Drew thought. A scheme to get her alone with Julianne, for whatever good they thought it'd do.

"I'll show Isaac around the lake while you're gone," Sherry offered. "We can check out the chicken coops, even if it's Todd's and Caroline's week."

"So?" Julianne said, nudging Drew. "What do you think?"

Drew swallowed her petty thoughts. She tried to swallow her distrust as well, but it wouldn't go down nearly so easily.

Finally she said, "Sure."

She followed her mother into the woods, meandering calmly through the trees, towels tucked under their arms and an awkward silence tucked between them. It was Julianne who broke the silence first.

"So... Isaac tells me you're still doing art?"

Drew clenched her jaw. Just a little.

"You were always such a talented artist," Julianne said. "Even when you were just small. Doesn't surprise me one bit. What kind of art do you do these days?"

She studied her mother from behind—her ebony hair pulled back into a swishing ponytail, her bronzed shoulders gleaming from beneath her tank top, muscular calves flexing with each step, her equally muscular feet collecting dark stains on their bare undersides. No one in this commune wore shoes. Except Kent.

"Mostly digital," Drew said.

"You mean on the computer?"

"Yeah, on the computer." Within the privacy of Julianne's shadow, Drew regarded her mother with a growing humor. "I'm in graphic design. It's my job."

"Oh!" Julianne said excitedly. "That's incredible. Good for you. Wow..."

It came out of nowhere. Truly. Drew's eyes were watering suddenly. Her humor quickly shifted into something else. That indescribable *longing* for something she'd always wanted but could never have—laced with bitterness, because what she longed for had been stolen by the very person she wanted it from most. She wiped her eyes on the back of her hand before her mother had a chance to see.

"So what does that mean, exactly? Graphic design?"

Drew smiled again. She couldn't help it. Her emotional state rose and fell as readily as the dirt path they followed.

"It's a pretty broad field. I do web design for a couple different online clothing catalogues. I also do some freelance stuff on the side now and then..." She stopped herself. All at once she realized how easy it was. How easy it could be. And for reasons she couldn't explain, that simplicity scared her the most. Her mother's ponytail continued to swish rhythmically. Hypnotically. In the distance, not far ahead, the sound of rushing water. "Is that the river I hear? We must be getting close."

Sure enough, the trail brought them to the head of a short downward slope, where the river waited at the bottom.

126

The water was a little more rapid than Drew expected, the river narrower than what she had in mind. Almost a creek.

"Here we are!" Julianne said triumphantly. "What do you think?"

"I mean, it's a river."

"You still good for a quick dip, then?"

Drew shrugged, nodded.

"Are you uncomfortable at all with your body?"

It was a very abrupt and peculiar question.

"No."

"Good," Julianne said. "Me neither."

And with that, Julianne began to undress. Drew hadn't exactly brought a swimsuit, but she had planned to keep her underwear on. There was no reason why she couldn't have stuck with that plan, but as her mother stripped nude—revealing her very natural and carefree grooming—and took her first steps into the riverside, Drew felt a strange impulse to prove herself.

She placed her towel in a weedy patch at the edge of the river and hastily undressed, before she could second guess herself. She glanced around sheepishly as she set her underwear aside, feeling exposed. The birds in the trees, and whatever else scurried in the woods, were already more eyes than she liked. Her mother waded into the middle of the river, which appeared to be deep enough that Drew could hide herself beneath its current, so she followed.

"It's cold," Julianne warned her. "But not too bad."

Her mother's eyes were upon her. Drew tiptoed into the current, the water climbing up to her shins, her knees, her thighs, at which point her entire body erupted with goosebumps. With another lunge into the water, she managed to conceal her sex beneath the flow, up to her navel, and from there she crouched down, letting the river wet her up to the shoulders. She shuddered violently.

"How is it?"

"Cold," Drew answered, and her teeth chattered as she said it.

Her mother smiled. Drew studied her face intently, eyes darting along each of her features. Were her mother's eyes her eyes, she wondered? Was her mother's smile her smile? Drew hadn't seen her own in what felt like ages.

"Be honest," she said, teeth still chattering. "How long's it been since you last did this?"

Julianne smirked mischievously. "There's really no need to bathe every day. Not out here, or in the city..."

"Agree to disagree."

Julianne focused on her daughter, still smirking, with a look in her eyes that said *I know you better than you think* which Drew didn't altogether care for.

"So tell me," Julianne said. "Are there any men in your life?"

Drew was slightly disappointed they'd already arrived on this particular subject—and yet she still felt an alien thrill in her mother's asking. There was so much her own mother didn't know.

"No," she answered. "Not currently."

Her mother continued giving her that knowing look, and suddenly Drew was certain she *did* know something. Something she shouldn't have known.

"Why, what has Isaac told you?"

"Not a lot," Julianne admitted. "Only... he says you're a bit of a serial dater."

"Oh, really? He said that?"

"A bit of a serial dumper, too?"

Thanks a lot, Isaac, she thought.

"What's that about?" her mother asked.

Despite the thrill of being an enigma, Drew deflated as the answer teased the tip of her tongue. A wet rag in a cold river.

Do you really want to know? she thought. It was a bit like having a conversation with a stranger on the train, or the bus. The question seemed straightforward enough, innocent enough, surface-level enough, but the answer—the *real* answer—would burden anyone who heard it with more reality than they bargained for...

Tell her the truth.

"I don't know. My therapist told me I'm afraid of commitment." She regarded her mother plainly, gauging her reaction. Julianne only appeared intrigued. "Apparently I have abandonment issues."

The quiet that followed was almost enough to mute even the river's noisy rush around them. Her mother's intrigue fell flaccid. Much less *slumber party gossip,* much more *family therapy intervention* than Julianne had probably expected. But the truth was the truth, and Drew had no intention of shielding her mother from it.

"Listen..." Julianne started. "I know... I'm one-hundred-percent aware it couldn't have been easy for you or your brother—"

"Why did you ask us to come here?" Drew interrupted, growing weary of the circular blame shifting.

Julianne's mouth hung open. "Because I wanted to see you again."

"But why now?"

Julianne tilted her head, gazing upon her daughter as if she already knew she wouldn't like the answer.

"Because it might be my last chance."

"And what does that mean? Where are you going?"

"Well, it's hard to explain..."

"Yeah, you said that in your letter."

"It's hard to explain because I know you'll think I'm crazy."

"That ship has sailed," Drew said. Her teeth were chattering less—her internal furnace eating *well* on the coals of her frustration.

"I've been with this group a little over a year now, like I said. That's about as long as anyone stays, before..." She paused. Drew's mind raced, not entirely sure where this was leading. "There is something truly special about this place, Drew. Maybe you've already felt it, during your short time here..."

Drew's first thought was of the cave, the figure in the dark, the voices in the woods, all potentially nothing more than harassment at the hands of their fellow campers.

"No," she said. "Unless you mean the locals all giving me the stink eye, then yeah, this place feels real special."

"What about what you saw last night?" Julianne asked. "On the lake?"

"You mean the weird light?" Drew said trivially. "What about it?"

Her mother couldn't have looked more disappointed. Which was fine by Drew. Unlike her brother, she had no intention of being a sucker just to earn some worthless brownie points.

"It's not *just* a light," Julianne said, trying her hardest to instill her words with weight, with meaning, which only sounded sillier to Drew's ears. "Whether you believe it or not, this place is *real*. The spirit we spoke of before... it's *real*. This isn't some hokey religion in the woods interpreting God's messages in the wind. The Mother of the lake is *real*..."

"Then what is it?" Drew asked, a growing hostility in her voice. "Why do you call it that?"

"Because that's what she is. The spirit of the lake. She's a Mother to us. *I know* how crazy I sound right now. But I've seen it with my own eyes."

"What have you seen?" Drew asked impatiently. "If it's real, then describe it to me, because I'm still having a hard time understanding what—"

"The light in the water," Julianne said, "it's not just a light. It's her. It's our Mother's embrace. That's where I'm going. Tonight, actually..."

Drew was reeling. She began shivering again. She looked around, at the surrounding shore, the woods, as if waiting for a crowd to burst out from the trees and announce that she'd just been hilariously pranked.

"That's why I needed to see you," her mother continued. "Because... I just wanted to make sure I gave you and Isaac some closure before I left..."

That word again. *Closure.*

Incredibly, Drew laughed. It was the only response she could muster, even when there was hardly anything funny about it—even if she was still trembling against the river's current.

"Where exactly do you think you're going?"

"Into the light," Julianne said matter-of-factly. "Into our Mother's embrace."

"Okay, but where do you think that'll take you?"

To this, Julianne shook her head like it didn't matter. "That's the mystery of it. The journey. To our Mother, wherever she is, wherever she's waiting for us."

"Superstitious bullshit..." Drew muttered.

"It's *real,* Drew..."

"Stop telling me that." Her anger resurfaced rather quickly. "So let me get this straight. You left us all those years ago, without a word of explanation or a goodbye... and now you've dragged us back into your life just so you can do it all over again? All because you've joined some suicide cult?"

"It's not a cult..."

"Figures," Drew said. "First dad, and now you..."

Julianne cocked her head back. "What do you mean..."

"You're like a fucking whirlpool, you know that?" Drew spat. "Destroying anything dumb enough to drift into your little spiral..."

"Drew—"

"This isn't about us. It's not about me and Isaac, or our *closure*. It's about *you*. It's always been about you. Nothing's changed. You left us because you were afraid your life wasn't what you thought it would be. Now you've come back into our lives because you're afraid death won't be all you imagine it to be, either? Trying to win some last-minute karma just in case? Is that it?"

"This has nothing to do with death. That's not what's happening—"

"I can't," Drew said. She turned her back to her mother, toward the riverside. "I can't talk about this anymore..."

As she waddled toward the shore, movement farther down the river drew her attention. Another arrival. Another body.

Of course, she thought irritably.

It was him. Charming poet boy. He must have followed a different path, arriving at a different point in the river. She froze momentarily, her nakedness still covered by the frothing water. It appeared Robert hadn't noticed them yet. He wasted no time stripping his own clothes, carelessly tossing his t-shirt into the weeds, followed by his sweatpants, under which he wore nothing at all. Even in the midst of her anger, and the tension pushing her from her mother like a repellant magnet, Drew's heart skipped a beat at the sight of him—his naked body unexpectedly muscled from a meager diet of soups and stews. He was knee-deep into the water when he finally glanced their way and saw them both. He paused there, unashamed of his nudity, and gave them an emphatic wave over his head.

"Jesus Christ," Drew muttered.

"I'll grab your towel," Julianne said, an urgent sympathy in her voice as she must have noticed her daughter's hesitation.

"No, thanks, I've got it."

She refrained from returning Robert's wave. Instead she stared straight ahead, toward the riverbank, and marched her goosebump-prickled ass from the water and onto the shore, folding her arms across her breasts along the way.

So much for being comfortable with your own body, huh?

She snatched her towel from the weeds, flung it around her shoulders, then grabbed her discarded clothes up from the dirt, her shoes included, and proceeded to hurry back along the path toward the lake.

10
THE WEDGE

She was met with a handful of bewildered stares when she arrived back at the lake. She didn't see Isaac anywhere along the way to their cabin, and was surprised not to find him when she stepped inside. As soon as the door was closed, she tossed her towel onto one of the vacant beds and dressed herself in some fresh clothes. While she did, she thought about what she might say to Isaac when she saw him next.

Grab your things, we're going home ranked the highest.

Then the cabin door opened and there he was. He stepped inside, and smiled at Drew with a guilt he couldn't hide.

When she refused to smile in return, he said, "What's wrong?"

"What's wrong?" She wanted to laugh. Instead she folded her arms defensively, wondering how best to put it. "Did she tell you already? About what's happening tonight?"

"Yeah," he answered truthfully. "She told me this morning."

Drew regarded her brother like he was a stranger—or a different species. How he could act like he didn't care was beyond her.

"We're not staying for this. We're going home. Today." She watched him carefully, searching for a twitch of the mouth, a daggering of the eyes. Instead he just watched her. "We're going home *now.*"

"You can do what you want," he said. "I'm not going anywhere."

"Isaac..."

"You don't know her half as well as you think, Drew. Mom's life wasn't easy, either. She's told me things about her childhood, her parents, about our grandparents..."

"I'm not interested in her excuses," Drew said. "It's time for us to go."

Isaac sighed defeatedly. "I've spent most of my life wishing I had more time with her. Like the time you got. This is my last chance to create meaningful memories with her..."

"And these are the kinds of memories you want? You're gonna let her taint the ones you *do* have with this bullshit?"

She couldn't help but think of their father again. Every time she thought of the man, the first memory that came to mind was the worst. The ugliest. The one she'd spent so many years in therapy trying to erase like a bad dream...

"She's not tainting anything," Isaac said. He watched Drew very closely, as if drilling into her skull with his eyes alone, and seeing the thoughts that wrestled inside. "This isn't like dad, you know. It's nothing like dad."

Drew shook her head disappointedly. "So you *do* believe it. You think these people here are—"

"I believe that *she* believes," Isaac said. "That's enough for me."

"Belief means *nothing* when her corpse is lying at the bottom of the lake with all the others."

Isaac flinched. His brows knitted in disgust of the imagery Drew's words conjured.

"We should go to the police and report these fuckers," Drew went on. "Report that creep, Blaine, for running a suicide cult."

"W-we're not reporting anyone," Isaac said, stammering. He almost never stammered. "And I'm not leaving. Not today. I want to see mom through this first."

"Why, because she needs your support? She's running away again, Isaac, like she did before. Only this time..." Drew stopped herself, before she could say something more upsetting. "I wonder what your therapist would have to say about all of this, if she knew. Something tells me she wouldn't have encouraged this trip."

"I'm not leaving," Isaac repeated. "End of story."

"Well I'm not leaving you here with these people."

Isaac shrugged. "Then I guess you're staying, too."

"Jesus, Isaac..."

"It's only one more night." Suddenly his tone was softer. Gentler."Then we can leave tomorrow. First thing, if you want. I know you already took the time off from work. Just stay with me one more night, and then we can go."

"I'm not gonna be a witness to whatever they're doing out here," Drew said.

"You don't have to. You can stay in the cabin if that's what you want. Just..." He adopted the sorriest, most pleading expression he could muster. "...let me be with her a little longer. Please."

Drew paced toward her unmade cot, where she sat with a heavy groan. Isaac joined her, sitting beside her, the heat of their argument dissipating as easily as the snap of a finger. Their shoulders brushed as he sat, and then he proceeded to lean against her slightly—an absolutely manipulative gesture, Drew was aware, but it still worked on her nonetheless. She softened.

"Has she asked you about dad *at all?*" she said.

"No," Isaac answered.

"And you don't think that's weird?"

"I don't know. I haven't really thought about it."

Drew didn't buy that at all, but she wouldn't press him. They'd argued enough already as it was.

Eventually Isaac stood up, and said, "I'm going back out there. Are you coming?"

"No. I'm gonna hang out here for a bit."

"Suit yourself."

He left her alone. In his absence, Drew spent another few minutes just sitting, thinking, ruminating, until she grabbed her backpack from the floor and pulled out her phone, which she hadn't checked in some time. Of course there was nothing new, as their phones received no service up here. But as she placed her phone back inside her pack, she noticed something was missing. She dug around through her clothes, her other possessions, not seeing it anywhere. As she searched with frantic hands, suddenly she heard the distinct jingle. She unzipped the outer pocket of her bag, and with immense relief found her keys inside.

I didn't put them in this pocket, she thought. *At least... I don't think I did...*

As a tremor of paranoia burrowed its way inside her, she eyed Isaac's bag beside his bed. She went to it, knelt beside it, unzipped the main pocket with trembling fingers. She dug through his clothes, and was once more relieved to find the gun still resting soundly at the bottom, undisturbed.

Just in case.

II

THE VICTIM

He wasn't doing so well. Not that he'd been doing well before, but now things were much, much worse, to say the least.

For starters, he didn't think he'd ever been so thirsty before. His mouth was so incredibly dry, it hurt to touch his sandpapery tongue to the soft palate. His gums throbbed, as if he could feel them receding from around his teeth, which were now so sensitive they were painful to simply *suck air* through. He felt his own skin shrinking around his body. Constricting. Thin. He was lucky he was paralyzed, or else he might have ripped from one end to the other trying to move. His head ached like he'd been bludgeoned against the back of his skull. Also like he'd dropped a heavy barbell on the bridge of his nose at the gym.

He wasn't the only one down here, either.

The offensive odor of decay assaulted him repeatedly, from one hour to the next, as his senses became dulled, desensitized, and then suddenly reawakened with a fresh,

140

ghastly reminder. The scent of death. Those who perished before him. Those he would soon join, certainly. If only he could move. If only he could untie himself. If only he could fight back the next time the basement door opened.

It had opened twice since he was first brought down here. Twice someone had come to visit. Twice he had been subjected to something beyond anything he could—

It opened again.

Quentin peeled his eyes—felt his eyelids slime their way up his sore, bloodshot eyeballs—and glimpsed the bright light of day coming through the door at the top of the stairs. How long had it been? With all his dreary hallucinations, he couldn't be sure. Couldn't remember. The doorway at the head of the stairs filled with a shadow. Footsteps creaked, one by one until they reached the basement floor. He blinked his eyes again, taking in the silhouette with its half-halo of fiery hair, lit by the scant sunlight coming from upstairs.

"You're awake," the man said. "Last time you slept."

Last time I slept? Quentin thought. *No. It's only been twice. Twice...*

The man moved closer. Away from the stairs, from the shaft of sunlight. Into the shadows where Quentin lay aching, shriveling up like an insect in a spider's web.

"Don't worry..." The man's bare feet whispered to a stop on the rocky floor just inches from Quentin's face. "I'll be quick."

Quentin opened his mouth to protest, but only twitched his jaw, releasing a dusty sigh.

In the dark, the man began to undress. And from beneath his clothes, something began to squirm.

12

THE JOURNAL

While her brother was off mingling with the enemy, Drew lay in bed struggling with her own emotions. Nothing new.

She entertained the possibility that she was wrong. That this place really was the sacred gateway between their world and some kind of *other*, where a majestic nature spirit beckoned them to cross its threshold not into an afterlife, but...

But what?

She hadn't allowed her mother to get that far. All Drew knew was that they believed something waited for them beyond the light in the lake. They were not *suicidal*, they were voyagers. They weren't running away from their problems, they were bravely entering a new phase of life, that was all.

Sure.

Drew couldn't help wondering if she was self-sabotaging her last chance at reconnecting with Julianne. Did Isaac have the right idea? Let bygones be bygones? Let go of *'resentments?'* Was her insistence on depriving their mother closure only depriving Drew of her own?

Her stomach gurgled violently. She still hadn't eaten anything.

As she lay listening to her body's requests, something scratched at the wood behind her head. Like little scurrying rat's toes...

She sprang up from her cot like it were electrified, her pulse already doubled. She stood absolutely still. The scratching continued. She dropped to the floor, peered under the bed like before, and once more found nothing there. Nothing scampering in the shadows. No glinting eyes peering back. No twitching nose or whiskers.

And yet the scratching persisted.

Like fingernails clawing at the wood.

A new fear pierced her heart. She straightened, sitting up, observing the top of her bed, her pillow, where her cot was pushed against the wall.

Scratch. Scratch. Scratch...

She got to her feet. She grabbed the end of her cot, and with both hands dragged it a couple feet across the floor, away from the wall. She observed the empty space left in its wake, the dusty floor and the wall behind it. Nothing. Nothing at all. Except...

With the cot pulled away, she was given a clear view of the mattress' end... and something flimsy sticking out from underneath it. She took a beat to simply stare at the thing, processing what she saw and the noises which had drawn her attention to it.

Don't think about it.

What she saw was the black and white pattern of a composition notebook protruding from beneath her mattress. Swallowing down her fear—and the implications— she pulled the notebook loose from its hiding place. Scrawled across the empty lines on the notebook's cover, someone had written their name in faded pencil. It read: *Olivia.*

She set the journal down on her bed, then pushed the bed back against the wall to its original place. She took a seat on the mattress' edge, brought the journal into her lap.

Olivia.

At that precise moment, the cabin door opened. Drew tossed the journal from her lap onto the mattress and pulled the blanket across it just as Isaac stepped inside and looked her way, none the wiser. He did stop and give her a funny look, though, sitting like she was, as if waiting.

"What are you doing?" he asked.

Drew shrugged. "Literally nothing. What are you doing?"

Isaac shut the door behind him. He regarded her with a sorry expression.

"Is this really how you want to spend your time here?" he asked. "Sitting alone?"

Am I alone? Drew wondered only to herself, her mind still occupied by the journal beside her.

"Mom wants to see you."

"I just saw her this morning."

"Drew..."

Yeah, yeah, yeah, she thought. She relented. "Okay."

"Okay?"

"Sure. Fine. Let her in."

Her brother gave her another funny look, this one even funnier than the last. He glanced around the cabin, as if wary of booby-traps she might've set while he was gone. Then he stepped outside again, and was soon replaced by the woman in question. Julianne entered on delicate feet, her eyes quickly finding Drew as if she *too* suspected that her daughter might descend from the ceiling in an ambush. She offered Drew a smile—a truce of the mouth—and closed the door behind her.

"Can we talk?"

Drew had no idea what more they possibly had to say to one another. What possible explanations had her mother come up with since their last encounter that could make any sense of it all? Either way, Drew supposed she'd be entertained, whatever it was.

Julianne moved toward the middle of the cabin, toward the table there. She paused, deciding where she might sit. Then she looked to Drew and said, "Would it be all right if I sat with you?"

Drew eyed the blanket, where the journal rested underneath. Thinking quickly, she scooted herself there, sitting on its flimsy-but-apparent shape. Then she gestured to the spot where she'd been, and her mother accepted the invitation, thinking nothing of the awkward behavior.

Seated side by side, shoulder to shoulder, Julianne said, "This isn't how I want to leave things between us."

Drew frowned. "Not trying to be a brat or anything, but... I'm not sure what else you expected. Did you think we'd come here and shower you with adoration? Did you think we'd be grateful that you decided to reveal yourself after all this time? As if it wasn't your choice all along?"

Julianne shook her head. "No. Not at all. I just wanted to see you again, truly. I wanted to say goodbye, and maybe allow the three of us to have some—"

"Please don't say it again," Drew said. She paused, struggling not to get angry, struggling not to storm off in avoidance of that anger. It couldn't be avoided, she knew. Not the anger, nor the cause of it. The only way to relieve it would be to speak her mind. So she did. "What about dad? What about *his* closure? I noticed you haven't even asked about him yet. Why is that?"

Julianne appeared caught off guard, which in and of itself was hilarious. Drew was beginning to suspect her mother *had,* in fact, expected this reunion to be much peachier than it was.

"I know you don't believe it, but I hated leaving you the way I did," she said, and looked Drew straight in the eye. "But your father on the other hand... I didn't love him. I've always seemed to attract these men who want to *control* me in some way. In the end, he was no different. I needed to get away..."

Drew could have laughed—she really could have—but found herself too offended on her father's behalf to do so. Was her mother really going to play this card?

"That's funny," Drew said. "Because dad sure loved you."

Julianne sighed. "I know he did. But it's not always so simple..."

"He loved you so much," Drew went on, and suddenly she felt herself vibrating with nerves, her heart performing against her ribs like a violent xylophone, words rattling up as an all too familiar lump tried to get in their way. "...so much that he blew his brains out a year after you left."

In speaking it aloud, Drew felt her own face drain of blood, somehow shocked by her own words. She turned to see her mother beside her, her sun-tanned face suddenly sun-bleached like a chalky skull, which was both satisfying and horrible. Mostly horrible. But the truth was now spoken, and Drew couldn't stop herself, lest she make herself sick again.

"And guess who got to find him?" she asked. She lost control of her voice. Up and down, her vocal cords becoming vocal *barbed wire* instead. The lump in her throat swelled, so that it felt like her head would explode from the pressure. "Guess who came home from school... and found him..." She tried to clear her throat, her voice turning wet and shrill.

Like throwing a fire blanket onto a burning victim, Julianne threw her arms around her daughter. She squeezed her harder than she'd ever squeezed her before. If Drew had any air left inside her, her mother's embrace would have squashed it out in an instant. Drew didn't fight her. She choked on her sobs instead.

"I saw the blood first... it was everywhere, and... and I found him at the table, and the gun was still in his hand..."

"I'm so sorry," her mother breathed into her ear. "Oh, baby... baby... I'm so sorry..."

"I hated you..."

"I know. I know you did. I know..."

"I hated you so much..."

Julianne said nothing more. She only continued to hold her tightly, and Drew only continued to allow it. The greatest relief she'd ever known came over her in those next moments —as if she cried her weight in tears, becoming lighter and lighter in her mother's arms until she could have floated up and away. She became limp as a cooked noodle as her mother rocked her gently, leaning into it, rocking a little herself, as wave after wave of relief, of *release,* came over her.

The ugliness was out in the open, and at last it wasn't hers alone to bear.

The quiet that followed was one of tranquility. The passing of a great storm. Julianne let her go, pulling back so that she could study her daughter's red and swollen eyes, her wet cheeks. Drew felt painfully vulnerable, but was too tired to care.

"I'm sorry," Julianne said. "I'm sorry I'm not a good mother. I never was. I'm still not. It's meaningless, I know, but I'm sorry."

"Why did you leave?" Drew asked. She'd already asked before, but still hadn't gotten a full answer.

"The truth won't exonerate me." Julianne pulled her dark hair back behind her ear. She looked into Drew's eyes with an earnest warning. "It'll only make you hate me more."

To this, Drew said simply, "More?"

Incredibly, Julianne smiled. "It had nothing to do with you or your brother. It wasn't even your dad, really. I loved your dad. I did. His love was just... something else. I never thought he'd do something like that. I swear I didn't. If I'd suspected that, I would have stayed..."

Drew was dubious, but said nothing to interrupt.

"Anyway, I don't know what you'd call it. I just had this... *bug* inside me. Restlessness. I felt like I was drowning all the time. I felt trapped. I had you when I was eighteen, like I said, and by the time I was thirty—thirty-one?—I saw the rest of my life stretched out in front of me, and it wasn't anything like I'd hoped it would be. Your dad wasn't anything I'd hoped he'd be. I know it's a terrible thing for a mother to say, but I felt doomed. Anyone would be right to tell me what an awful person I am. What an awful mother I am. What I did was unforgivable, and maybe that's why I finally ended up in a place like this. I fluttered around aimlessly for years, getting burned everywhere I went, burning others along the way. But then I found this place, this mystery—or it found me. Maybe I'll get burned again, I don't know. There is no *knowing*. All I know is that I don't belong here anymore. And maybe I've done another terrible thing asking you to come and see me off. I've just had a lot of time to think all these years, and... I didn't want to leave without you knowing what became of me."

Drew was at a loss for how she felt about her mother's story. It was still difficult to reconcile her reason for leaving them and her reason for wanting them back. Apparently she loved them, but not enough to stay for them. She missed them, but not enough to want to be part of their lives in any meaningful way. She left because she needed more? And now she was leaving again because *more* wasn't enough, either?

Sitting alone just the two of them, Drew was only certain of one thing: Julianne was *afraid*. Of so many things. And she'd learned to conflate her fear with a need for *freedom*.

149

She wasn't a frightened little animal fleeing from all semblance of responsibility, no! She was just a *free spirit* who couldn't be tied down—not by her children, not by her marriage, not by any job, not even by the limits of their mortal world, apparently. It was all beyond Drew's ability to understand. So she decided she wasn't going to try any longer.

Which left her with one last thing to worry about.

"Are Isaac and I going to be in danger for coming here?" she asked.

Julianne, incognizant of Drew's inner thoughts, appeared wholly derailed by this question.

"Huh?" Her mother squeezed her eyes shut tight, as if trying to physically realign her train of thought. "I'm not sure what you mean..."

"I have a bad feeling about this place," Drew said. She looked to the cabin door, where she imagined her brother waited outside, anticipating the outcome of their conversation. "I get the feeling we're not supposed to be here, and... call me crazy, but I'm worried about them not letting us leave."

"Oh, Drew," Julianne said, and gave Drew's leg a squeeze, just above her knee. "I asked Blaine if I could invite you here, and he had no problem with it. He encouraged it, actually."

"Really? He did?"

"He knew I needed this. I couldn't take the next step without seeing you both first." A quiet pause for consideration. "Will you come tonight? To see me off?"

Drew hesitated. "I don't know if I can handle that."

"That's okay. I'll understand if you don't." Julianne

sniffed, and a pregnant silence followed, until finally she said, "Do you still hate me?"

Drew was reminded of her brother's words, yet again. He had so many good ones, after all.

...you can try to understand someone without having to like them, you know...

"No, I don't hate you."

Julianne leaned against her daughter, and placed a kiss against the side of her head.

"You don't have to come tonight, if you don't want to. I'm just glad you came at all. Permission to hug you again?"

Drew shared a gentle embrace with her mother, before Julianne stood up with a heavy sigh and asked, "Your brother and I were going to join Sherry in some guided yoga lessons. Would you be interested in joining us for that, at least?"

"Maybe in a bit," Drew said. "I think I need a moment alone. I'll come find you, though." Julianne smiled warmly, and astonishingly Drew was able to reciprocate it. "Tell Isaac to leave me alone for a bit, will you?"

"I'll do that."

Drew waited a minute or so after her mother left, expecting her brother to come barging in to complain that she was staying cooped up in their cabin. But her mother must have stayed true to her word, as Isaac did not reappear.

In their absence, Drew produced the journal from beneath her bedcover.

Olivia's journal.

She flipped through its pages and was surprised to find so many filled out. Quickly checking the dates, it seemed Olivia was with the commune for at least seven months. Her last entry was dated only a couple months ago, which for some odd reason struck cold fear into Drew's heart.

Here and gone.

She skimmed the final entry, which detailed Olivia's own nervousness for *'the journey ahead.'* Like Julianne, Olivia knew nothing about where she was headed, or what waited for her there. Only that she'd been *'chosen by our Mother'* and was lucky for that alone.

> *I wish Cameron had stayed to see me go. I miss him already... and that stupid mullet of his...*

This line caught Drew's attention. She skipped back a page, then another, skimming for another mention of this Cameron. Someone who had left the commune, apparently? Someone with a mullet.

She was instantly reminded of the man she'd seen in Blaine's cabin, immediately after their arrival. With his blond mullet and his unblinking stare. Now that she thought about it, she hadn't seen him again since. Not at dinner last night. She would have noticed him for sure.

When she came across his name in the journal again, it was in the wilderness of another week's entries entirely. She started at the beginning:

> *I honestly can't believe what just happened. I*

was feeding the chickens. I stepped out of their coop, and I barely took two steps when a sparrow landed on my shoulder. I literally gasped, it scared me so bad, but it just sat there like it didn't care. And then another bird landed on my other shoulder. I froze, holding perfectly still, and then I nearly screamed when something else landed in my hair. John was watching. He saw the whole thing. I could hear them. Birds in the trees. So many of them. I held up my arms and it seemed like every other second a new one landed on me. At first I thought it was the chicken scratch they wanted, but they just kept coming. A blue jay landed on my wrist! I think there must have been twenty birds perched on my body (and not a single one took a shit on me). And while it was happening, the most incredible sensation came over me. You know that intensely warm feeling you get when you drink on an empty stomach? It was kind of like that, except all over.

I feel like I'm dreaming. It's been a few weeks since anyone was chosen, and I thought for sure it'd be Julianne next. She's been here longer than I have. Longer than most of us, now that Charlie and Alex are gone. Strangely Cameron seems upset about it? I thought he'd be excited for me, but he's *acting like he's done with this place. I can't tell if he's just jealous or if he's gotten impatient about the whole thing. He's been skeptical since we got here, despite the things we've seen with our own eyes. I told him he needs to take a moment and just listen for it. Really listen, I mean. He's too closed off. Even Blaine told him it's a self-fulfilling prophecy. If you're always looking for reasons not to believe, you're never going to see the proof right in front of you.*

Drew stopped reading there. Whoever this Cameron was, he was gone now, which obviously meant it couldn't be the same man she saw. That would be impossible. Obviously.

Forget it.

She regarded the journal in her lap. She considered skimming back further, maybe to learn more about the others who had already come and gone, perhaps about the journey itself. Instead she closed the journal and set it aside. She didn't want to know any more than she had to. She had enough horrors living rent-free in her mind as it was.

One more night. That's it. Just one more night.

She was content to suffer some yoga lessons with Sherry in the meantime.

13
THE FAREWELL

It wasn't so bad. Not as bad as she expected, anyway. She joined Isaac and their mother back at Julianne's and Sherry's cabin, where Sherry led them in some downward dog and other poses with similarly stupid names. They did them right there in the patchy grass on the cabin's eastern side, as the sun crossed over their heads and began its slow descent toward another fast-approaching nightfall.

When yoga was over, Drew tagged along with the three of them—Isaac, Julianne, and Sherry—out into the woods to practice what Sherry called 'listening' which immediately reminded Drew of the entry she'd just read in Olivia's journal. Apparently this was something Blaine taught everyone at the lake, a means to connect with their surroundings and grow closer with 'Mother.'

"It's simple, really," Sherry said, walking them into the trees in what seemed to be a randomly selected direction. "Just as it's important that people connect with each other, and nurture each other through physical touch, it's important that we do the same with the natural world around us. Our Mother. We might not be able to speak to her with our voices, with our human language, but we can communicate with our bodies."

Standing in the thick of the woods, Sherry chose a tree of her own and encouraged them to do the same. Sherry leaned against hers, her shoulder blades against its trunk, and she lifted her arms over her head and caressed the tree behind her with both hands. Drew glanced at her brother, thinking *come on, are you seeing this right now, are you kidding me?* But Isaac didn't indulge her. He was too busy deciding which tree he thought was sexiest, or something.

"It's okay, Drew," Sherry said, peeking at her through slitted eyes, an expression that made Drew's skin crawl. "Whatever your reservations... let them go... let it *all* go..."

Julianne and Isaac were already following suit. Even more than Sherry, Isaac's participation disturbed Drew to her very core. She'd be letting *that* go as soon as her memory allowed...

Give it a chance.

She approached the nearest tree and did her best. Except Sherry kept stealing glances at her and reminding her that she wasn't letting herself go enough.

"Hands on the tree, Drew," she said. "Like you're embracing a close friend."

Never in a million years would she treat a close friend like this, if she had one. She wrapped one arm around the tree, as if she and the tree were posing to have their picture taken. Julianne was full-on wrapped around her tree, hugging it possibly tighter than she'd hugged Drew earlier on her cot. Isaac appeared to just be mimicking her approach.

Oh, what the hell, Drew thought finally, and decided to do the same. At least if she copied their mother, Sherry couldn't reprimand her for it.

She wrapped both arms around the tree's smooth trunk. She held on as if a tornado were bearing down on her, threatening to yank her up off the ground. She pressed her face against the smooth, cool bark. She continued watching the other three, as Sherry talked them through the ordeal.

"That's it," she said, writhing awkwardly against her tree. "Become part of it. Become one. Listen to the woods around us... her breath in the branches, her heartbeat beneath our feet..."

Drew listened. The leaves whispered with a breeze, sure enough. She also heard the chirp of birds. She peeked upward into the branches overhead and saw them—sparrows hopping to and fro from one twig to another. She focused her eyes on one quite close, and could have sworn it focused on her likewise. Its beady little eyes seemed to stare. Its tiny little head and body cocked this way and that, repositioning its little claws on its branch left and right, and its black eyes remained on her. Except... they weren't so black, were they? Perhaps it was the sun in the sky, but Drew could have sworn the little bird's eyes glinted with an unusual light. A distinct, amber glow. Or a reflection, perhaps?

"Let's close our eyes," Sherry said, "and listen..."

As Drew closed her eyes, she still thought of the birds in the trees. She imagined them swooping down, landing upon her head, her shoulders...

It's all crazy. All of these people are crazy...

"Deep breaths," Sherry said, and blew a long, steady wind from her pursed lips.

Right. Deep breaths. Listen... listen to the sounds of nature, listen to the sounds of...

Her stomach growled ferociously and she prayed the others couldn't hear it. She focused on the tree. She held it tighter, pressed her face more firmly against its slightly knobby surface. She took a deep breath and smelled the humidity in the air, the living wood against her cheek. And she felt... she felt...

By God, she felt *something*. A pulse. Was it her own? It had to be. Probably her posture, her grip around the tree, the lack of food in her belly. She felt a steady thump through the heels of her feet, up through the trunk of her own thrumming body. A boom, boom, boom in the deepest part of her, in her skull, with her ear pressed to the tree's wooden flesh...

A flutter in the trees. She opened her eyes again. She glanced up, to the same bird on the same branch as before. Except it wasn't alone now. The branch which had previously held one bird now held five. Five sparrows, all watching their little tree-hugging party. At the sight of them there, Drew tensed, and the sensation she'd been feeling vanished, dried up like sweat. She pulled back slightly, and felt the sticky sting of tree sap pulling against her cheek likewise.

"What the..."

She stepped back from the tree, a hand to her face, tacky with sap which she was sure hadn't been there moments ago.

"How are we feeling, Drew?"

At the sound of Sherry's voice, the birds overhead fled in a panic. Drew looked to their departure, then to Sherry, then to the tree which had just secreted all over her face for some reason.

"Oh. You picked a sticky one, didn't you?"

"Not a second ago, it wasn't," Drew said.

Sherry stepped away from her own tree finally, and stretched with a great big yawn. "I think that's enough for me today, too."

Julianne separated from her tree, and Isaac did the same, always mirroring. Only now did Isaac give Drew a funny look. Only ever at her expense.

"Gross," he said, and then smiled deviously. "I think you might have hugged your tree a little—"

"Watch it," she told him. Then she looked at his shirt, and saw his chest was stained with the very same yellowy sap. "Looks like you got some, too."

Isaac pulled his shirt away to see it for himself. Then he noticed it was on his arm as well and grimaced. For whatever reason, in spite of all her conflicted feelings, Drew couldn't stop herself from busting out laughing.

After yoga and tree hugging, Drew and Isaac headed back to their cabin while their mother headed to the main lodge by the pavilion to help prepare dinner for that evening—her final dinner with the commune. She came to collect them when she was finished, and much to Drew's relief said they could be first in line for stew if they wanted.

"Caroline's not serving again, is she?" she asked.

Julianne appeared perplexed. "No, Marcus is serving tonight. Why? What's wrong with Caroline?"

"Nothing."

The sun was dipping below the horizon when they started toward the pavilion, setting the treetops ablaze in its descent. Following the curve of the shore, at their mother's heels, Drew peered out over the lake, its placid surface reflecting the fiery sunset in full, and felt another worrisome pang in her gut. The dread. Time running short, the end drawing near.

Lo and behold, they were nearly the first in line when they arrived. Marcus proved much friendlier than Caroline, going so far as to offer Drew a wink with her three ladlefuls of stew.

"Did I just see what I think I saw?" Isaac muttered as they chose their table.

Staring at her bowl filled to the brim, Drew said, "Hey, I'll take it."

They sat together, and Julianne sat with them, sans stew.

"You're not eating?" Isaac asked.

"Not tonight," she said. Then she joked, "Not supposed to swim on a full stomach, after all."

As Drew focused on satiating her hunger, she listened to their conversation with a great deal less hostility than the previous day, and even caught herself smiling here and there at a few of their mother's quips.

Every now and then they were interrupted by other members coming to share their excitement for Julianne, and her fast-approaching journey. Each time it happened, Drew felt another cold stab of anxiety—like remembering a class presentation you were supposed to give later. But with everyone's attention on her mother, it meant fewer scowls thrown her way, at least.

And then Robert appeared, and Drew tried to bury her entire being into her dwindling bowl of stew.

"Good luck tonight," he told Julianne, giving her a pleasant squeeze on the shoulder.

"Hopefully there's no luck involved," Julianne joked, beaming up at him as he passed behind her.

Drew allowed herself one flick of the eyes in his direction, and was horrified to find him watching her. She looked away again—burning up with feelings she truly loathed. Why should she be nervous? Because he'd seen her naked before? Like that meant anything? She felt like a child, but couldn't help her embarrassment regardless.

By the time she was nearly finished eating—Isaac had already beaten her—Blaine arrived at the pavilion and called for everyone's attention. The chatter died down in an instant. All eyes on their glorious leader...

All hail the Holy Goatee.

"As we all know," Blaine said, pacing along the edge of the pavilion, the calm lake at his back turning darker under the twilight, "tonight we give our final farewell to another of our flock. In a matter of moments, Julianne will be leaving us for greener pastures, so to speak... though we won't begrudge her for it..." A collective laugh worked its way through the pavilion. Oddly, Drew only found herself growing more anxious. Short of breath. Her full belly didn't help matters. Blaine turned his attention entirely to Julianne. "It's been an honor having you here, Julianne. And as happy and excited for you as I know we all are, saying goodbye is never easy."

Julianne had tears in her eyes—glistening wetly in the light of the kerosene lamps. Watching her, seeing her overcome with her own emotions, Drew was reminded of things long forgotten—memories of childhood, before the Great Vanishing Act. When life was simpler, or seemingly so.

The woman seated across from Drew hadn't always been the terrible mother she now claimed to be. The first twelve years of Drew's life hadn't been spent neglected, or wanting. She'd *had* a mother then. A good one, she thought. Good enough, at least. And she still *had* a mother now, she realized, but something had obviously changed along the way. Julianne called it restlessness. A *bug*. Could it be so simple? Drew had wanted to believe the worst—that their mother had absconded from her responsibilities in favor of a child-free life. Was it possible there was more to it than that? Perhaps more than even Julianne herself could admit?

The look in her eyes now, listening to Blaine and his quackery, concealing some trace amount of fear behind her hopeful smile, told Drew another story. Her mother had been honest. It wasn't her or Isaac, or even their father she'd fled. But it wasn't freedom she was after, either—as she herself might have believed. Seeking freedom didn't lead a person to a place like this, after all. She was chasing something else. Escaping something else. Something maybe even she couldn't put a name to.

"I hope you'll give our Mother my love when you see her," Blaine said.

"I'll give her *all of our* love," Julianne corrected, and swabbed a tear from her eye on the back of her finger.

It was all so sickeningly heartfelt, Drew thought, and still she couldn't shake the disturbing implications of it all. Observing the others under the pavilion, she found expressions of envy, perhaps a couple instances of bitterness. All of these people wanted what Julianne was about to get, and not a single one of them knew what that was, exactly. All they currently had was a promise. Blaine's promise. Blaine's confidence. Everything on a feeling.

"When everyone's finished here," Blaine said, his voice falling into a somber reverence, "you know where to find me."

Drew finished the last of her stew. She and Isaac and their mother shared a strange silence then, looking between each other and smirking as if something was funny when in reality nothing was.

"You both ready to follow me over?" Julianne asked.

No, Drew thought.

"Yeah," Isaac said, and stood with his empty bowl.

Drew simply followed their lead. She and Isaac took their empty bowls back to the table where they'd taken them from. Along the way, Drew caught a couple of those distrustful glares she'd been missing, coincidentally from the same faces who'd appeared bitter during Blaine's speech. Perhaps it was less hers and Isaac's trespassing and more that they were the spawn of the woman they envied, or believed undeserving of tonight's proceedings.

One more night, Drew thought again.

Placing her bowl with the rest, she turned to her mother

waiting for them both, her fingers clasped loosely together in front of herself like a lone woman waiting to be asked to dance. She then held out both hands. Isaac took one with a sheepish grin. Drew took the other to be agreeable, and thought *I guess I'm attending after all*, and together they started toward the large dock, the lake now inky black with nightfall. The moon was missing from the sky, hidden behind a thick blanket of clouds on the far horizon whose fluffy edges were traced with its silver light.

Blaine waited at the end of the dock, like the first night. Holding her hand, Drew felt like she was escorting her mother down the aisle toward her groom, and a whole new kind of heebie-jeebies physically shook her, enough that Julianne glanced her way as they stepped onto the dock.

"Front row seats for you two," Blaine joked as they neared. They stopped before him, still hand in hand. "It's a beautiful thing, your coming here for your mother like this."

Julianne gave Drew's hand a squeeze.

There came the noise of multiple footsteps behind them, and Drew looked back to see the rest of the community gathering on the dock, forming a single file line. Julianne released Drew's and Isaac's hands. She gently pushed through them both, and approached the forming line.

Blaine said loudly for all to hear, "The time has come to say farewell. To send another of our flock into our Mother's embrace. Let us make Julianne our vessel, so that she may bring word of our love directly to our Mother's ears..."

One by one, Julianne proceeded to hug each and every member of the commune, all of whom whispered secretly into her ear—their farewells, as well as their messages for the *sacred Mother of the lake.* As each person parted from Julianne, they circled back, allowing the next to step forward, until soon they were all finished and gathered at the start of the dock.

Then Julianne turned to Drew and Isaac.

I don't know if I can handle this, Drew thought.

Julianne hugged Isaac first. Drew watched with a heavy heart as her brother's face rested on their mother's shoulder, and spilled fat tears from his eyes, struggling to maintain a smile on his trembling mouth. She could hear her mother's voice, whispering unintelligibly into her brother's ear. Then they parted, and she turned to Drew next. Cheeks glossy with tears, Julianne opened her arms, meeting Drew halfway. Drew shivered, legs weak as a newborn foal. She stepped into her mother, felt her arms wrap her firmly. She hugged her back.

"You're stronger than I ever was," Julianne whispered in her ear. "Thank you for taking such good care of your brother. I'm so proud of you. I love you."

Drew hardly recognized her own voice as she replied, "I love you, too."

They separated, fresh tears still streaming from her mother's eyes. Strangely, Drew's eyes remained bone dry. Perhaps she was too anxious to cry—her tear ducts as dry as her mouth. But like her brother, she tried to smile and felt her mouth contort with the effort. Julianne broke into a tearful, toothy smile. She stepped back, enough that she could see both her children side by side, and she held both her hands to her mouth as she took them in one last time. Then, unable to find her voice, Julianne simply mouthed, *'goodbye.'*

There was a great deal of movement behind them. Drew glanced in the others' direction, and was startled to find them all stripping naked. They dropped their clothes at their feet. The moon remained hidden behind the building clouds, and so their naked bodies appeared eerily flat in the night's shadow. Drew averted her eyes. She faced forward, tense as hell with the knowledge that a couple dozen buck-ass naked bodies stood at her back, and watched as her mother stripped out of her clothes likewise. Drew, Isaac, and Blaine were the only clothed people on the dock. Drew regarded her brother with a pleading stare, begging from the depths of her soul that he would not join in, and was unfathomably grateful to find him looking at her much the same.

Blaine crouched and picked something up from the edge of the dock which Drew had failed to notice before. He held a bowl in his hands—the same ceramic variety they ate their stew from. He dipped his bare thumb into the bowl, and produced a wet, yellowish globule. He held up his thumb, dripping with amber ooze. Julianne opened her mouth, unfurled her tongue like a red carpet. Every muscle in Drew's body clenched as Blaine placed his thumb upon her mother's tongue, and pasted a sticky line there. Julianne retracted her tongue with a mild shudder. Then Blaine gestured toward the edge of the dock. Julianne nodded obediently, looked again to her children—each of them struggling to hide their bafflement—and exchanged with them one final, bittersweet smile. Then she bent down, swung her legs over the dock's edge, and dipped her toes in the water.

As if waiting on her cue, the lake began to steam. White vapor rose off the black surface in soundless wisps, starting at

166

the lake's center and growing outward, toward their dock, toward Julianne. The soft wave of its heat reached Drew and she broke into an immediate sweat. She glanced around nervously, then peered across the lake in all directions, as if she might spot somebody, somewhere, manipulating something to achieve this impossible effect.

The light reappeared. In the lake's deepest center it bloomed, a golden glow rising up to the surface, spreading out wide like a blooming flower. Pleasant sighs escaped the others watching.

Our Mother's embrace, Drew thought warily.

Despite the new warmth, she shivered with the thought. She wondered what Julianne must have felt in that moment, looking out over the steam and the strange light, preparing to swim into it—preparing to never return from it. And as Drew wondered this, something touched her hand. Isaac's hand. He reached for her, his fingers scrabbling over her own, and she took his hand into her fist. His tearful eyes were full of that amber light as he watched their mother sit at the dock's edge.

"Go on, then, Julianne," Blaine spoke. "It's time to make your journey."

Julianne's shoulders tensed as she put her weight onto her arms, her hands, and pushed herself gently from the dock and into the water. She let go with a final splash.

It's happening. It's actually happening.

Drew felt as if she'd swallowed someone's drum set. Isaac squeezed her hand even harder. Or maybe she was squeezing him.

They watched as their mother waded out into the lake.

The steam obscured her slightly, but the light ahead revealed her silhouette, her bobbing head, even as the sounds of her movements in the water faded with distance. Drew could hear the sorrowful sniffling of her mother's audience, stifling their tears. Farther and farther Julianne swam, shrinking, pressing into the light like it were a physical thing closing around her... until its bright glow overpowered her silken shadow.

Until Drew lost sight of her completely.

14
THE GHOSTS

She was gone again. Without a trace. Without any clue as to what happened to her.

Like nothing's really changed, Drew thought, lying in bed.

After their mother had vanished into the lake, and darkness reclaimed the water's surface, Isaac had become quite distraught. *Inconsolable* was the better word, actually. Drew held him to herself, clutched him securely in her arms as he clutched child-like to her. The others gawked momentarily, as if realizing that not only were the outsiders indeed human like the rest of them, but that the outsiders had a greater claim to Julianne than they ever did. Then eventually everyone shuffled back to their cabins, murmuring amongst themselves. A bit of an anticlimax, Drew thought.

Blaine remained, however—long enough to meet Drew's gaze as she held her brother, offering her wordless condolences with his frowning mouth and his sympathetic eyes which Drew felt no true sympathy from.

169

Then, as Isaac hitched with sobs, Blaine said rather flatly, "I'll see you both in the morning," and excused himself.

Drew might have cried, too, if it wasn't imperative that she be a rock for Isaac instead. He needed it more than she did, she thought. She believed her brother had maintained a laudable denial about the whole situation thus far, and now their mother was gone, truly gone, he could let that wall crumble accordingly.

Now Drew lay in that familiar, unnerving silence, listening as her brother lay completely still, lulled into a deep sleep with the aid of post-sob fatigue. She could only wish for the same. Her mind was relentlessly awake, replaying the night's events again and again—their mother swimming out, slipping into the light, then gone. Drew's morbid imagination showed her the *mountain* of bones under the lake's surface, her mother's body added to the pile. But even that didn't make sense. Their mother didn't spontaneously drown. They'd have heard it. So where did she go?

That's the whole point, Drew thought. *There is no way to know.*

She tossed and turned herself dizzy, until finally she sat up in the sweaty dark, jealously eyeing her brother across the room.

She climbed out of bed. She slipped into her shoes, grabbed the flashlight from the table, and tiptoed to the cabin door, where she stepped out into the quiet night.

The clouds which previously hung over the horizon were on top of them now, masking the sky with lumpy grays and crushed blacks. Drew peered warily up at them, but sensed no immediate threat of downpour. She studied the individual cabins sprinkled all around, all of them dark once again except for Blaine's. It seemed he kept a lantern burning all hours.

Hoping to wear herself out some more, Drew began a steady walk around the lake. The water rippled gently off the top of the lake against the shore, moved by a strong breeze that pushed through occasionally, shivering the surrounding trees. She drew deeply upon the breeze, into her lungs, and could taste the forest.

Eventually she arrived at the dock again. The image of her mother repeated in her mind's eye, naked at the dock's edge, poised to jump into the water, the amber light waiting for her like a sentient beacon. Drew walked onto the dock, alone this time, and peered over the edge into the murky water below. There was *something* out there, wasn't there? Something besides the light. Something which had to have *created* the light...

Another strong gust of wind came. Hidden beneath the roar in her ears, Drew heard movement. Or sensed it. She turned and observed the dark pavilion, the main lodge beside it. Nothing. No one. Alone. She rolled the flashlight in her hand, still off. She looked once more out onto the lake, its black surface lapping softly at the dock under her feet. No steam. No light. No reflection of the sky above, for the dark clouds there. The longer she stared, the more she sensed that something was staring back. Something in the water, perhaps.

Our Mother?

She shook with a sudden, violent shiver. Whatever she felt, it wasn't desirable. It was—

A wooden plank groaned. Drew's breath caught in her throat.

"Can't sleep?"

She turned to see a handsome face in the muted dark. Robert stopped as he noticed she was startled, and smiled for reassurance.

"Sorry," he said. "Didn't mean to sneak up on you." He joined her at the end of the dock, and together they stood silently for a moment. "I can't imagine how weird you must feel, after watching your mom disappear like that."

"Yeah, well... at least I got to watch this time," Drew said, halfway joking, halfway serious—although she was beginning to wonder if that was something to be thankful for. "Honestly I wish I could think about literally anything else."

She turned to look at Robert, and he turned to look at her. A shared silence. She unabashedly appreciated his visage —the easiness on the eyes, so to speak. The awkwardness of their last encounter was already forgotten. In retrospect, there was nothing to be embarrassed about, she realized. Soon she would be gone, and would never see him again. And along that train of thought...

Nothing to lose...

Looking at him now, the expression with which he regarded her in kind was anything but subtle.

"Where's your cabin?" she asked him.

The corner of Robert's mouth quirked. "That-a-way," he said, and nodded in its direction just around the curve of the lake. "I don't have it all to myself, though."

Drew nodded, thinking.

"Where do you go then, when you want to be alone?"

Robert peered around them in a mocking fashion. "I mean, the woods are as good a place as any for that."

Surprising even herself—desperate for that distraction—Drew turned entirely toward the man beside her and said, "Show me."

～

He led her into the woods by the hand, and there under the gloom she explored him. She pressed him to a tree, his body as solid as the tree itself. She put her mouth to his, as his hands smoothed their way up her back.

In the branches overhead, the frantic motion of little claws and little wings. Hopping, fluttering. Watching.

Drew's focus was ensnared by their sounds. So lively in the middle of the night? She imagined them darting down, perching upon hers and Robert's bodies as a flock. As she imagined this, she forgot her mouth, her tongue, as Robert tried to remind her. His guitar-string-plucking hands pulled her against himself. He placed his face into the crook of her neck, and she opened her eyes with an involuntary gasp.

And it was then she saw them. Their shapes. Not the birds in the branches, but the shadows in the forest. Silhouetted figures erected between the trees. Drew gasped again, louder than before, and Robert's hands groped harder in return. The figures in the trees were moving. Slightly swaying in place. Drew pushed against Robert, forced him back against the tree.

"Stop," she said.

Hands falling away, out of breath, Robert said, "What's the matter?"

She scoured the dark with darting eyes. The shadows were gone in an instant, or had simply become what they'd always been—nothing.

She looked over her shoulder, seeing only the numerous pillars of tree trunks in the darkness. Then she looked up into the spidery canopy above them, where the empty branches whispered with another breeze.

Impossible.

Robert followed her gaze. "What are we looking at?"

"I thought I saw something..."

"Something?"

Drew squirmed as her body crawled with goosebumps. Robert stepped away from the tree, toward Drew, and his hands moved toward her waist, not yet given up. But even as he stepped against her, she could only look to the shadows, to the trees, to the *things* hiding in them, muscles tense and ready to spring at the first sign of trouble. She ignored the furnace-like heat of Robert's body as she brushed his hands away.

"I'm sorry. I can't."

"What is it you think you saw?"

I don't think *I saw anything,* she thought. *I saw it.*

"I don't know." She paused, doubting the words even as she spoke them—doubting the words that followed even more, though she failed to stop them. "Do you believe in ghosts, Robert?"

He laughed, taken by surprise.

"Oh, you're serious?" He scratched the back of his neck

as he considered it. "Well, I'd be a hypocrite if I said no, considering the other crazy stuff I believe. I've never seen one myself, though. Why, have you?"

Drew hesitated, loathing the thought. "Years ago." Then, after some reluctance, she said, "This is going to sound random as hell, but I have to ask..."

"More random than if I believe in ghosts?"

"Did you know Cameron?"

Robert was taken once more by surprise, but instead of laughing he simply appeared confused. "Cameron? You mean *from here,* Cameron? Yeah, I knew him. But he left a couple months ago. Why? Where'd you hear about him?"

"Describe him to me," Drew said. She regarded Robert soberly, no hint of humor. "Please."

Robert's confusion gave way to something else. Apprehension?

"Uh, okay..." He thought about it. "I guess he stood out mostly thanks to his hair. He had a pretty bitchin' mullet. But he was one of those dudes who's good-looking enough to pull it off. You know?"

"Was he blond?"

Robert nodded. "Yeah. How'd you know that?"

"Is there anyone else currently here who looks like that?"

Now Robert smiled again, like he was missing a punch-line. "No, nobody else with a blond mullet, sadly. Why?"

Drew took a long, shuddering breath, watching the woods around them distrustfully.

"I think I've seen another ghost. A few, actually..."

"What, here?" Robert glanced left and right. "Just now?"

Drew nodded. "This place is crawling with them."

Isaac was awake when she returned. Not just awake, but sitting outside near the water with a blanket wrapped around his shoulders. Drew was relieved to see him there, as the eeriness of her time with Robert clung to her like moss to a tree, following her the whole way back around the lake to their cabin. She scuffed her shoes in the dirt as she approached to warn Isaac of her arrival.

"Where did you go?" he asked.

"I couldn't sleep." She took a seat on the dirt beside him. "Thought maybe a walk would help."

"I couldn't sleep, either..."

"Really? I could have sworn you were in a deep coma when I left." To this Isaac said nothing, neck deep in his own thoughts. Despite the obvious answer, she asked, "What are you out here thinking about?"

"We just witnessed..." Isaac shrugged. "I don't even know how to describe what we just saw."

"Weird shit, you mean."

"And yet I don't feel all that weird about it. Like, any of it. Maybe it just hasn't fully sunk in yet? I don't know. I still just wish I had more time with her first."

Drew watched him discreetly, as he fidgeted under his blanket, and wondered if they were stable enough to speak her mind in the moment. She was going to regardless.

"I mean... mom must have thought the time we got was plenty, or else she'd still be here. Right?"

She expected Isaac to raise his hackles at this, but staggeringly he nodded in agreement. Then even *more* staggeringly, he smiled at Drew and said, "I heard you say *'I love you'* though. Does that mean you forgave her after all?"

"I said that because I thought she needed to hear it..." Drew hesitated. She and Isaac both knew perfectly well that wasn't the truth. "And maybe because I do love her, a little... or did... even if I hated her just as much."

"It's okay if you forgave her," Isaac said. "You can be honest."

Even solemn as he was, it was clear he was quite pleased with himself. Drew could have argued this much later into the night, but instead she only said, "I have to pee."

"Story of your life."

"Story of my life..." she said, and groaned as she picked herself up off the dirt, flashlight in hand. "Wait up for me, okay?"

In case I don't make it back.

She made her way to the trees, where she flicked on her flashlight to reveal the hidden path which narrowed into the woods until the darkness swallowed it, where the light of her flashlight couldn't reach. She eyed the cabin at her back, and considered dropping trou there instead, even if it was against the rules. Anything to avoid going back into the woods.

There is something wrong with this place.

Another strong breeze *whooshed* through the woods, rattling the branches before her. Taking a deep breath, training her wobbling beam on the path, she started in. She walked briskly. The trees creaked and groaned, and the underbrush rustled and tittered with movement as critters darted through them, out of them, scared away by the petite woman who in actuality was much more frightened of them.

You're being a baby.

She told herself to keep her head down, her feet moving, the light shining. Until eventually her light revealed the lone shape of the outhouse at the path's end, its charmless door a gray, dull slab. She hurried inside and closed the door before the darkness could follow her in.

One more night. Gone first thing in the morning. You can do this.

The intermittent breeze moved through the gaps of the roof, creating a horrible drone as it passed, filling the outhouse with cool air that broke Drew's legs out in goose-flesh. When she finished, she pulled up her shorts, readied the flashlight, and without a second thought pressed back out into the night, slamming the outhouse door at her back along the way. Her feet scuffed the dirt in her haste. The breeze picked up momentarily, into a howling wind, and Drew lowered her eyes to the ground as dirt picked up from the path. Then her ears perked to the abrupt sound of something nearby.

"You."

She looked. She couldn't avoid it. She turned to the voice, her whole body pivoting stiffly in its direction, and was wholly unsurprised to find the dark mouth of the cave staring back against the light of her flashlight.

"Not this again," she muttered under her breath.

"Help us."

Drew flinched back wildly, as if a hornet had buzzed against her earlobe, and of course there was nothing there. Nothing but the breeze in the trees. Her entire body seemed to sing out then—a rush of chills, which she imagined if she followed like braille across her skin would repeatedly read: *get out of here, get out of here, get out of here...*

She shined her light on the cave once more. The flashlight beam shook terribly in her grip.

"Who are you?" she asked.

Along with the urge to run, some part of Drew struggled against the urge to cry. It came out of nowhere. Or perhaps everything she'd bottled up from her mother's departure had simply decided now was the perfect time to manifest.

"Please."

It was ahead of her now. Somewhere between the path and the cave, though the darkness appeared empty. Against all reason, Drew moved into the trees, cleaving the dark left and right with her flashlight as she approached the cave's mouth, repeating a single mantra as she went: *What are you doing... what are you doing... what are you doing...*

Meanwhile, another, quieter voice in the back of her mind told her to run, return to the cabin, back to Isaac.

"Please."

The word echoed hollowly from the cave's belly, finding Drew at its entrance, shaking her like a dry, brittle reed. She pointed the flashlight inside, and found that the tunnel curved, showing her nothing from where she stood. Her feet were rooted in place, unable to flee like her fear insisted, unable to venture onward like her curiosity demanded. This was something else, she knew. Something not even Julianne had known about. Nor Robert, nor Sherry, nor probably even the stink-eyed Caroline.

This was something beyond their routine, beyond their

system of belief. But in the deepest pit of Drew's belly, she knew this had something to do with the *truth of it all*.

"Fuck it," she muttered, and took her first step into the cave.

The tunnel entered the hillside at a slant, and she followed it, pointing her flashlight along the glistening, rocky walls ahead. She stepped around a single bend and it turned in on itself, snaking deeper. The chittering noises of the forest and the wind faded behind her. All she heard now was the hollow breathiness of the cave. Dank and muted. She thought back to that first conversation with Robert, wherein he'd seemed so sure this wasn't a bear den, and she morbidly considered how funny it would be if he was wrong, if she found something hungry and waiting at the tunnel's end.

But of course the voices weren't leading her to a bear.

The tunnel soon brought her to a small, oval-shaped chamber. She aimed her light across its rounded rock walls, and found no other branching paths. This was it. Then she pointed her light to the ground, and discovered she was wrong. Another path lay at her feet, this one dropping straight down into the cave's floor... filled to the brim with water.

No way I'm going through—

A series of tiny bubbles broke the water's surface as Drew shined her light there, and every thought in her mind scattered, leaving her in a frozen stupor. More bubbles appeared. The watery hole gently popped with them. Then a larger bubble floated up, large enough to gurgle as it broke upon the water's skin, and with its arrival the cave erupted in a deafening choir of voices which screamed out—

"HELP US!"

Drew stumbled back, bumped against the cave wall with a scream of her own, shrill and brief. She aimed her light at the cave's ceiling, swept it along its every contour, still alone, no sign of the voices' origins except for the watery hole which was beginning to burst with so many bubbles that it appeared in a boil. It was then she listened to her fear. She ran.

Her light was a strobing slideshow against the rocky tunnel walls as she fled, arms pumping, shoulders bumping left and right through the snaking tunnel as new voices continued to bellow from behind her all the while.

"PLEASE!"

"HELP US!"

She burst from the cave's entrance in a flurry of slapping sneakers. She chased through the trees, back to the smoothed, hard dirt of the path, and proceeded to sprint back toward the cabin, back toward the lake, against the strengthening wind of what had to be a coming storm—though she would refrain from thinking about that just yet.

What the fuck... what the fuck?

There were no more voices behind her. Just the movement of the trees all around, and the scuff of her feet, and the hectic shadows her aimless flashlight threw in all directions. The cabin appeared beyond the tree line. Almost there. Already she felt bursting at the seams to tell Isaac what she'd seen—what she'd *heard*. There was no misinterpreting this, she thought. No doubting the difference between what was real or imagined.

She emerged from the trees and felt the forest's darkness

pull away like a hood from around her head. She hurried past the cabin, came around the corner in full sprint... and then slid to an immediate halt.

No.

Isaac remained by the lake shore, but he was standing now. The blanket which had previously been wrapped around his shoulders was now pooled around his ankles. His arms were held out, as if basking in the warm sun.

No, no, no...

Every inch of Isaac's upper body was aglow with blinking, swarming fireflies.

15

THE CHOSEN

"No," Drew said aloud. "Isaac..."

Isaac turned in a slow circle. His face was illuminated by the fireflies clinging to his forehead and around his jaw like a bizarre chin strap. He was grinning like a fool.

Drew dropped her flashlight carelessly as she rushed to him. Without hesitation, she swept at his clothes, swept the fireflies from his body in a hurried panic. Suddenly Isaac's beaming face turned dour with shock.

"What are you doing?" he said. He tried to step back and nearly lost his footing. "Stop it, Drew!"

She beat at his clothes, at his arms and shoulders, felt the fireflies squish and smear beneath the palms of her hands as others took flight to save themselves. She looked wildly around them, at the dark lake and the surrounding cabins, praying no one else saw as she continued to swipe the fireflies from her brother's body.

"What the fuck are you doing?" Isaac exclaimed.

He shoved her and she hardly registered it before she was at him again, this time swiping around his face. He slapped her hands away.

"I said knock it off!"

"We have to get you inside. Oh my God, Isaac…"

But it was too late. From the shadows—where Drew failed to see him coming—a man approached with a slow clap and a smug laugh that involuntarily curled Drew's hand into a fist.

"Well I'll be damned," Kent said. "Isaac… you lucky dog, you…"

"No," Drew said lamely, as if she could argue what she knew was coming.

"Do you know what this means?"

By now, Drew had either killed or frightened off all the fireflies, leaving Isaac to stand in his shirt and boxer briefs, his blanket abandoned by the water. Overwhelmed, Drew grabbed Isaac by the wrist and pulled him toward their cabin. He followed for a bit, feet stumbling, before he pulled away.

"What are you doing?" he asked again.

"We're leaving tomorrow," Drew blurted. She glanced toward Kent, watching with great interest. "Promise me, Isaac. We are leaving *tomorrow.*"

"Did I see what I think I saw?"

This was not Kent, but another voice Drew dreaded to hear. Blaine appeared from just over Kent's shoulder, the two of them gazing at Isaac as if Drew didn't exist. She could hardly believe it—that they were both so conveniently *around* to witness Isaac's strange little miracle. Blaine whispered something into Kent's ear as he stepped by, which sent Kent off in the other direction.

"Unbelievable," Blaine said. "I've never seen anything like this before. Only here a day, and... chosen so quickly."

"Chosen?" Isaac said.

"This doesn't mean anything!" Drew shouted. She grabbed Isaac by the wrist again, and with angry spittle flecking from her mouth barked, *"My brother and I need to talk in private."*

Isaac pulled back again, but was ultimately unprepared as Drew dragged him to their door. His bare feet scraped the dirt along the way. His voice cracked shrilly as he ordered her to stop. She opened the door and, like the overbearing mother he never had, pulled Isaac inside behind her, yanking him across the threshold with all the strength she could muster. She slammed the door shut on Blaine's ridiculous goatee advancing on the other side.

"What the hell is wrong with you?" Isaac asked, pulling free again.

Drew put her back to the door, blocking the way as Isaac stood mostly stunned before her.

"He's trying to keep us here," she told him point-blank. "This is all meant to keep us from leaving."

Isaac shook his head, bewildered. "You think this was planned? How *the fuck* do you plan something like that, Drew? Explain it to me."

"I don't know. I don't know what they're up to, or how they did it. But they did it. This is what he wants, Isaac..." She clenched her jaw, grinding her teeth as she felt the weight of the world crushing her down. "Goddamn it..."

We were idiots to think we could just waltz in here, say goodbye to mommy dearest, and go merrily on our way...

At her back, Blaine rapped his knuckles on the door, and his muffled voice said, *"Is everything all right?"*

"Isaac, promise me." Standing in the dark, she could hardly make out the expression in his eyes, only that they were looking her way, listening. "Promise me we're going home tomorrow. First thing. Promise me..."

"You're being crazy right now," Isaac said.

"No. Fuck you. I'm the only one here *not being crazy* right now."

Once more, Blaine knocked on the cabin door, harder this time.

"I'd like to hear what Isaac has to say," Blaine said.

"Drew."

"Isaac, please..."

"He is his own person, is he not?"

Blaine was a master manipulator, Drew had to give him that. These words rang Isaac like a bell, loud and clear, shaking him at his very core. Even without the light to reveal his features, Drew knew her brother's expression then—his embarrassment, shortly superseded by the anger he felt for her in that moment.

"The others want to hear about your experience, Isaac!" Blaine shouted. *"Won't you come tell us what it was like?"*

So that was what he sent Kent to do, Drew thought. Round up the other sheep. Manufacture some excitement, some peer pressure—where no peers actually existed.

"It doesn't mean anything," Drew said.

Isaac sighed irritably. Her insistence was having the opposite effect than what she hoped.

"Move out of the way."

"Are you kidding me? Isaac, these people don't give a shit about you. About either of us. He's just trying—"

"Get out of the way," he said, harsher this time.

"You're not going out there."

Isaac stepped close, close enough that Drew could feel the heat of his frustration as he said, "You're not my fucking mom, Drew."

She felt something terrible in that moment. Her spirit leaving her body. Utter shame. Isaac's words struck her in places she didn't even know were exposed, didn't even know were so tender. She sagged with her back against the door, until Isaac physically made to move her, to push her aside. She moved willingly, wounded and reeling. When Isaac pulled the door open, the others' voices reached them—just a few people by the sounds of it, probably from the nearest cabin Kent had reached so far—and their quiet murmuring lifted into an intoxicating round of cheers as he appeared.

Most horrifying of all, as Isaac stepped outside to meet them, she glimpsed his plain-to-see agitation melt away in favor of something warmer. An unexpected delight, as the others welcomed him with open arms. She followed him into the doorway and watched as the others circled, their sleepy faces lit with excitement. They started away, talking as they walked. Only Blaine stayed behind for a moment.

"Are you coming?" he asked Drew.

She regarded him with open-faced hatred, eyes darting between him and her brother getting farther and farther away. When she gave no answer, Blaine simply smirked and left her there, standing like a fool in the dark.

Drew returned inside and had herself a panic party. Just a little one, replete with plenty of pacing back and forth and pulling at her hair like someone on the edge of insanity. She went to her cot, where she produced Isaac's switchblade from under her pillow. She pressed its little metal nub and watched the blade appear with a satisfying *shwick.* She stared at its sharp edge in a daze, thinking *ugly things,* before finally she remembered herself. She folded the blade back up, then took a seat at the table in the middle of the cabin where she thought for a while, popping the blade out and folding it back up again and again. It was almost soothing. The repetition, the noise it made, the way it felt in her hand. Eventually she set it down, propped her elbows on the table, steepled her fingers against her mouth, and stared off into the shadows, imagining the worst and trying to plan against it.

This isn't happening.

She lay her head in her arms, like she'd done through so many morning lectures in college following late nights of general degeneracy.

This can't be happening.

Surely he wouldn't want to stay. Not alone, not without her. Leave everything behind for these people? There was no chance in hell he was that naive, she thought.

With her head down, eyes closed, she saw her mother again, a silhouette in the glow of the lake, wading into its unknown... into her unknown. She saw the figures in the trees standing like faceless sentries, watching and listening. She replayed their voices from the path in the woods, from the cave, from the strange watery hole therein. Calling for help. *Begging* for help. Nothing here was *ever* as it seemed, not from the moment they set foot in this commune. Not even the others knew, she thought. They acted on faith. Faith in the lake. Faith in *Blaine,* who peddled its mystique. More than ever, Drew believed her morbid assumption was right. A pile of bones *did* rest at the bottom of the lake. Past victims lured to their doom by some impossible hoax Blaine somehow managed to fool them with.

And Isaac would soon be next.

He returned unexpectedly. Drew wasn't sure for how long she sat with her head buried. She jerked upright as the door opened. The switchblade lay on the table before her. She snatched it up and shoved it into the small but stretchy pocket of her sweat shorts. Isaac closed the door softly behind him. Without even looking at his sister, he moved to his cot, where he paused, head bent in thought, before finally turning to see her in the dark. He had something terrible to tell her, she could tell.

"So we're leaving in the morning, then?" she asked, giving him no chance to voice the dreadful news.

He sighed. "Don't you even want to know what happened?"

"I already know what happened. I already know what Blaine wants you to think. Trust me, I know. But it doesn't even matter, does it? Because we're going home first thing tomorrow morning."

Isaac turned away slightly, avoiding her gaze which he probably couldn't even see anyway, not any better than she could see his.

"What home..." he muttered.

Drew's stomach plummeted out from beneath her, went *splat* on the wooden planks beneath her chair.

"Home, Isaac. Where we live. Where our lives go on after we leave this place."

"Right..."

"Don't tell me they've convinced you to stay. You're *smarter than that,* Isaac."

"Don't tell me how smart I am, or how naive I am, or whatever you think will—"

"He's manipulating you!"

"*You're* manipulating me," Isaac said. His shadow stiffened at the shoulders as he tried to keep his composure. "Call it whatever you want, but our lives back in the city... that's not *home* to me. It has never been home to me."

"Are you serious? What are you saying? You *want* to stay here?"

"I don't want to stay here," Isaac said, and for an instant Drew felt a hint of relief, until she realized how naive *she* was. "I... I want to go with mom. I want to be with her, wherever that is."

"You mean at the bottom of the—"

"No, that's not what I mean," Isaac interjected, a vicious bite creeping into his words. "Why do you have to be such an asshole? You'll ignore *anything* just to cling to your cynicism. Because that's how you cope. That's your own little defense mechanism, assuming the worst about *everything.*"

Drew stood up, the feet of her chair squealing across the floor as she did. She moved toward Isaac, and barely stopped herself from grabbing hold of him, wishing to shake some sense into him.

"There are no such things as forest spirits, or gods, or whatever these people believe. There is no such thing as a magical lake, or a light that transports you to... wherever the hell these people think they're going."

"Blaine didn't rig an entire lake to steam up on command. Or light up on command. He didn't gather up and train a bunch of fireflies to swarm me at the snap of a finger. This is *real,* Drew. There comes a point where *you're* the one who looks ridiculous for not believing in something that's right in front of you."

"I believe in things," Drew said. "I've seen plenty, trust me. There very well might be something going on here, but it's not what these people think it is..."

She was torn. Telling Isaac the truth about what she'd witnessed the last couple nights felt like too little, too late—out of left field, especially, because she'd never shared with him the one other experience she'd had all those years ago. What she'd seen on that horrendously ugly afternoon... the day of their father's passing...

"And what makes you think you know better than all of us?" Isaac said.

Us. It hit Drew like a fist. He was gone. Not just standing at the edge, but already mid-dive. No bringing him back. And in that case... she supposed she had nothing to lose.

"I've seen and heard things the last couple nights," she said. "Things I didn't tell you about because I thought you'd think I was crazy, but apparently it turns out you'll believe much worse..."

Even in the dark, Drew could read his expression. The *too little, too late* in full effect.

"You've seen and heard things..." he said, his tone unimpressed. "You know... I've been in therapy for years, too. You and I don't talk much about what happened, even though my therapist has repeatedly told me it would be good for us both. But I avoid bringing anything up because I know... I'm *aware,* that you saw a lot worse than I did. I know you've got plenty more to forget than I do. I also know you think I'm lucky, somehow, because I didn't know mom as well as you did, and I didn't get to be as close to dad as you were. I know you think because I got six years less than you, that somehow means the loss is easier for me. You think you're the only one who's fucked up. You think you're the only one dealing with shit. What you call *home?* It's just an endless routine for me. How many years has it been now? And I'm still going to therapy every other week, and I just keep talking about the same old shit and nothing ever seems to change or get better..."

"Isaac..."

"It's like I'm just living for my next session. And I'm tired of it. I'm so tired of it. It doesn't feel like living. And nowhere feels like home. Not with grandma and grandpa, not in my college dorms. I feel like I'm a *shell,* Drew. I thought I was coping, pretending I have some grasp on the situation with all my therapy bullshit, but the truth is I'm barely holding it together day to day. And yeah, I know I'm only nineteen, but... it's like I can already see the rest of my life stretched out in front of me, and it doesn't ever get any better..."

...my life stretched out in front of me...

Isaac's words were chiseling away at her poise with incredible speed, unraveling all her preconceived notions with surgical precision—but this phrase stuck out like a sore thumb above all the rest. Because she'd already heard it before, very recently...

"Mom's letter was like a lifeboat, Drew. Like I'd been waiting for something all these years and didn't know it, not until that letter showed up in my mail, and suddenly I had something else to think about, something to look forward to. I know you think I'm crazy for buying into these people's superstitions—or whatever you want to call it—but this is the first time in my life I've ever felt excited about something. I'm telling you, this is *real*. Or at least... it's real *for me.*"

He watched her intently, waiting for her to say something. But she found she had nothing to say. Well, that wasn't true. She had loads of things to say, but she wasn't anywhere close to knowing how to properly express them.

"You don't have to stay," he added. "You don't need to watch me go, if you don't want to..."

The emotions which had failed to overwhelm her at their mother's farewell found their way to the surface now, overwhelming her to the point of breathlessness.

"I'm not leaving you here," she said. She snorted back the tears which had flooded her eyes, her nasal passages. "I'm not letting you do this..."

"It's not for you to decide what I can and can't do—"

"I'm not letting her take you away from me, too!"

She threw her arms around him, squeezed him against herself hard enough to turn him into a diamond. Isaac didn't struggle. She even listened as his breath strained out of him from the pressure, and still he didn't pull away.

"You can't do this," she choked into his ear. "You can't just leave me..."

The panic returned tenfold. It washed away all thought, all reason. She held onto her brother with the intent of never letting him go. Perhaps she could squeeze him hard enough, she thought, to collapse them both like a dying star.

"Please. I promise you... when we leave this place... when we get back... you'll realize h-how f-fucked up all of this is..."

"Drew, I'm not—"

"You'll realize how c-crazy these p-people are, and... and..." She swallowed with monumental effort. "Please don't do this. Please don't..."

Finally Isaac grabbed hold of her, tried to push himself away, tried to separate them.

"Drew..."

"There's something wrong with this place," she said, clinging to him like putty. She spoke quickly, as if blurting out the same things all over again could convince him. "We'll go right now. Please. We'll leave tonight, and..."

"Drew, stop it!"

He forced her away. She staggered but didn't fall. She wiped both her eyes with violent swipes on the backs of her hands. She stepped toward him again, and he stepped back, nearly against the wall, and raised his palms defensively against her approach.

"Stop," he said firmly.

Drew stopped, but she could hardly keep still. She held herself, hands around her biceps.

"Please don't do this," she begged. *"This is crazy, Isaac..."*

Blinking through tears, she saw his expression and it was *crushing*. A clear desperation to escape her melodrama. If he could fast-forward this whole encounter, he would. His mind was made up.

"I'm sorry, Drew. I... I really am. I wish I had something better to tell you, but..."

As her panicked mind realized all was lost, she found herself moving through the stages, until she arrived at the stage she knew best—the one that had fueled her through most of her life thus far, and had served her well enough. She wiped more tears from her face. The last of them, if she could help it.

"You care more about her than me? You'd rather chase her into *oblivion* than stay with me?"

"This has nothing to do with you, Drew. This is my decision. I'm doing it for *me.*"

"Oh, believe me, I know," Drew said. She swallowed yet again, and this time succeeded in ridding her throat of its melancholic frog. "All you think about is you, Isaac."

"You know that's not true," he retorted, which Drew didn't think was much of a retort at all. "Listen... maybe we should both sleep on this. We'll talk about it more in the morning. Okay?"

Drew tried to scoff, but it came out sounding more like she was laughing with someone's hands around her throat.

There were so many more unproductive things she wished to say, accusations to blindly lob, knees yearning to be begged from. She couldn't simply stand by—couldn't bear the thought of another night listening to her brother fall into an easy sleep, as if his actions didn't keep him up at night. Despite not seeing him well in the darkness, he looked different now. She *saw him* differently now. Her baby brother wasn't such a baby after all. He was meaner than she thought. Sadder, too. More lost than she ever could have guessed. It was hard to tell which of these attributes informed the other...

"Like hell I'll be sleeping on this," she said.

And she promptly removed herself from the cabin.

She stopped outside. She was shaking again. Not out of fear, but wrath. She closed her eyes, lifted her face to the clouded sky, and breathed in deeply as the wind whipped around her, tussling her hair and cooling the sweat which had broken at her temples. She allowed her mind to slip into any dark place it might—too exhausted at this point to fight it. Where it went surprised her.

She thought of the gun in Isaac's bag. She thought about using it. On Blaine. Force him to reveal the charade to Isaac at gunpoint. She thought about forcing Kent to take her back to town, where she would call the police and tell them about this place, this suicide cult, have them perform a raid before Isaac could make the stupidest mistake of his life. The *last* mistake of his life.

Or maybe just use the damn thing on myself. For being stupid enough to come here. Stupid enough to climb into Kent's truck. Even stupider for submitting to the blindfolds. All of it.

She opened her eyes to the sound of thunder in the distance, just in time to see the distant clouds ignite with soft golden light whose thunder would reach her again shortly. An omen, she thought.

Before she even had a plan in mind, she started moving. She marched along the edge of the shore, the lake lapping hungrily beside her feet, heading toward the only cabin with a lantern still glowing out front.

She would tell Blaine he couldn't do this. Not to Isaac. She'd beg him if she had to. Beg him to deny Isaac the *'journey.'* Beg him to let them go, send them home where they belonged.

The closer she came to Blaine's cabin, the more she wished she'd brought Isaac's gun after all. The switchblade remained in her pocket, however—stiff and awkward against her upper thigh as she hastily swished one leg in front of the other. But would she need it?

They might all be crazy, but that doesn't make them murderers.

She told herself this, but was ultimately unconvinced.

Every other cabin along the way was dark and quiet. Had everyone already returned to bed following the excitement? Judging by the lack of celebration for Julianne's departure, Drew was beginning to think this community was fairly lukewarm on celebration in general.

Lightning flashed again as she neared Blaine's cabin, and revealed Kent's pickup parked beneath the nearby trees. She stopped a few paces from Blaine's door. The windows were faintly illuminated, suggesting that a lantern was lit inside. He was still awake.

Why am I here?

Three more steps brought her to the door. She raised a fist, then hesitated.

What am I going to say?

She knocked four times. She waited. After twenty seconds or so, she raised her fist again. A fresh wave of anger, impatience, and desperation flooded her. She was prepared to take it all out on the door, to bruise her knuckles pounding if she had to.

"Screw it," she muttered.

She tried the door instead, and it opened with a soft click. Hand on the knob, widening the gap in the door, she glimpsed the table in the middle of the room where the lantern sat, casting its modest firelight around the cabin. She opened her mouth as if to call Blaine's name, and then said nothing, pushing the door inward all the while until finally it stood open, and she stood in its threshold. Inside Blaine's cabin were two other doors—one to a separate bedroom on the left, and one to a small pocket in the far right corner, which Drew had previously assumed to be a closet. Both doors were open.

Drew called softly, "Blaine?"

When he didn't answer, she moved inside. She left the entrance open behind her, stepping quietly toward the table and chairs, sitting neatly on a square, green rug. From there, she could see into the bedroom which was mostly too dark to make out, save for the foot of Blaine's bed inside. She looked to the other door then. The closet. She started toward it, until she glanced in passing at the rearmost chair at the table, pulled out slightly at an angle, its seat cluttered with items. Upon spotting those items, she paused, and there her eyes lingered for a prolonged moment. Processing.

On the chair were a set of keys, a wallet, and a phone. Drew recognized one of these items right away, though her mind took a few seconds to believe it. The wallet. She'd seen it before. An otherwise unremarkable black bifold, except for the engraved leather on the bottom corner—the letters 'QN.' She regarded the other two items. The keys and the phone. If not for the wallet, the keys could have been anybody's. Anybody's BMW key fob, with its signature blue-and-white insignia in the middle. Not that she needed any more confirmation, out of curiosity—dreadful, heart-pounding curiosity —Drew bent toward the phone lying screen up, and tapped her finger twice upon its black glass. It illuminated. She was presented with her own face, positioned affectionately beside the face of the phone's owner. Her and Quentin, their visages bathed in the intense pink-and-blue glow of night club lights.

Drew flinched to the sound of a voice close by. A loud, *pained* moan, which echoed from the second open door. The door which did not, in fact, lead to a closet. She stood frozen by the table, by the chair holding Quentin's possessions, as another moan rose up from some place down *below*—the moan of someone in distress, someone who could do nothing *but* moan. Helpless. Trapped. Hurt. As the second moan thinned weakly into a rasp, the unseen stairs beyond the open door creaked with movement. Climbing footsteps. The nape of Drew's neck prickled with terror.

Get out of here. Now!

She pivoted blindly in the direction of the front door, one foot chasing the other, and screamed as she bolted straight into Kent's waiting arms. He grabbed her roughly, spun her around, wrangled her against himself, and slapped a firm hand across her shrieking mouth.

"Shh, shh, shh," he spoke into her ear, as he wrestled her down onto her knees, then down onto the floor. She wriggled and fought as he grabbed each of her wrists, pinned her arms behind her back. She screamed again, his hand no longer over her mouth, to which he simply let out a terrible laugh. "No one can hear you."

Ahead of them, the footsteps reached the top of the stairs. Someone moved toward them with slow, plodding movements. With her face against the floor in the other direction, Drew couldn't see who it was, though she had a decent idea.

"A little late for a visit, isn't it?" Blaine said.

Kent held Drew with little trouble, strain as she might. The switchblade prodded uncomfortably against her thigh inside her pocket. So close and yet so far. Blaine knelt beside Drew. As Kent held her down, Blaine proceeded to tie her wrists with twine. Tight enough to smart. Then he did the same around her ankles.

"Please," she said. "I... I won't say anything. I won't tell anyone. I didn't see anything. I didn't..."

"Let's not fool ourselves, Ms. Prescott," Blaine said, standing upright. "If it makes you feel any better... you were never going home."

She wanted to scream some more—maybe beg some more—but instead she asked, "Why is he here? What are you doing to him?"

"Who? Your boyfriend?" Blaine laughed softly. "He's

here because he followed you here. Kent found a GPS tracker inside the trunk of your car. Did you have any idea?"

Drew had no words.

"Anyway, lucky you, you'll have some company down there..."

"Wait," she said, as Blaine moved across the cabin, fetching something else. "What about my brother? What about Isaac? He'll wonder where I am. He knows I wouldn't leave him here..."

Drew shrugged uselessly on the ground, pulled her wrists within their restraints to test the twine's give and found no give at all. Then Blaine was stomping across the cabin toward her again.

"Isaac knows no such thing," he said. "All he knows is that the women in his family have a tendency to run when things get serious. Isn't that right?"

Drew opened her mouth to argue and in an instant Blaine was down on his knees, shoving something terribly wet and sweet into her mouth with his bare hands. She might have bitten him had she not been so surprised by it. He scraped it off behind her teeth, a thick wad of something both sugary and bitter, like congealed cough syrup. Only it wasn't that. It wasn't anything Drew could place. She immediately gagged. The warmth of her mouth softened it instantly, turned it runny and melting down her tongue, her throat, where she couldn't help but swallow and choke in equal measure, sputtering uselessly as what remained in her mouth stuck there like glue.

"There," Blaine said. "That should have you feeling rather good shortly. Don't fight it, Drew."

The more it drained down her throat, the more of its bitterness she tasted, until she reflexively convulsed from the taste alone.

Then, with a wordless order from Mr. Goatee himself, Kent hoisted her up from the floor. It was difficult, balancing her up onto her feet which she offered him no help with. Irritated, Kent simply dragged her under the arms. The heels of her sneakers rubbed and bumped against the wooden floor, until he brought her into that open door, to the dark stairway beyond, and one by one he walked her down each precarious step into the hidden basement. Blaine swung into the doorway, watching from the head of the stairs as a soft silhouette, and it was only then Drew realized he was entirely nude.

"You have her?" he asked.

Voice straining with the effort, Kent said, "I've got her..."

At the bottom, he dragged her into the deeper dark, where the floor was hard as cement but scratchy against the rubber heels of her sneakers. Natural rock. She was vaguely reminded of the cave earlier, wandering its glistening tunnel...

Kent dropped her onto the ground at last. Then he returned to the stairs and *hurried* up them, as if he couldn't escape the basement a moment too soon. After she swallowed the rest of the substance—what she now assumed was the same substance given to her mother before her journey—Drew understood why Kent hurried. The basement smelled *rank*. The unquestionable scent of flesh rot. Something dying, or already dead. And then she remembered the moans she'd heard.

"Sweet dreams," Blaine called.

The door shut. The basement fell into absolute darkness. Near-absolute silence, too, except for her panting. She blinked her blind eyes. Something moved in the darkness with her. The rustle of clothes. A dry-throated, rasping breath. She tried to sit up, lying on her side, and was strangely unable—as if her muscles had all been suddenly turned into lead. The *other* continued to breathe, to rasp, and soon let out a hacking cough, which was so dry their throat squealed like a rusted hinge. His name flirted with Drew's mouth, her lips twitching to form the word, but she was too drained to even speak.

Quentin?

She lay perfectly still. She stopped fighting. She relaxed onto the jutting ground beneath her body, the rock not as cold as one would expect. There was a humidity here, the air warm and thick, which only served to make the spoiled meat smell that much worse. Stomach-turning. Inescapable.

She stared into the shadows, in the direction of her invisible company, and marveled as her vision began to change. The darkness filled with strange hues. Strange lights. Blues and greens and golds bled like inkblots—an illuminated Rorschach test in her mind's eye. A weightlessness settled over her, lifting her up even as the rocky floor remained firm underneath. Like flying and going nowhere...

Paralyzed. Helpless. Doomed.

16

THE MANIPULATOR

The light coming through the cabin window was dull and gray when Isaac opened his eyes, but well beyond that of early morning. He'd slept in later than he intended. As he lay blinking, he felt the subtle throb of a headache. Or a migraine. Sometimes he forgot which was which.

The previous night came to him in a rush. Their mother's journey. The fireflies. The whirlwind of emotions that followed. He'd never felt so swept up in something before. Like *something* in the universe was finally aligning for his sake.

And then he remembered his fight with Drew.

He rolled over to face her cot, and frowned upon seeing it empty and unmade. *Weird,* he thought. She almost never woke earlier than he did. He glanced to the floor beside her bed and noticed something else. Or rather, a *lack* of something else. Her things were missing. Her clothes, her bag. All of it.

Drew was gone.

He slipped toward the edge of his bed, and reached for his own bag on the floor underneath. Still there. Hanging awkwardly off his cot, he rummaged through it, through his remaining clothes, until he found the pistol nestled inside. Why he needed it now, he wasn't sure—but some part of him had to check, had to *know*.

It won't matter much longer, will it?

A cold pang of fear went through him at the thought. To rid himself of it, he climbed out of bed and got dressed. He did another cursory check around Drew's bed to make sure he was right, that all her things were gone, and confirmed it. Perhaps she'd requested another cabin, unable to sleep in the same room as him.

Stepping outside, the overcast sky greeted him with its gloomy kindness, gentle on his aching gaze.

"Morning!"

He hardly made it two steps from his cabin before he was greeted by Sherry—like she was waiting for him to rise.

"Morning," he said, his voice still croaky with sleep. "Hey... you haven't seen Drew this morning, have you?"

Sherry cocked her head like a floppy-eared dog. "Drew? No. She's not in bed?"

Isaac shook his head glumly, then forced a half-smile and said, "What about Blaine?"

Sherry pointed toward Blaine's cabin around the curve of the lake.

"He's waiting for you at his place," she said. "He asked me to tell you when you got up."

"Oh. Okay, thanks."

Somehow in talking with Sherry his headache had become worse—the impact of each footfall sending a faint throb along the top of his skull. Probably dehydrated, he thought.

When he arrived at Blaine's cabin, the door opened before he could even consider knocking. Blaine emerged, his red hair loose around his face instead of pulled back in its usual bun.

"Isaac!" he said jovially. "I was hoping you'd swing by soon."

Isaac squeezed his eyes shut, a very slow blink, trying to clear the fog from his mind as he skipped the niceties and said, "Yeah. Hey... have you seen Drew this morning?"

When he opened his eyes, he found Blaine watching him with a furrowed brow. Confused.

"Oh," Blaine said. "I thought..." He hesitated. "Isaac, your sister left last night. I thought... I thought you knew."

"Left?" That cold fear which had graced him earlier in bed returned with a vengeance. "What do you mean *she left*?"

"Drew came to me last night and demanded she be taken home right away. I tried to talk her into staying, but she refused. Kent drove her back into town."

...I'm not leaving you here...

Drew's words echoed cruelly in Isaac's mind. After the headache, and the icy grip of anxiety, a third pain struck him then, ringing his aching head like a hollow bell. An unsettling guilt. It flared like indigestion, a bleak fist around his heart.

"I told her we'd talk more in the morning. She..."

It occurred to him how selfish that had been. Thinking he could string her along another night, like she didn't already know he'd made up his mind. She knew him better than anyone. Sometimes he thought Drew knew him better than he knew himself, though he would never give her the satisfaction of admitting that.

"I'm sorry," Blaine said. "I'm sure that's not what you wanted to wake up to this morning..."

"Maybe..." Isaac didn't know what to say, or what to think. More than anything, he wanted these thoughts put away before they consumed him. "Maybe it's for the best," he said. That was it, he thought. Pretend to accept it, until pretend became reality. The ol' *fake it til you make it* strategy. He could be quite good at convincing himself of things, he knew. "I know it was hard watching our mom go. I can't blame her for not sticking around to see me do the same."

"Some people would rather run from their problems than face them head on," Blaine added. He said this gently, kindly, but Isaac couldn't help but prickle at his words. Blaine didn't know the first thing about Drew. He hadn't earned the right to make an assumption like that.

But he isn't wrong, Isaac thought. In fact, it sounded just like Drew—running before she could get hurt.

"Is that all she said? That she wanted to leave?"

"She said quite a few things, actually..." Blaine considered this morosely. "Hurtful things, mind you. She was upset."

"What kind of hurtful things?"

Blaine grimaced, then shook his head with a mournful attempt at a smile. "You should focus on the positive right now, Isaac. Have you thought more about it? About the journey?"

Isaac was at a loss for words. He bent his head slightly, ran his fingers through his untidy hair. He didn't think he'd ever felt so alone before. And with that loneliness—that fresh sting of abandonment—he was surprised by the sharp little flame that ignited, what his therapist would undoubtedly tell him was a defense mechanism, grasping for a new light to shine upon the situation, anything to distract from his guilt —anything to redirect fault.

"What hurtful things?" he repeated, not letting it go. "What exactly did she say to you?"

Blaine regarded Isaac with pity. "That won't help anything, Isaac. Truly, it won't." Then before Isaac could insist further, he said, "I have something else I'd like to show you. *Give* you, actually. I think you'll appreciate it. Wait here a moment."

As Blaine left inside, leaving Isaac to stand alone, he felt the tiniest drop of rain on his face. He peered upward into the rolling clouds, dark enough to threaten rain but not promise anything. Then he looked over his shoulder at the lake behind him, and could see the sporadic ripples of the drizzle.

Blaine reemerged in a matter of seconds. In his hands he held a notebook. He handed it over and Isaac took it absent-mindedly, until he saw the name written on the cover.

"That was your mom's journal," Blaine said. "I thought maybe you'd like to have it. You know by now that I encourage everyone here to keep one, detailing their experience, their spiritual journey, their *enlightenment,* as it were..." Blaine cleared his throat. "I suspect your mother's thoughts could be a great comfort to you now—and perhaps fill in some of the gaps you must be feeling. Most of the others have a chance to find themselves here, to truly connect with our Mother before they're chosen. Your selection was... much more abrupt and unexpected than even I'm used to. I think she must see something great in you, Isaac. Or, who knows... maybe your mother already put in a good word." Blaine gave Isaac's shoulder a friendly squeeze. "Get yourself something to eat, then read that and we'll talk again. All right?"

Blaine's hand rested on his shoulder as Isaac simply gazed at his mother's notebook, lost in thought. Then Blaine squeezed him a second time before he headed off. Isaac turned and watched him go, and as he did he noticed Kent's truck parked under the trees nearby.

Must have been driving all night, he thought.

Not only could he not believe his sister had left him so suddenly—he could hardly believe Kent of all people had indulged her.

Isaac grabbed a bite at the lodge by the pavilion, where the commune kept a modest stock of packaged foods—which Kent must have supplied via his errands into town. Isaac heated up some coffee and took some biscuits from the pantry, which he ate at one of the two tables inside the lodge, hopeful that he might avoid too much conversation that way. He was partially right. A few people wandered in, saw him there, congratulated him again rather dryly—without expression or any hint of warmth in their voices—and went about their business.

He'd already gotten the sense the previous night that their excitement had much less to do with him, and much more to do with their own fascination with the spirit of the lake. With *our Mother*. Now that the others had slept on it, digested it, it seemed the whole camp was a little more comfortable letting their jealousy sit front and center—their disdain for the new kid, who clearly didn't deserve the opportunity he'd been granted so prematurely.

Isaac finished up his biscuits and coffee and hurried back to his cabin, avoiding any further attention if he could help it. He was halfway there when someone called for him.

"Hey!"

With a sweaty sheen, Robert caught up to Isaac, joining him.

"Congrats on being chosen," Robert said, panting. "I wasn't awake to see you last night. I couldn't believe it when I heard..."

Isaac glanced at Robert from the corner of his eye as they walked—a man who was exactly Drew's type, Isaac knew. Objectively attractive, with dark features and a lean, wiry body. Personally, Isaac was unimpressed. Such men were a dime a dozen, he thought.

"I can't believe it, either," he said, and left it at that.

"Some of the others think your mom must have whispered in the Mother's ear and convinced her you were next. Apparently nobody's ever been chosen so soon after the last. Kinda crazy..."

"Yeah..."

Robert sighed heavily as he caught his breath. "What's that?"

He eyed the journal in Isaac's hand.

"Oh. It's my mom's journal. Blaine thought I should read it before making a final decision."

Robert pursed his lips, nodding understandingly. "Makes sense, I guess. How's your sister taking it?"

Isaac swallowed nervously. They arrived outside his cabin, where they stopped and faced one another, though Isaac continued to look elsewhere, avoiding Robert's gaze.

"She's gone," he answered truthfully. "Left last night."

"Oh. Shit. Seriously?" Robert cocked his head back, as if he had a hard time believing it. "Just up and left?"

"Just up and left," Isaac said, and tried not to sound too bitter about it. "Didn't say goodbye. Nothing."

"I wouldn't have expected *that*," Robert said, like he knew Drew very well at all. "Huh. I was kind of hoping she'd stay..."

Isaac couldn't help but laugh at that. Bitterly, of course.

"She was never going to stay here. Not in a million years."

"Yeah, I figured as much. But a man can hope..." He smiled sympathetically. His tender eyes rested on Isaac for a moment, long enough to make him uncomfortable again. "I'm sorry, though. That's gotta be rough. Are you..."

"I don't know. I don't think I've made up my mind yet." With a frown, Isaac held up his mother's journal and said, "I'm gonna take Blaine's advice and do some reading first. See what my mom had to say about it."

Robert returned his grimace with a friendlier one. "Sounds like a plan. I haven't been here the longest by any stretch, but you can ask me anything, too. If you want."

"Sure. Thanks. I think I'm gonna keep my head down for a bit in the meantime, though."

And with that, Isaac broke away and returned to the isolated *'comfort'* of an empty cabin. He set his mother's journal on the table, and then stood there pondering whether or not he wanted to read it. *Of course* he wanted to read it, he thought. But at the same time he could hardly force himself to start. *Julianne* was scrawled across the blank spot, carved in pencil which didn't do a very good job of marking the notebook's smooth cover. He eyed Drew's unmade cot near the back of the cabin, and felt a stinging new wave of loneliness crash over him.

She thinks she's the only one suffering, he thought. *I've just been better at hiding it, that's all...*

He wished Drew had stayed, but ultimately couldn't blame her for going. As angry as he felt, he was entirely aware he'd been asking a lot of his sister, expecting her to watch him follow in their mother's footsteps, so to speak. Drew had only left him first, before he could do the same, which was painfully typical of her, he thought.

We all do what we have to do.

And with that in mind, Isaac took their mother's journal to his cot, where he lay and started reading.

At some point the hallucinations transitioned into sleep. In and out, in and out. Drew dreamed a little. Or she thought she did. When she wasn't sleeping, she *remembered* things, remembered them vividly enough that they felt like dreams. Like she was really there again...

She dreamed of That Day. The ugliest day of her life. That which set the standard for all ugly days to come. None would ever amount to being so ugly, not even close. It was the day she learned that rainstorms were not tranquil or cozy as many believed, but omens of terrible things on the horizon, literally and figuratively. They were not to be trusted.

She was thirteen years old.

School let out, and some part of her had hoped due to the torrential downpour—the windows in her classrooms had nearly become *opaque* with rainwater—that her father would be waiting outside in his truck to drive her home. But there was no such luck. He was working, after all. So she pulled the hood of her jacket over her head and *ran* the four blocks to her brother's elementary school to pick him up like she always did.

Isaac was seven years old.

She took her brother by the hand and led him five more blocks in the deafening rain. That was how far home was. Five blocks. Not too far, really, but in a rainstorm it was *leagues*. He droned on and on about how there was no recess that day, at least not outside because they would have *drowned*, and so they got to watch some animated movie in class he'd never seen before. Drew wasn't paying enough attention to hear what movie it was. Isaac could talk the ears off a stalk of corn, even when the heavens were flooding down upon them. Every other sentence out of his mouth, she urged him to *hurry* so they wouldn't be completely drenched by the time they got home, even though she was already drenched before she picked him up from school.

She was all the more surprised to see their father's truck in the driveway when they arrived home.

"Dad's home!" Isaac shouted.

He ran ahead of Drew but the front door was locked. Drew kept their key, which she fished out of her pocket and opened the door. They both stepped inside sopping wet. Drew told her brother to take his jacket and shoes off by the door when she noticed through the kitchen doorway red specks on the white linoleum, and suddenly she found herself ignoring her own advice. Even Isaac took offense at the hypocrisy as she crossed the living room, calling after her, *"Hey, what about YOUR shoes!?"*

Each step revealed more red specks. Wet and shiny. Until there was more than just specks. Then she was standing on the kitchen's threshold and she saw him—a moment that only lasted a few wide-eyed seconds, but burned into her mind's eye so vividly that it was all she saw even after she turned around, rushed toward her brother who was still kicking off his second shoe, took him by the hand, and pulled him wordlessly out into the storm once again. He whined about his socks getting wet as they ran across the lawn, down the sidewalk, along the neighbor's driveway, and to their front door where Mrs. Boyter answered to Drew's frantic knocking. The elderly woman barely got a chance to ask Drew what was the matter before she burst into tears and bawled, *"Can we use your phone!?"*

Mrs. Boyter let them inside without complaint, where she tried to get a coherent story out of Drew with great difficulty, telling her to calm down and tell her what happened. Isaac had no idea, but he was crying now because *Drew* was crying. Then Mrs. Boyter's retired husband came into the living room to see what all the commotion was about, at which point Mrs. Boyter told him to phone the police.

Drew couldn't calm herself. She couldn't breathe. Mrs. Boyter took her jacket and told them both to sit on the sofa. Drew had very little memory of what happened after that. Mostly because the few seconds she'd spent standing in their kitchen doorway were stretched across the rest of the day like a veil she couldn't pull from her eyes.

She'd seen their father at the kitchen table, his head leaned back, his mouth full of blood, the wall behind him spattered with the same. A plaque hung on that wall, obscured with these fleshy bits of their father—a nicely framed, homey sentiment their mother had hung a few years prior which read *'Life is short, DANCE in the kitchen.'*

Worse than the wall, however, was the ceiling overhead. Or rather, the ceiling *fan*—the reason those red specks had reached the other side of the room where Drew had first noticed them. Thin red tassels of congealed blood clung to the undersides of the fan wings—round and round they went.

And yet still none of this was the worst part.

The absolute worst part—or more appropriately, the most shocking—was the second man in the room. The man who looked just like her father, his spitting image, only without the blood in his mouth or the hole through the top of his skull. The man standing in the rear corner between the window and the pantry door, gazing over the scene with the hollowest expression Drew had ever seen, even more hollow than the dead version of him sitting at the table. His eyes twitched upward to see Drew in the doorway. Other than that, there was no change in his expression. She looked between her father's corpse, the mess he had made, and the phantom he'd become standing in the corner like a director on a film set, and something in her mind *snapped.* Or *switched.* Something innate, dormant, coming to life. A gift she wouldn't realize again for another twelve years, at least.

Not until she arrived at that damnable lake and its grave-yard of unrest.

When she opened her eyes there was nothing to see. No remnants of her dream, nor the illusions of her drugged mind. Just the darkness. She stirred, and realized she could move again. Barely. Her body was still *heavy,* like every limb weighed more than its muscles could support. She could no longer hear the struggled breaths of the body sharing this space with her. Quentin. The putrid scent of decay still hung in the humid air, thick and pungent as ever.

As she came to, and flexed her tired muscles and strength-less fingers, she remembered the terrible substance that had been forced into her mouth—the goo which stiffened her body and unraveled her mind—and knew suddenly that she'd been right all along. Right about everything. About the lake and what waited there for them. A pile of bones under the water's surface. The goop was the secret. A drug of some kind, one they willingly took, no questions asked. A drug which soon paralyzed them, stunned them out of their wits. Her stomach knotted with an awful image—Julianne swimming out into that light, tongue swabbed with Blaine's funny sauce, losing control of her own body and mind until the lake claimed her, sinking into its darkness without a struggle, without a scream. Unable to resist it...

Footsteps upstairs. The ceiling creaked with them. A single pair. They traveled overhead, clomping and creaking, until the basement door opened and the faintest trace of light appeared. A soft, fiery glow. A silhouette started down. Drew fidgeted on her back. She turned ever so slightly onto her side, and felt the prodding shape of the switchblade handle in her pocket. The silhouette reached the last stair, then stepped onto the rocky ground and stopped. One side of the figure was given shape from the light upstairs. The other side blended seamlessly with the dark, so that all Drew saw was half a person.

"You're awake," Blaine said. "Surely you haven't been all this time?"

There came a *click* in the dark, and suddenly the basement was cut by a swath of LED light from the flashlight in Blaine's hand. He pointed it directly into Drew's face and she winced. Then he swung the light across the floor, toward something nearby, and he said, "How's your friend holding up..."

Squinting, Drew peered into the light and what it revealed. A few feet from where she lay another body lay on the black rock, on its back, its head turned toward her. Its head was *wrong*. All its features were sunken, shriveled, as if its very flesh had been vacuum-sealed against the bones underneath. Even still, it was undoubtedly Quentin. His half-lidded eyes peered toward her lifelessly, the yellowed whites shot through with blood. What had been done to him, exactly, was anyone's guess.

Blaine pointed the light at her again. Like a vampire in the sun, she tried to turn away from it. His feet swept the damp rock as he came near. Then he crouched beside her.

"I am sorry about the smell. Like your friend, you'll get used to it soon enough."

With the energy of a zombie, Drew mumbled, *"...fuck you—"*

The moment her mouth was open, Blaine stuffed his hand inside. Another dollop of hazy. He scraped the goo behind her teeth like before, only this time she returned the favor by scraping the skin off his fingers in kind. He pulled his hand out with a hurt gasp.

"You fucking..." He didn't finish the thought. Shining the flashlight on his fingers, he scoffed—an irritated little laugh—and said, "I guess it's only fair you get a taste of me. It'll be my turn soon enough."

While Drew gagged and fought not to swallow the second dose of goo, Blaine left upstairs again. She failed as spectacularly as before. It was too thick to spit, and yet too quick to melt not to swallow. But as the fog seeped back into her mind, and those lovely colors spread across the darkness once again, she was a little grateful.

Because as Blaine climbed the stairs and shut the door behind him, the last thing Drew saw in the low light were the many, incredibly faint silhouettes surrounding her in the dark, of those who perished before her.

Much of what Julianne had written in her journal she'd already covered in their conversations. Like how lost she was before Blaine found her. Or the lingering guilt she felt all these years later for leaving her family behind. Isaac understood that Drew believed their mother to be remorseless, but these entries repeatedly hammered home the fact that not a day went by that she didn't think of them.

In skimming through the entries, Isaac also got a sense of their mother's growth within this community. Not only thanks to the others, but the place itself. The forest, the lake, and the *presence of something larger than them* behind it all. The *'Mother.'* Our Mother.

> *And it's not just us. It's like the wildlife senses it, too. Everything is drawn to the lake.*
> *Sometimes I swear I can hear the whole forest breathing.*

As the days in Julianne's journal went by, Isaac noted the solidification of these beliefs. From an abstract concept into something more absolute, into the doubt of preconceived notions, into the suspicion that *'this might be greater than I ever could have known.'*

In the latter half of Julianne's entries, things like guilt and fear made fewer appearances, until they weren't mentioned at all in favor of her faith that something about this place was truly special.

For the first time in my life, I know that I am on the right path.

These words hit Isaac like a cement truck. He lowered the journal in his lap to reflect on them, staring across the quiet cabin, and in that moment of utter silence there came a knock on the door. He flinched. Then, as he made to stand up, the door opened regardless.

"Have a moment to talk?" Blaine said, poking his head inside.

"Okay. Sure."

Blaine entered the cabin, drawing his gaze first across Isaac's bed, then the other where Drew had previously slept, still unmade.

"How are you feeling?"

"Okay, I guess."

Isaac watched Blaine as he paced toward the middle of the room, before noticing Julianne's journal in his lap.

"Have you had a chance to read very much?"

"Yeah. Not all of it, but some."

"And?"

Isaac shrugged. He hadn't had much time to process everything he'd read. He supposed he *did* feel a little differently now than when he'd last spoken to Blaine. The crushing loneliness in Drew's absence seemed to have alleviated some, but that had more to do with his own thoughts than anything he'd read in their mother's journal.

"I still wish I had more time with her. My mom, I mean."

Blaine turned to Isaac with a bright expression, as if he had very good news.

"Isaac, that's the beautiful part," he said. "You have all the time in the world. I know it's still probably hard to wrap your head around, but... it's real, what we believe. Your mother isn't *gone*. She's waiting for you. I mean... if that's what you decide you want to do, of course."

Isaac chewed his lip. Drew's cynicism nagged in the back of his mind, telling him what an idiot he was for entertaining these people's *lunacy*. He only knew one thing for certain: that their mother was *not* a lunatic. Nor was she an idiot, he thought. She didn't believe because she was *told* to believe, or because she *wanted* to believe, but because she'd experienced this place and its majesty and had no other choice *but* to believe. Isaac trusted her. And despite the goatee that he agreed was a little too *'circus tent'* for his tastes, his mother's trust in Blaine had to count for something, didn't it?

"You think I'll see her again?" Isaac asked. A rhetorical question, if there ever was one. "If I make the journey?"

"Oh, I guarantee you will," Blaine said. With a glimmer of sympathy in his eyes, he nodded reassuringly. "She's waiting, Isaac. That's not a metaphor. She's waiting for you. Right alongside our Mother."

Even Isaac had to admit Blaine's words sounded too religious for his liking.

"How do you know that?" he asked.

"Because I've met her," Blaine said. "When I first discovered this place, years ago. She's everything I describe and more. Mere words could never do her justice, to be honest."

"And what about you? Why haven't you made the journey?"

Blaine smiled. "One day I will, like the rest of you. But

for now, I am her shepherd. And I'm truly joyous to be trusted with the task." He continued staring at Isaac with those gentle eyes of his, trying to read him silently. "But you're still feeling conflicted. It's your sister, isn't it..."

Feeling especially vulnerable—as Blaine seemed to succeed in reading him like an open book—Isaac averted his eyes, looking down at Blaine's bare, dirt-stained feet instead.

"I feel like Drew wanted me to chase after her..."

"I'm sure she did what she thought was best for her," Blaine said. "Which makes it that much more important, I think, that you do the same." Blaine smiled thoughtfully. "You're a kind soul, Isaac. I see that in you, just as I saw it in your mother. Join us for dinner tonight. I think the sense of community will do you good. I also happen to know there are several members who didn't hear your story last night who would *love* to hear all about it. What do you say?"

Isaac hardly listened to Blaine, as an unexpected question had leapt into his mouth. He held it there momentarily, tasting it. His pulse quickened with the mere thought.

What's best for me?

Meeting Blaine's gaze again, he said, "How long before I can make the journey?"

17
THE BRINK

She had no concept of time as she faded in and out of sleep, in and out of dreaming. The moments between were spent in a waking fantasy, which the pitch black basement provided the perfect backdrop for. Visions of the past. Visions of a nonexistent future. Her body was stiff, muscles tensed, as she recalled sweet things she'd forgotten.

Memories like day trips to the library with Isaac and their mother, taking all the time in the world to sift through books, deciding what they wanted—Drew with an armful of Goosebumps, Isaac with a stack of his favorite picture books. Drew always marveled at how many books she was allowed to check out at one time, asking herself, *'you trust me to take THIS many home?'* and never managing to read them all before they were due, anyway.

She recalled being stuck in bed with the flu once—much like she was now stuck on Blaine's basement floor—and Julianne fussing over her all day long, bringing her soup and crackers and even lying in bed with her for a time while she shivered with fever chills. She remembered Isaac coming back from kindergarten and being jealous of Drew staying home from school despite how clearly miserable she was, sweating through her bedsheets all day long. But his jealousy was quickly forgotten, as he'd dragged some kiddie board game up onto Drew's bed and insisted that she play with him despite having lost half the pieces to the damn thing months ago.

She remembered their older teenage babysitter, Jackie, whom they were left home with for their parents' anniversary a couple years in a row, and how Jackie had invited her boyfriend over to join them for the evening. Except Drew and Isaac were left alone with a movie while Jackie and her boyfriend disappeared upstairs to have what they called "serious discussions" in their parents' bedroom. Drew and Isaac had abandoned their movie to listen from the head of the stairs, Drew covering Isaac's mouth when his giggling became too loud.

She also remembered their parents' last anniversary together—returning home in complete silence, Julianne immediately excusing herself upstairs while their father sent Jackie home and ordered Drew and Isaac to bed... so that he could make the couch into his own. Drew had heard their mother's weeping that night, even from across the hall like she was. Isaac, whose room was directly beside their parents, had tiptoed into Drew's to get away from the noise—tiptoed directly into bed beside her all that night.

Their boat was already on rough waters, but their mother's disappearance had sent them capsizing. Then their father's death had sent their lifeboat sinking just the same.

All that was left were the waves and their hands, holding desperately onto one another as the currents relentlessly threatened to separate them.

When Drew surfaced from this bout of fantasy, and the basement's darkness appeared to her like a curtain closing on a stage play, one thought entered her mind above all the rest:

I miss you, Isaac.

"Wake up."

She roused to the sound of a voice in her ear. Then, as she opened her eyes, she heard the footsteps. Not upstairs, but *on the stairs,* someone coming down. She closed her eyes. The footsteps moved noisily toward her, making no attempt to be quiet. Before she even knew *why* she did it, her instinct was to play dead—or asleep, rather. She focused on relaxing her face, her breathing, even as her heart went *boom, boom, boom* against her lungs. The footsteps drew near, and suddenly a painfully bright light was shined into her face. Miraculously she managed to keep her expression still, not wincing or squeezing her eyes or anything.

A terribly drawn-out moment.

Then the flashlight pointed elsewhere. A man sighed, and those footsteps carried back to the stairs, up them again, creaking and groaning all the way to the top. With the door left open, she heard their voices.

"She's out cold."

"Good. Maybe I'll be ready for her after we're finished with the kid..."

225

"That's really tonight, then? So soon?"

"Surprised me a little, too. It's just as well. This whole family has been nothing but a pain in my ass." There was a pause, and the floorboards above were scuffed and stomped upon as someone paced around. *"Let's get this over with before the rain comes. Lock that before we go."*

The basement door shut. The lock clicked. Their footsteps shuffled around some more overhead before she heard what had to be the cabin door slam shut. Then silence.

Drew lay for a moment, just listening. Confirming. She briefly considered the voice that had awakened her. Bodiless. Unfamiliar. If not for that voice, she might have instead woken to the flashlight pointed in her face, and would have been unable to hide her consciousness...

The hallucinations were gone. Not only that, but her paralysis seemed to be wearing off. She wiggled her fingers behind her back, then her toes. Her muscles were still fatigued—like pins and needles after a limb goes to sleep. She still felt the switchblade stretched awkwardly in her pocket, and was amazed they hadn't even bothered to search her. In her shirt and sweat shorts, she supposed she probably did look like she'd just rolled out of bed.

She managed to push herself off her side and onto her stomach, her face against the rocky floor, hands behind her back working at the air like an overturned crab. Then she rolled slightly onto her other side, and with great effort crunched herself inward, and reached her bound hands around her waist toward the pocket containing the switchblade. She strained until she had to stop for a moment. Her muscles ached. She caught her breath—a horrid exercise all on its own as she huffed and puffed the warm, putrid air.

She reached again. Her fingers played against the lip of her pocket, but couldn't quite reach inside. She pinched the waist of her shorts and managed to hike them farther up her body, bringing the pocket closer in the process. She reminded herself to breathe. She reached for the pocket again, for the switchblade stuffed inside. Her blind, wiggling fingers found their way. She touched the cool handle. She tried to grasp it between two fingers—between the nail of her index and the pad of her middle finger, which afforded no purchase at all.

"Come on," she whispered.

In the midst of all this mild strain, she could already feel her strength returning, little by little, her blood flowing, her muscles waking up from the nameless drug she'd been given. She shrugged where she lay, leaning farther to the side of the switchblade, jamming her hand deeper into the pocket. This time she grabbed hold of it, for a moment at least, but found it stuck—the corners of her pocket stretched on either end of it.

"Come on," she muttered again. *"You've got this..."*

Noise up above. A low, growling rumble. Drew paused, listening, until she realized it was the sound of thunder.

She grabbed the switchblade again and twisted it, pulled it, her fingers hooked around its slender body, until finally she yanked it loose from the fabric trapping it in place and freed it from her pocket entirely. About as satisfying as pulling a splinter from one's flesh, she thought. Breathing hard, she lay for a moment. A short rest. The switchblade was solid in her fist. She squeezed it, pressed the little metal nub, and listened to the spring-loaded blade extend.

The next difficult bit was arranging the knife in her hands without dropping it, and angling its blade against the twine around her wrists—again, without dropping it.

She *did* drop it, multiple times. And multiple times she paused to rest, to steady herself. But she never paused for long. The same thought repeated in her mind: *Isaac is swimming out tonight.*

She got the blade beneath the twine, against her wrist. Here was the most awkward part of all. At first she simply tried to *pry* —to leverage the blade against the twine and hope the pressure against its edge would be enough to break it. Maybe if she had more strength. Maybe if the twine were slightly finer. Unable to get a good look at it behind her back, she soon resorted to rapid *fidgeting*. Pressing, prying, sliding, focusing all this movement in the same direction, at least, until she thought she could feel the vibrations of splitting threads against the blade.

Yes. Just keep going. Eventually...

A louder crack of thunder sounded, loud enough that it was clear to her ears even underground, under the solid floorboards of Blaine's cabin. It didn't surprise her, the storm. It felt natural that such weather should coincide with such horrors.

Come on already you fucking—

With a satisfying *snap*, the rest of the twine broke against the knife and her wrists were free. She sat up in an instant, then felt immediately loopy for it. Lightheaded. The darkness swirled with dizzy lights, fading. She reached for her ankles,

found the twine that tightly bit them, and sliced it through
with one pull of the knife.

She was free.

Isaac was given spare clothes to match the others. Gray sweats
and a t-shirt. He put these on, even though he'd be taking
them off again in just a couple hours.

And never putting them on again.

Despite Blaine's suggestion, Isaac didn't join the others
for dinner. As cynical as Drew could be at times, sometimes
she was right. For instance, Isaac also sensed that many in the
community were not happy about his being chosen. Those
who were had already gone out of their way to congratulate
him, or to ask him about his experience over the course of the
day. The rest were cold, avoided his gaze, or seemed altogether oblivious to him. In their eyes, he supposed, he was an
undeserving unbeliever. A tourist.

"I won't force you to join the others," Blaine told him.
"Tonight is your night. Do what feels best."

And so he did what felt best. He spent most of the day
alone with his mother's journal, reading her thoughts in
search of comfort and reassurance. Drew's doubts nagged
him all the while, but that couldn't be helped. His guilt
couldn't be helped, either. Nor the intense feeling of *missing
her,* nor the disappointment that she'd left him in the first
place.

As the clock ticked by, and the storm outside gathered

more wind and thunder, he soon found himself overcome with an eagerness to get it over with.

The stormy light of day faded into the darkness of night, and there came a knock on the cabin door. Isaac answered the door to Blaine, hands clasped reverently in wait, a soft warmth upon his goateed mouth with a mischievous wrinkle between his fiery brows.

"Are you ready?"

Thunder rumbled across the night at Blaine's back, almost comically, and Isaac couldn't help but ask, "Is it okay we're doing this in the middle of a storm?"

Blaine glanced over his shoulder at the blackening sky. "We should be all right." Then, with a slyness behind his crystal blue eyes, he added, "It isn't storming where you're headed, anyway, right?"

"I wouldn't know," Isaac said, and laughed nervously.

Blaine blinked like a relaxed cat.

"Come. The others are already waiting."

Isaac cast an anxious glance into the cabin behind him, at his mother's journal on the bed, at his bag on the floor with the rest of his possessions, as a sudden rush of panic set in.

"Leave it all behind," Blaine said. "You entered this world with everything you need."

That was an oddly comforting thought. Disturbing, too. Both these sentiments coiled around each other like an awkward handshake in Isaac's mind.

Mom did it. I can do it.

He stepped outside, where the breeze was warm and bellowed across the dark, shivering treetops on all sides of them. He peered across the lake toward the dock, where the others' figures waited, standing in little clumps amongst themselves. Even from afar, their body language seemed reluctant. Impatient.

He followed Blaine around the lake, flinching every time lightning flashed them, or the subsequent thunder cracked overhead.

They arrived at the dock and he was relieved to be greeted with a few smiles from the others. Sherry was beaming, naturally. Robert offered him a brotherly smirk. Plenty of the commune, however, gave him nothing at all. A few were in a circle of their own conversation and after glimpsing his arrival returned their attention to said conversation. Blaine walked Isaac onto the dock and toward its end. Then, with a hand on his back, they turned to face the queue of followers forming behind them, just as they'd done for Julianne the previous night. Their faces lit up with a flash of lightning but nothing more. Perhaps he was projecting, but Isaac felt a general sense of *let's get this over with'* from all involved— Blaine included.

"The time has come... *again...* to say farewell," Blaine said. "To send another... into our Mother's embrace. Let us make Isaac our vessel... so that he may bring word of our love directly to our Mother's ears..."

Isaac barely recognized those who approached. Faces he'd seen around, but hardly knew. They opened their arms to him with bored expressions—mouths fighting not to yawn—and he hugged them each very lightly, hands patting against their backs. Then Sherry appeared at the front of the line and she smiled *for real,* like an oasis in a cruel stretch of desert, and she whispered into Isaac's ear, *"Tell your mom hi for me.*" This filled Isaac with a modicum of comfort...

Which was quickly stolen away as the next stranger approached him. Not entirely a stranger. Caroline was next, penetrating him with her dark eyes surrounded by blood-like freckles, like she'd just finished with her favorite pastime— cold-blooded murder. She wrapped her arms around Isaac and unlike the others actually *squeezed him* against herself.

"*It should have been me,*" she whispered, and then released him rather roughly, pivoting away in the same breath.

Then Robert was next. Another warm light in the stormy dark. In Isaac's ear he said, "*Good luck, buddy.*"

Then the line was finished. Isaac sighed with relief. He turned and faced Blaine behind him, who stood waiting with a ceramic bowl in his hands. Beyond Blaine, Isaac noticed that the lake was already swelling with its amber light, its steam spreading fast. Blaine followed Isaac's gaze.

"Seems our Mother is ready for you, Isaac. Are you ready for her?"

Isaac swallowed nervously. He looked into the bowl, where the gooey substance seemed to shine with notes of that same amber light.

"What is that?" he asked.

"This is the very blood of the forest," Blaine answered. "The blood of our Mother. Are you ready to receive it? Are you ready to submit yourself to her majesty, Isaac?"

Isaac nodded that he was. In the midst of that gesture, a stray thought floated into his mind, which was: *Why aren't you here, Drew?* and he swatted it away like the annoying fly that it was, and forced himself to think something else. He nodded again, more emphatically this time.

"I'm ready."

Blaine stuck his thumb into the bowl, into the amber sap, and pried up a thick wad. Then he presented that thumb to Isaac, gravity pulling the substance down the fleshy pad of his thumb, and Isaac presented his tongue in kind.

Just do it, he thought. *Just do it already...*

He closed his eyes, his whole body tensing as he anticipated the taste of Blaine's dirty thumb.

They don't even have soap or hand sanitizer in their outhouses, Isaac thought to himself, and physically winced as Blaine swabbed him in that same instant. He tasted both the sap and the salt of Blaine's skin. The sap was much sweeter. It tingled on his tongue as he pulled it back into his mouth. Sweet, tangy, and bitter all at once, not quite like anything he'd tasted before. He opened his eyes and Blaine gestured with an open hand to the edge of the dock.

"Now you'll disrobe," he said in a low, instructive tone. "And present yourself to our Mother as you were born."

Now those dispassionate souls behind Isaac felt like a million watchful eyes upon his back, judging his every move, his every hesitation. He caught himself trembling and wobbling on his feet as he stripped, first his shirt and then his shorts, stepping out of them like a locker room nightmare from middle school gym class. Even the storm erupted with its sharp laughter, illuminating his lanky, naked body. He couldn't sit down fast enough, plopping himself down on the splintered planks, feet dangling to the water underneath. The water was warm. As his toes settled into it, the light in the center of the lake expanded greedily, throbbing open. Isaac's heart responded by quickening its beat. His breaths were shallow. He listened to the movements of those on the dock behind him, shedding their clothes. More lightning in the distance, strobing the lake with daylight.

"Go on, then, Isaac," Blaine said. "It is time to make your journey."

18

THE JOURNEY

There was always another hurdle.

After breaking loose from her restraints, Drew stood shakily, felt herself swaying, her equilibrium failing her. With the switchblade in her grip, she pressed her other hand to the dark and navigated her way toward the stairs, stumbling and tiptoeing until she kicked the bottommost step with the toe of her sneaker. She started up, climbing on all fours until she touched the base of the door at the top. She pushed herself up against the door, felt for the knob, already knowing it would be locked. She jiggled it anyway, which didn't feel so sturdy in her hand.

She headed back down the rickety steps and began her search for something to *smash* with. Something that could break a doorknob with a solid strike. She folded her knife, replaced it in her pocket, and proceeded to probe the dark with both hands outstretched. She felt for the basement wall. She touched it, nothing but cool rock, and began feeling her way around its perimeter.

She happened upon a stack of wooden planks. Leftovers. Too long and unruly to wield. She passed those, kicking her feet blindly into smaller stacks she found. She kept moving. In the back of her mind, she kept a mental tab on the general whereabouts of Quentin's corpse. No risk as of yet, stumbling over him. She wanted to avoid that, if possible...

Then she kicked another lumpy thing at her feet—something that wasn't a stack of wood. She bent down to touch it, and her hands touched upon old dusty cloth, and her fingers felt up, up, up the fabric until there was a hole in the cloth from which something hard and knobby protruded, and her fingertips played delicately along the little knobs until they connected to something larger, something sitting atop the narrow row of knobs like a large...

Oh... oh no...

She touched the smooth, sharp shelf of its jaw. Then the bumpy surface of its neat rows of teeth...

Drew bolted upright, took a step back. Panting in the dark, eyes wide and blind as ever, she stared down at the second corpse she couldn't see. A much older corpse. Bones and not much else. She moved past it, pressed toward the wall again, and her foot found another soft sack of something. She kicked it. The toe of her sneaker met it with a mild *thump*. Not hard as bone. Something meatier, perhaps? Something fresher? She didn't want to know. Didn't want to touch it. The rancid smell of decay overwhelmed her now. Their decomposing particles hung in the warm air like dust motes and she was breathing it in all this time. She felt sick. How many others, she wondered? She kept moving. She found the wall, the cool stone, feet shuffling onward. She kicked another shape, stepped over it. Or tried to, anyway. She stepped into it, felt a hollow crunch under her foot.

Shit. Fuck. I'm sorry.

She kept moving. Kept shuffling. Her hands whispered on the rocky wall, patting gently.

Give me something.

The rocky wall became something else. She touched wood, finally. Not a stack of it, but something built. Something constructed within the rock. She felt its frame, butted up against the rock itself, and touched the flat surface of what was hung inside the frame. A door in the dark. She stood before it, placed *both* hands upon its hard, slightly warm surface. She searched with fumbling hands until she touched a latch. A padlock hung from the latch. As she stood there, a silent gust of warm air plumed out from beneath the door around her ankles. She stepped back again, tensing in the shoulders.

Where does this go? What's hidden behind it?

Her mind jumped to *'more bodies.'* That seemed logical. Although, why Blaine would keep a stockpile of corpses in his basement when he had a perfectly good lake, Drew couldn't fathom.

Because the lake is reserved for believers. These are the bodies of dissenters.

Cameron. Friend of Olivia. A skeptic. Was it his skeleton she stumbled upon? Or perhaps the fresher corpse was his. There was no way to know. Quentin's visage flashed before her mind's eye, sucked dry like a human sponge. She'd been unable to rationalize that, to make sense of it, and so she

237

simply ignored those details. Like how she ignored the fire-flies. Or in Olivia's case, the birds.

Quit your fucking lollygagging, your brother is about to drown himself.

She skirted past the door, found the continuation of the rock wall on its other side, and then promptly kicked something else stacked there. Not a body, nor a pile of wooden planks. She bent, touched something cool as the rock itself. Something with hard edges, rectangular, with an empty middle. Or empty pockets in the middle.

A cinderblock.

That would do, she thought. That was perfect. She grabbed the topmost cinderblock, hoisted it into both hands. Carefully, she trudged back through the thick, warm shadows toward the stairs, or at least where her spatial awareness remembered the stairs. She kicked ahead, cautious not to trip with such a heavy weight in her arms. She kicked the bottom stair. She began to climb. Her calves trembled. Her whole lower body cried out, wishing to buckle then and there, to collapse and take a rest on the fourth step. She mounted the fifth. She jostled the cinderblock in her arms, shifted its weight from one arm to the other then back again. A kink in her neck which had always been there made itself unpleasantly known, as she strained not to topple backward —or forward, for that matter. On the ninth or tenth stair— she'd lost count—she bumped into the door with the cinderblock and threatened to spill backward from the recoil. She bent slightly at the knee, pressed fully into the door, resting the cinderblock against it to save herself.

"*Shit,*" she muttered.

She straightened. She touched the doorknob with the back of her hand to locate it. Then she proceeded to lift the cinderblock higher, then higher still, turning it in her grip until she had a comfortable hold on it. Then she swung it downward, hard and fast, clobbering the door along the way to the knob, which the cinderblock glanced off from with a solid *thunk.* Another smack would do, she thought. A better smack this time. Her arms were already weak under the block's weight. She raised it again, shaking all over. She heaved it downward a second time, onto the knob, jolting it with a good, heavy *bang,* and felt it give a little, rattling violently in its housing.

One more time, she thought. *You can do that. Can't you?*

She lifted the cinderblock again, and bumped the door-knob against her knuckles along the way. She felt the metal knob budge aside as she did, as if it were already only hanging on by a thread. She didn't bother lifting the block as high as the last couple times. She dropped it down, gave the protruding knob a third and final bludgeoning, and listened as it fell out of place—as it broke onto the stairs and tumbled down behind her.

Thank God...

Carelessly, she dropped the cinderblock aside, and listened as it tumbled down the stairs after the broken knob, crashing all the way down the wooden steps until it clattered to a stop on the rocky ground below. She touched the place where the knob had been and found only a perfectly round hole in the door's wood. She gave the door a push. It opened silently, until it bumped against something on the other side. Something small and trivial. The other half of the

239

doorknob. It rolled and scraped as she pushed the door further.

Blaine's cabin was dark. Drew stood in the basement doorway for a hesitant moment, surveying the empty cabin with bated breath until she was certain there was no one there, no one keeping watch. Thunder gently growled outside, more audible now than it'd been down below.

Go already. Stop him.

She paced to the front door, then paused with her hand on *its* knob, only for a second until she proceeded to pull the door open slowly, discreetly, peeking out into the stormy night.

She was immediately flashbanged by lightning on the other side. A cool breeze whipped around her, and the sound of a million fluttering leaves of the forest. Stepping out, peering toward the lake whose surface was already masked beneath the eerie glow of its steam, she saw them—dark figures crowded at the dock on the other side. She crossed the dirt toward the shore, eyes on those figures as they shifted in place, as they suddenly became *paler* under the gloom of the storm. Naked. Taking off their clothes. It was happening, she realized. Right now. Not a second to spare.

She gave chase. Her sneakers slapped the hard dirt. Her switchblade bounced within her stretched pocket. Lightning flashed, exposing her. Thunder cracked, startling her. Oddly not a drop of rain. Not a single sprinkle. She ran along the shore, gasping for air as she went, heart thumping wildly, with no plan in mind on how she might stop them when she got there. Would she arrive with her knife unsheathed, with an accusation lobbed at their glorious leader?

He locked me in his basement and fed me weird goo!

She wondered what kind of story the others had been told. What Isaac had been told. The same story they'd been told about Cameron, perhaps? Judging by the gathering on the dock, Isaac had believed the story, whatever it was. He believed she'd left him. The idiot. The punk. The absolute nincompoop...

If we survive this place, I'm going to kill him.

Thunder growled menacingly overhead once again, and as it faded Drew heard something else beneath the stirring wind and the lapping lake water. Something close, getting closer. Louder. Scuffing in the dirt.

She cast a wary glance behind her as those noises stalked right up on her heels, and suddenly he was there in her ear, huffing and puffing with his groping hands extending around her body, baring his teeth like a feral thing from the woods.

Kent wrapped his arms wide around Drew's shoulders and tackled her clean off her feet. They fell together. She landed on her side with a terrible jolt, a terrible wheeze, the air going out from her lungs. They squirmed together, feet kicking in the dirt. Kent forced her onto her back and pinned her there, just as she ripped her hand from her pocket, just as she clicked the metal nub on the handle in her fist and plunged the extending blade straight into his throat. The switchblade barely winked before it vanished into his flesh. He reared back, eyes bugging out of their sockets. She pulled the knife free as she wriggled out from beneath him, and his blood jetted in a narrow stream upon her until he clapped his hand to the wound, where it seeped through the cracks of his fingers. Drew picked herself up, shivering madly with adrenaline.

In a daze, she left him there, sprinting once more in the direction of the dock, the knife squeezed in her slippery palm. Lightning bloomed in the sky again. Those naked bodies illuminated underneath.

Isaac's naked body illuminated underneath, sitting at the very end of the dock, on the edge, pushing himself off and into the murky water.

He hesitated even after Blaine told him to go. He stared into the darkness beneath his toes, then lifted his gaze to the glowing vapors beyond him, waiting for him, the mystery of another world calling. Beckoning. Promising things this world couldn't reasonably promise. And yet Blaine had promised them. Isaac's mother had promised. He wanted nothing more than to believe. He wanted to *let go.* There was so much to let go, to leave behind. Most of it he was glad to be rid of, but some of it... some things held onto him as tightly as he held onto them.

"It's okay, Isaac," Blaine whispered. "There's nothing to fear. Nothing to hold you back. She's waiting for you with open arms..."

In a desperate bid to *let go,* Isaac thrust himself off the edge of the dock and into the lake's warm waters. Impossibly warm. His plunge sent a surge of bubbles around his splashing body, and then he resurfaced, his limbs tearing through, arm over arm, legs kicking, blinking the moisture from his eyes, gasping with his mouth half submerged in the lake. His head was buzzing. Actually his *entire body* was buzzing, and he was reminded of the sensation he got sitting in a dentist's chair huffing the nitrous, the laughing gas, like his limbs could start lifting up from the earth of their own accord. Except he didn't feel at all like laughing at the moment. He felt like crying. A terrible beauty wrapped itself around him like a wet cloak, an unshakable sadness. There was no turning back from this, he knew. This was final. This was *the end* of everything he understood. Relief and terror hand in hand. He swam ever onward, into the lake's steam which clung to him like fresh perspiration, the dock somewhere behind him growing smaller, the light ahead growing brighter, closer, expanding like the flashing muzzle of a gun.

There wasn't time for any climactic confrontation. Isaac was already in the water, swimming out toward the light—toward certain doom. Drew folded up her knife as she ran, stuffed it back into her pocket. The dock drew near. A few heads turned in her direction as she raced toward them in a flurry of scuffing sneakers and pumping arms and wild-eyed panic. Their naked bodies turned to see her as she kicked off her sneakers and pressed into them, through them, meeting nary a gaze as her eyes remained focused on the steaming waters ahead.

"Drew?" she heard a voice say. A familiarly charming voice, now pitched with disbelief.

"Get out of my way," she snapped. *"Get the fuck out of my way!"*

She shoved until she broke through the other end of their crowd. There Blaine stood, rooted in his own shock. She felt a mild tremor go through her, expecting another fight. Her feet carried her onward. He moved, one foot sweeping apart from the other as if he meant to cut her off, and with an angry growl escaping her she shoved him aside with both hands and sent him off the side of the dock, crashing into the water. A collective shout rose from the others. Then she reached the end of the dock herself...

...and she dove straight in.

She swam like a madwoman. Like a bloodthirsty predator was on her tail. Or perhaps like *she* was the bloodthirsty predator, swimming desperately to catch up to her prey, which she could actually see through the glowing steam ahead, his body visibly moving at a slower pace, arms cycling through the water almost leisurely.

Because of the sap, she thought distantly. *He's tiring out, slowing down, paralysis setting in.*

Soon he wouldn't be able to support himself and he would sink to a watery grave. She swam harder, faster, if that were even possible. The kink in her neck screamed something fierce with her efforts, aching and burning as she swam with her head above the water in order to keep Isaac in her sights. She caught up to him much quicker than she believed herself capable.

"Isaac!" she screamed.

The amber light was underneath them, powerfully bright and just as mysterious, impossible to tell its source, how far down it was, or perhaps *how close it was*. By the time she reached her brother, his movements were beginning to devolve into lazy thrashing, like an animated statue returning to its natural state at the stroke of midnight.

"Isaac," she said, panting and spitting water as she tried to wrangle him into her arms. "It's me. It's me. Please..."

She tread water as best she could as she tried to take him against herself, tried to swim them backward. He relented to her touch. His eyes rolled fearfully in their sockets, full of that amber light as he clearly lost his ability to work his mouth, his tongue.

It's okay. I've got you. It's okay.

And then something touched Drew from the water's depths.

Trying to keep Isaac afloat, trying to keep herself afloat, she couldn't very well look down into the water beneath them to see what it was, but something definitely touched her. Not in passing, either. Something in the water, in the light, *touched* the side of her leg, from her calf down to the protruding bone of her ankle. Then it was gone.

With so much else to worry about, Drew hardly registered the sensation. Across the water was a dock full of naked people, watching, waiting, readying to unleash their bewilderment upon them when they returned. All hell was about to break loose, she thought, when she revealed what Blaine had done. What he'd *been doing* all this time. There was proof of it still, down in his basement. Quentin's corpse, among others. This whole community was in for the shock of their lives...

Then it touched her again. Something met the *back* of

her leg this time, a strangely tacky pat against the crook of her knee, then the back of her calf all the way down to her heel, and in an instant it was folded around her, circling her leg like a rolled-up newspaper. Her first instinct was to grab hold of Isaac even tighter, to clutch herself to him like a buoy as her leg was tugged gently from below, in the grasp of something she couldn't place. Couldn't imagine. Then it tugged her again, harder this time, and she plunged. She let go of her brother as the thing around her leg dragged her under the water's surface. She jerked and pulled to no avail. She opened her eyes in the illuminated depths, the lake water as clear as a swimming pool's, and glimpsed the strange, flat pad of flesh that was wrapped around her leg. Shining flesh, glowing hot, the source of the light. And in the same instant she saw it, the water below bloomed with further movement. Larger movement. Another billowing *thing* reached up from beneath her —a second, much *wider* petal opened to receive her. A silky curtain of tissue. It closed around her much like the first, swallowed her up to her ribs, around her waist and thighs and everything else, rolling her up like a corpse in a rug as she reached fruitlessly for the black surface overhead. She sank farther and farther, the lake much deeper than she ever could have imagined, until finally she was pulled into something else that waited below, enveloped on all sides like an insect sucked through a pulsing straw.

Everything became a disorienting mess. The farther out he swam, the more tired his body became. Impossibly tired.

246

He'd never felt so out of shape in his life. It was as though his limbs lost their ability to receive commands, churning the lake water like it was butter until he couldn't even make the proper motions anymore. He slapped uselessly. His legs *felt* like they were kicking, but it was only the memory of what they'd been doing a moment ago. Then, just as he was about to give up, to sink, someone screamed his name. A body arrived next to his, and it was Drew.

Drew? he wanted to say, but couldn't say anything at all. His lips wouldn't move.

He couldn't resist as she pulled him against herself—not that he *wanted* to resist, but it might have been his panicked reaction if not for the strange paralysis settling over him. Wading gently, Drew took them back in the direction of the dock. The orange-yellow light throbbed brilliantly underneath them. He peered up at the dark clouds overhead, still flashing with hidden camera bulbs... and was amazed as the darkness bled with color, like watercolor paint leeching across wet paper. Swirling green, powdery blue, and something between pink and red curling in around them. He became entranced... and remained entranced even as his sister let go, as her arms fell away.

Drew?

He bobbed on the water's surface, floating serenely, trapped in his observation of the stormy kaleidoscope.

As quickly as Drew had departed, another body took her place. Another pair of arms tucked Isaac into themselves, carrying him through the wet warmth. Then, staring up into the sky, his vision obscured with faces. More hands took hold of him. They hoisted him up from the water like a dead fish, dragged him onto the hard, dry planks of the dock.

A man hunched over him, his dripping, orange goatee sizzling in Isaac's vision like the heat off asphalt on a hot summer day.

"You're all right," Blaine said, except his voice was sizzling, too. Then, to the numerous voices rising up behind them he said, "He's in shock, that's all. Something went wrong. I don't know... I haven't the slightest idea. She *did* leave, last night. I have no idea how she's back, or what... why..." The other voices overcrowded him, drowning out the answers he did or didn't have. There were more questions about Isaac, what was wrong with him, which only inspired further non-answers. "The spirit of the lake took his sister instead. I don't know what it means, or what happens now. I swear I'm as lost as the rest of you..." Then Blaine snapped his fingers at someone nearby. "Let's get his clothes back on. Then let's get him inside the lodge. Put him in one of the beds there..."

Just then Blaine turned to see something else, something that caused his face to turn white as a sheet. With the vaguest of interest—and ability—Isaac rolled his eyes up to see what it was, and saw a man staggering toward them, upside-down in his vision. A man even paler than Blaine was, with his hand to his throat, and a vivid spill of crimson up his body.

Down his body. You're upside down—no, he's upside down...

And then Kent collapsed onto the dock beside them.

PART THREE
THE ROOTS

19

THE DWELLING

For the first time in her life she knew what it was to be completely vulnerable. *Truly* vulnerable—at the mercy of something she didn't understand, her brain lighting up with warnings and flight responses which she couldn't do anything with because she was quite literally trapped, passed through some rubbery esophagus which ushered her through with its flexing, caterpillar movements. Through the whole process, through the jostling and gasping for air and clawing mindlessly at the choking walls on all sides, she only formed one coherent thought, which was: *It's alive!*

Not even *that* did she fully understand. Nor was she entirely correct in her assumption, anyway.

She abruptly spilled out into open air, her insides recoiling nauseously into themselves from the fall, until she landed painfully upon hard, rocky ground. Her feet hit first. Her legs folded beneath her as she rolled onto her ass and then finally onto her back where she lay in a puddle of lake water, blinking it from her eyes, spitting it from her mouth as more *drip, drip, dripped* from the ceiling overhead. She was surrounded by a grim, muted glow. That same yellow-orange light as before, but turned down to that of a child's nightlight.

As her vision cleared, she found herself face to face with a puckering monstrosity in the rocky ceiling. Round, fleshy lips were embedded there, smacking lightly, pulsating grotesquely from the rock like an enormous tumor, shedding droplets of lake water onto the ground beside her. The mouth she'd come through—where the lake had quite literally swallowed her whole.

Where the hell am I? What the hell is going on?

She pushed herself up onto her elbows. She was in a dimly lit chamber. A *cave,* judging by the jutting, irregular walls, but no ordinary cave. No ordinary walls. In and out of the rock, weaving through its surface like burrowing worms, was a network of what appeared to be roots of some kind. Tree roots? Impossible to know, except that again, these were not ordinary roots. They were everywhere, scrabbling over the rock like a mesh, with pockets of glowing fluid that swelled from them like amber-filled pustules—the source of the low light by which Drew's surroundings were made barely visible. Like the throbbing mouth in the ceiling above, the roots pulsated as well, quivering as though they felt Drew's gaze fanning over them.

I was wrong.

There were no bones at the bottom of the lake...

Something moved nearby. Something besides the mouth in the ceiling, or the roots on the walls. Approaching footsteps. Loud, thumping, *scuttling* footsteps. Sitting on the ground soaking wet, beads of lake water yet to dry from her fear-stricken brow, Drew turned rigid as those footsteps clambered nearer, echoing off the cave walls from an adjoining tunnel. And with them, the distinct whisper of something dragging behind—an immense body slithering in her direction.

Drew sprang to her feet. Her jittering hand unleashed the switchblade from her pocket once again. She ejected the blade, still stained with Kent's blood, and held it toward the darkness as the *thing* arrived at the chamber's threshold with a sudden, scraping halt. Concealed in the tunnel's shadow, something stood. A hulking body, filling the tunnel to its brim. A circular rim of many, gleaming eyes hovered there in the dark, green orbs raised high toward the ceiling. Watching. Hungering. Drew met its bodiless gaze, watching within the tunnel's obscurity, its eyes becoming slits. Wary. Confused, perhaps.

Prefer your meals frozen, don't you?

She fought to hold still as her skin crawled with wild horror, body shivering with goosebumps, and all the while the thing in the tunnel remained still as ever. Observing her with cold, calculating patience. She wasn't the victim it anticipated. Nor was she incapacitated from Blaine's wacky sap.

Which looks suspiciously similar to the fluid filling up the roots on the walls here, she noted.

With the switchblade trembling in her grasp, keeping her eyes on the thing before her, she said, "Stay the fuck away from me."

The lake continued to drip softly from the mouth in the

ceiling. The roots in the walls rustled gently. The thing in the tunnel stood still as a figment, its eyes unblinking, until finally there came an inhuman groan—oddly feminine in its tone, with an impossible layered quality, like many voices speaking in unison. With that, the hovering eyes retreated. They sank into the dark like beads into muddy water, vanishing entirely. Drew stood frozen for a while longer, and listened as its footsteps retreated likewise, shuffling and padding backward until they faded from earshot.

Its absence gave her no relief whatsoever.

She turned and peered into what appeared to be a second tunnel behind her, sparsely illuminated by the same infected roots along its walls. Horrifyingly convenient. She cast a final glance toward the opposite tunnel, where the *thing* had retreated, confirming it wasn't simply waiting for her to turn her back.

How the hell do I get out of this?

Only one way to find out, she supposed.

She started into the second tunnel, moving slowly as the roots on the walls tittered and flinched in response to her passing. She struggled to reconcile that any of this was real—that she wasn't simply still hallucinating in Blaine's basement. Her various bruises and the chafing of her thighs within her sopping wet shorts were evidence enough that while this was certainly a nightmare, it was no dream.

The roots were leaking. She noticed the luminescent sap oozing down the walls from some of their ruptured bulbs. She could smell its tangy sweetness on the muggy, cavernous air. Once or twice she gasped as she was touched in the darkness, and turned to find the roots shrinking away, their hairy-tipped ends probing the dark like tiny fingers. She kept the switchblade secure in her fist, just in case.

As the tunnel twisted and looped and sloped, she doubted her chances of escape. She imagined the *thing* making its way toward her from another direction, some other route in its network of tunnels which it surely knew by heart. All Drew knew was that she needed to keep moving, however hopeless it was.

I've gotta get back to Isaac.

She hoped he'd been saved, that the others pulled him from the water in time. *Isaac, the Chosen But Not Taken.* What would the others make of all this? Her mysterious reappearance? Or what about Kent's fate?

I hope I killed him, she thought mercilessly.

Turning the next corner, Drew barely stifled a scream as she was abruptly faced with a human skull. It was embedded in the wall, fastened beneath a thin lattice of roots. Its dark sockets peered emptily. A partial spine trailed beneath it. Nothing more.

With a hand to her heart, she continued on. She soon emerged into another small chamber, where her already tripping heartbeat began playing hopscotch against her ribs.

"Shit..."

Multiple remains decorated these walls. Skeletons suspended against the dark rock. Unlike the last, most of these were whole. Skulls, spines, and all four limbs splayed out in all manner of poses across the chamber.

So I wasn't entirely wrong about the pile of bones at the bottom of the lake...

The closer Drew studied them, the more she realized

some weren't nearly as old as others. Then a weak, debilitated moan sent her body rippling with chills all over again.

From her left, a haggard voice ground out what sounded like its last breath. She turned toward the sound, and was dizzied by something between horror and despair.

Not every corpse here was fully decomposed. Not every corpse here was a *corpse,* though they very well should have been. She faced the victim in question, roped to the wall by the glowing, fluid-filled tendrils, and found a body nearly skeletal, except for what appeared to be a thin skin still clinging to the bones' surfaces, barely any flesh to separate the two. And the skull—*no, the face, it's a goddamn face*—still contained eyes, dull hazel eyes, which now peered into Drew's very soul.

"Oh my God," she said.

A woman's body, judging by the shriveled details of her sex and the deflated remnants of what were once her breasts, and the long, stringy, dusty hair hanging about her sunken face. The poor woman's eyelids fluttered minutely, as those dreary hazel eyes struggled to make sense of the much more lively woman before her.

Olivia? Drew thought.

Before she knew entirely what she was doing, she reached for the roots around the woman's body, across her chest and arms, which were pinned up on either side of her head. She grabbed the roots, felt them budge gently under her grasp like sleeping snakes.

"It's okay," she said. "I'm gonna... I'm gonna..."

I'm going to do absolutely nothing for you because you're obviously within an inch of your life, and I don't even know how you're still alive like this, and I know I'm probably not even going to be able to save myself let alone someone in your condition...

She cut at the roots with her knife. They cut easily enough. Most disturbing was the manner in which they *whined* as she severed them—little mice-like squeals in the dark. And was she mistaken, or did the amber fluid in the surrounding pustules strobe brighter? She continued to cut, to slice and dice, until the woman's left side was freed from the roots holding her in place. Her body fell forward slightly from the wall, shoulder slack, and Drew screamed as the woman's arm detached like a poorly glued popsicle stick. A bloodless break. The skeletal arm dropped to the ground at Drew's feet. She stumbled back. The woman hung awkwardly there, those sad hazel eyes wincing.

"Oh my God," Drew said. "I'm sorry. I'm so sorry... I..."

The roots strobed again. The amber light brightened, like lightbulbs surging in a thunderstorm. Then they dimmed. From someplace far off in the cavern, there came a stampede of movement. A rush of limbs and feet echoing through the tunnels as something raced to meet her.

"Shit," Drew muttered. "I'm sorry, I... I can't help you."

The half-dead body simply moaned as Drew turned away, fleeing onward into the next available tunnel, leaving the chamber of corpses behind. Her bare feet slapped the warm, damp rock as something larger, something *unreal* fought to catch up. She bounced from wall to wall in her haste. The roots lazily crept toward her hands as she planted them, pushed off from them, chasing into the dimly lit shadows ahead. Her thoughts scattered. Aimless as her stumbling gait.

She came to a fork in the tunnel and bolted right without consideration. There was no time. She pressed deeper, felt the ground rise and fall in gentle slopes, felt the odd trickle of water from the ceiling upon her shoulders, the nape of her neck, where the lake above seeped through the rock. All the while, the sounds of her pursuer never faded, only followed, keeping pace if not gaining.

She arrived at a second fork in the tunnel, this one something of a split-level stairway, in that one path aimed downward, the other upward. A thick cluster of glowing pustules hung over the forking path, which allowed Drew to quickly make the distinction. She chose the upward slope. Anything that might bring her closer to the surface.

She regretted her decision ten seconds later when the path she chose dove downward again. Steeply. Sloping, sloping, sloping farther into the earth. She had no choice but to follow it. There was no turning back. The slope provided some additional speed, at least.

When at last the tunnel evened out, and spilled her around a sharply twisting bend at the bottom, she caught herself against the wall there, bruising her palms with the impact... and there she noticed a deep indentation in the lower wall. She peered farther ahead where the tunnel snaked out of sight. A split-second decision. She ducked down. Like a child crawling into a plastic playground chute, she scrambled into the hollow pocket in the wall on her hands and knees, feeling blindly so as not to ram her head into any sudden barrier.

I don't know what I'm doing. I don't know where I'm going.

Her knees ached against the rock with every shuffle.

Surviving. That's what you're doing. Don't think too much or you'll get yourself killed.

She knew the entity in pursuit was large. Larger than her, larger than any person. She'd seen its green eyes floating near the ceiling. Seven feet tall or more, she thought. Beyond that, there was no telling the true shape of it. Was it humanoid in *any* respect? Did it hunch? Was it a thirty-foot centipede slithering through these tunnels? All she could do was hope that it was too large to follow through the crawlspace behind her...

Please tell me this doesn't lead to something worse...

She looked over her shoulder, and listened as those footsteps came closer. A scrambling rush of feet or hooves or whatever made those pounding, scuttling noises. Then it was *there.* It passed by the crawlspace's opening, and she glimpsed its movement. A flash of dark, dangling limbs, and the rough, scratching whisper of leathery skin over the rock as it propelled its body ahead. Then it was gone. Its noises continued, settled into the cave's distance, echoing faintly until she heard nothing at all.

Nothing but the cavernous silence.

She continued through the crawlspace. Like the tunnels it branched from, the crawlspace possessed twists and turns of its own, and Drew's knees grew sore and bruised. She bumped her scalp painfully on the rock a couple times. When at last she reached the other end, and wiggled into another dim, rocky corridor, it was a struggle to climb back to her feet. Every joint seemed to pop and crack. She braced herself on the tunnel wall, pushed herself upright, then rested there a moment, breathing heavily.

She looked to her left, and to her right, and wondered pitifully which direction she should choose. She was utterly aimless by now. She tried to imagine the lake sitting overhead, and wondered which direction would take her out from under it, if possible. Closer to the surface. Closer to salvation. She thought she'd like to see the look on the others' faces when she returned from their so-called Mother. Was that the name of this creature, living beneath their feet? They had no idea.

Only Blaine knew.

Stop thinking. Get moving. Now.

She picked a direction and did just that. Moved. Shuffling and aching the whole way. Every now and then she paused and listened, checking for the sounds of the *other*. She heard nothing. Just her and her sad-sack of a body, straining to keep itself upright with each and every step.

Eventually she wandered into yet another small, round chamber, decorated with many throbbing roots on its walls as well as corpses tucked neatly underneath them. Across the chamber were two branching tunnels. Another haphazard choice to be made. She started toward them immediately, avoiding the corpses if she could help looking. Between the two tunnels, her gut feeling was to choose the left this time, although...

"*Drew...*"

A soft voice stopped her. Ice water trickled through her veins, through her marrow. She stiffened from head to toe, could barely turn her neck to see them, to see the face she knew she would.

She turned slowly, and lifted her gaze toward the chamber's upper wall. Displayed in a nest of dark roots, naked and trapped against the rock like a pinned moth, Drew met the gaze of one Julianne Prescott.

20

THE FOOLISH

They carried him to the main lodge, to one of the vacant beds inside. Robert and someone else, someone whose name Isaac never learned. Setting him down on the bed, and adjusting the pillow under his head, Robert looked concernedly into Isaac's eyes and said, "Hey buddy, how ya feeling?" to which Isaac didn't say anything at all because he couldn't. His mouth didn't work. But those swirling colors remained, now dancing across the cabin's dark ceiling, and Isaac was vaguely reminded of one of his favorite childhood movies—*Fantasia*. He watched the colors play across the shadows of the rafters overhead, looping through them, weaving in and out between each other. At any moment he fully expected a gang of crocodiles to pirouette into view, but nothing so absurd as that happened.

Then there were other voices. Other bodies shifting about, moving around him and the bed beside him. Someone else was set down in the bed to Isaac's left. He didn't possess

262

the ability to turn his head to see. But the voices were very grave. Very concerned.

"He's bled a lot..."

"Looks like he was stabbed with something..."

Then he heard Robert's voice again, but farther across the room.

"I thought she left? How did she get back?"

"I already told you, I don't know. Kent could probably tell us something, if only he were in any condition..."

And then their voices faded into the rest, into the murmurs and aggressive muttering of those trying to patch up the body on the other bed. Kent's body. Isaac listened to all of this very distantly, his half-lidded eyes glued toward the shimmering shapes on the ceiling.

Someone appeared beside him, hovered over him. The Goatee.

"You're all right, Isaac," Blaine said. "Sit tight. You'll be all right..." Then Blaine turned away and said to the others, *"Stay here and watch them while I go check on some things. I'll be back. I'll be right back..."*

Then Blaine was gone. Isaac wasn't certain how many others were in the cabin with them. He was growing rather tired, his eyelids heavy and draping down his eyes slowly, slowly, slowly as the colors continued to splash and bloom across his vision.

"Look what I've got, Isaac..."

Isaac turned his head then. Or at least, he *perceived* himself as turning his head. He looked toward a new voice in the room, a familiar one, and was surprised to see something more revealed in the cabin's shadows. A familiar place.

This isn't real.

His old bedroom. Not his early childhood bedroom. After that. In his grandparents' house. After everything had already happened. And the voice... the voice speaking to him was...

"I found this in one of my boxes. I don't know what it was doing in there, but..." Her voice faded out suddenly, then faded back in, like a bad service connection. *"...I can read it to you, if you want..."*

Then there was another voice. Another *terribly* familiar voice. A young child, a young boy, struggling not to cry and failing fantastically. It was *his own* voice. He remembered. He could even feel the lump in this throat now, like he was there again, living it. Swallowing it. He remembered this moment, remembered his sister, remembered the sad look on her teenage face—a face which looked much too sleepless for someone her age, much too darkened by things no child should endure—and how the hint of kindness there deteriorated miserably in light of his petulant answer.

"That's a baby's book," he heard himself say, even as his voice tremored with emotions. *"I don't want that. I'm not a baby anymore."*

The truth was, he'd already been crying before she came into his room that night. Probably why she brought the book in the first place—could probably hear him going on and on from the next room. She'd probably had that book for some time, worrying whether it was appropriate or not to let him have it, if it would soothe him or remind him of painful things he'd yet to process. She was too young to be worrying so much about her baby brother, and yet she did. Every day she did...

Isaac couldn't keep his eyes open anymore. As the colors overtook his vision again, he closed his eyes and could feel the world fading, could feel himself falling out of it.

And then he snapped awake as someone returned to his bedside. It was Robert. Again. Isaac had no idea how long he'd closed his eyes—a minute or two, or an hour—but suddenly he felt sensation returning to his face. Barely. And the colors were gone.

Hovering over him, looking into his eyes once more, Robert said, "Still with us?"

Isaac puckered his lips, or at least felt them puckering, and managed to say, "Drew..."

Robert nodded understandingly. "We all thought she left, but..." His gaze flickered elsewhere, and even in his delirious state Isaac sensed controversy in Robert's unspoken words. "Anyway, she swam out into the lake to stop you. But then she vanished. You know, like the lake took her instead." Robert peered deeply into Isaac's eyes, as if he couldn't tell whether Isaac was *there* or not, if he could hear him, and then he sighed heavily, looked toward the next bed, and then in the direction of the cabin door. "Between you and me... I think something's definitely not right here."

Robert chewed his lower lip, thinking, speaking to Isaac how someone might talk something over with their pet cat.

"I don't know Drew like you do," he went on, "but something tells me your sister isn't a violent person. Or a lunatic, for that matter..." He looked to the next bed, where Isaac gathered Kent must have still been lying. Was he alive?

"She must have had her reasons for doing a number on him like she did."

Listening to Robert, another wave of loneliness settled over Isaac. And under that loneliness was another fear. Another realization. His sister *wasn't* a violent person, nor a lunatic, although she could really get inside her own head about things at times, Isaac knew. While she was undoubtedly upset about his decision to stay, there was zero chance she would *'solve'* that problem with a knife in someone's throat. Even if they'd drifted apart a little over the years, he knew her well enough to know that. He knew her better than anyone, really—a helluva lot better than Blaine or Robert or any of them. From the sounds of what had transpired, there was really only one logical explanation Isaac could think of, which was: *Blaine is a fucking liar.*

And I'm a goddamn moron.

His despair threatened to undo him. Drew was now *totally* gone, and he was at their mercy. So he latched to what he considered his last resource left, one he couldn't utilize in his current state, but would feel immensely reassured to have on hand, at least. He struggled to move his lips—was unsure if he succeeded or not, until his voice made use of them—and told Robert concisely, "My bag..."

Robert furrowed his brow. "Huh?"

"My bag," he repeated. Then he swallowed. "Please."

At that precise moment the cabin door opened. Although Isaac still couldn't turn his head, Blaine's voice appeared clear and distinct as ever.

"How's he doing?" he asked Robert, shutting the door behind him.

Robert glanced between Blaine and Isaac, his gears turning, still processing Isaac's last words.

"Fine, I think. He's awake." Robert's eyes narrowed as Blaine approached them, and he said, "Did you run here? You're covered in sweat."

"Maybe," Blaine answered nonchalantly. Dismissively. "Has he moved at all? Said anything?"

After the briefest hesitation, Robert shook his head. "No, nothing yet. I was thinking..." He paused. "I was thinking maybe I'd go grab his things from his cabin, if he'll be spending the night in here. Are you good to—"

"That sounds like a great idea." Blaine groaned as he took a seat on the edge of Kent's bed. "I'll keep an eye on them while you do that. Give you a bit of a break, huh?"

Robert lingered a moment longer, watching Isaac carefully, and then left. The cabin door shut behind him just as another bout of thunder rumbled through the storm outside. In Robert's absence, Blaine stirred, twisting around to see the wounded man beside him, in the bed beside Isaac's.

"Hang in there, Kent," Blaine muttered. He turned back toward Isaac, hunching over from the edge of Kent's bed toward him. "You too, Isaac. If you can hear me at all."

Isaac's lips were parted, and he felt increasingly able to move them now, but he remained silent. He stared emptily up at the ceiling, even as his hallucinations were long behind him now. Blaine didn't need to know. It was Blaine who had done this to him, he thought. It wasn't shock, it wasn't to do with what happened in the lake, it was whatever that substance was that he'd swabbed Isaac's tongue with. With most of his body still petrified by its effects, Isaac couldn't help but wonder how no one else had figured that out, or at least *asked* about it.

What's this gooey stuff you're feeding us before sending us off into the lake? Oh, Mother's blood? All right, then, no further questions!

And yet he understood the lapse in judgement, because he'd made it himself. He'd trusted just like everyone else. He couldn't help but wonder what the intended outcome was, sending him off into the lake with some paralyzing agent leaking into his bloodstream. Had Drew been right about everything? Her paranoid fantasy of bones piled at the bottom? But if that were true, where had *she* gone, then?

"What do you think happened, dear Isaac?" Blaine grumbled just out of view. Isaac flicked his eyes in Blaine's direction but gave no answer. Blaine shifted where he sat, then gave a casual sniff. "I suppose your sister must love you very deeply, going to such lengths to stop you from leaving her. There's that, at least. I'm sorry it's gone down this way. This was supposed to be a sacred night between you and our Mother, and... well, it would seem that your sister has beaten you to it. But maybe that's not such a bad thing. Maybe this is how it was meant to go all along. There is still time for you to join them, of course. Your mother and sister. The three of you, together, in the embrace of our Mother..." Isaac wasn't entirely certain, but he thought Blaine might have laughed softly to himself at the thought. "Maybe that's what fate has always had in store?"

21
THE ECHOES

"Mom?"

Julianne peered down at her daughter, her worn face softly aglow in the amber light, enough that Drew could see the sunken hollows of her cheeks, as well as the dark circles under her eyes—which appeared bulging due to the shrunken nature of the rest of her face. Not yet as drained as Quentin had been, but nearing it. It wasn't the roots draining them, Drew thought vaguely. There hadn't been any roots in Blaine's basement, after all.

"Hold on," Drew said. "I'm gonna... I'm gonna cut you down..."

She stood on tiptoe, and reached with her knife toward the roots around her mother's naked waist. As she pierced the first, it made the same eerie whine, as if she'd stabbed a baby animal. The other roots appeared to tighten across her mother's body, visibly squeezing her ribs, her breasts. Julianne winced. Drew continued to cut and saw against them, severing them, listening as they cried out.

269

Then there was movement overhead. Drew glanced upward to see the ceiling *bowing* downward—or rather, the roots there descending, creeping steadily toward her. Their feeble little tendrils grasped at her, at her hands, her arms, at her *hair,* and she shrugged them away, ducked out of their reach. A shudder went through her, listening to their movements, their continued cries.

"It's okay," she muttered, as her mother let out a pained cry of her own. "I'm gonna get you down. We're gonna..."

An echoing disturbance in the nearby tunnels gave her pause. A slithering, stomping pursuit. The *thing* was coming again. It was all connected, she realized. These roots, sending signals—*pain, pain, she's hurting us!*—to the *thing* lurking somewhere close.

Shit.

Those frail tendrils caressed the side of her face and she flinched away. She stepped back from her mother entirely, whose fearful gaze pointed toward the tunnel behind her, sensing the *other's* approach as well.

"Go," Julianne gasped. The roots around her middle continued to constrict, and she bared her teeth against their smothering. "Just go, Drew..."

Drew shook her head. She swiped the tendrils away, stepped toward her mother again, and began to cut at the ones around her ribs. She sliced into a glowing pocket of amber sap, which dripped warmly down her wrist, her elbow. Behind her, the tunnels came to life with echoes. That strange, womanly choir of voices slipped through the cavern in the thing's approach.

"I just... I just need to cut a little more..."

She couldn't cut them fast enough. Her mother was just too ensnared—too many roots holding her back. Drew felt them reaching for her now, slipping beneath the sleeves of her shirt. The *thing* in the distance was getting closer all the while. Too close. No time left.

"I'm sorry," Drew said. She felt like crying, but was too afraid to even start. "Fuck. I'm sorry. I can't... I can't save you..."

"Go..." Julianne said, her voice an angry rasp.

Drew obeyed.

She left her mother where she hung, tore herself out from beneath the net of roots attempting to keep her as well, and started for the two branching tunnels on the chamber's other side. She chose the left like she'd originally planned— nothing but a gamble—and again regretted her decision near instantly.

Footsteps echoed in the gloom ahead. Not monstrous ones. Human. Bipedal. Coming her way. Thinking quickly, she retreated back into her mother's chamber and this time slipped into the righthand tunnel instead. She followed its twisting length, and barely got out of sight before the human visitor announced his arrival in the chamber behind her.

"Oh, Julianne!" Blaine spoke genially, like greeting someone at the supermarket. *"I didn't expect to see you here..."*

How had he gotten down here, Drew wondered? She tried to steady her breath as she listened. At last, the immense movement of the *other* spilled into the chamber as well, arriving in a stampede of scuttling limbs. Julianne moaned with fright, involuntary, as though the thing's mere arrival instilled in her uncontrollable terror. There came a series of unusual sounds. A low, creaking noise, intertwined with a deep, droning hum, followed by clicking and grumbling in one disquieting breath.

"Yes, yes, I know," Blaine replied. *"This wasn't planned. Things have just gotten so out of hand on the surface. But..."*

To this, there came another deep, drawn-out groan. A sickly baritone whimper, underlaid with the same feminine breathiness she'd heard before. Something about it sent chills up Drew's shoulders. The thing fidgeted, its body rubbing and rustling dryly, and in response to its movements Julianne cried out. Drew stiffened. She couldn't see them, but her mind did a fine job filling in the blanks.

"No, no, I can't stay," Blaine went on. *"I must return to the surface. The cattle are in a proper tizzy and I must put their small minds at ease..."* He sighed heavily. *"She's still down here somewhere. Keep looking. I'll be back as soon as I can."* His words were met with more shifting, more groaning, and what now reminded Drew of tree branches wobbling in a breeze, clacking against one another. *"I'm dealing with a lot more up there than your one little cockroach down here, believe me. Don't be so goddamn dramatic. I'll be back soon, I said..."* As it seemed he was making to leave, Blaine paused and said one last thing: *"When you do find her, mother, do us both a favor... and tear her apart."*

And with that he departed, presumably back the way he came—back to whatever entrance he'd used, which Drew knew she had no hope of finding on her own. She remembered the padlocked door in his basement, in the dark, breathing warm air from underneath, and instantly knew it must have been the one. Only she couldn't exactly follow him there, with the *thing* lingering in the chamber like it was.

Out of sight, Julianne gave another agonized moan. The creature tittered its approval. It moved, its body groaning like a settling house, and Julianne cried out again, louder, distraught, before her voice rose sharply into a piercing whimper. There was little Drew could do for her. Little she could do without getting herself killed in the process, anyway.

Resting with her back against the tunnel wall, clutching the knife in her fist, Drew tensed as she felt something wiggling against her scalp—dry little feelers creeping into her hair. She stepped away, or tried to, and discovered the roots on the wall had lightly, and stealthily, secured themselves around her forearm. They constricted, pulled her arm tight against the rock. She pulled once, but they held fast. More roots reached for her, rippling from the wall like a curtain in a breeze. She tore herself away in a panic, tore the roots violently out of place and freed herself, staggering and empty handed as the tendrils pried the switchblade from her grip. They mewled like milk-starved kittens. From around the corner, the *thing* in the chamber fell silent. As did Julianne...

Shit...

She bolted. Again. The thing's movements erupted into a frenzy behind her, entering the tunnel not far behind. It let out a low, hollow screech in pursuit. She propelled herself on sore, now-bleeding feet, cut up against the rough rock of the cave floor. She shouldered the wall a few times, careening left to right and back along each of the tunnel's wild bends, her vision only *just* adequate for the gloom, for the sparse amber light provided by the roots which now actively grasped for her in passing.

Let me go, she thought uselessly, pleadingly. *Just let me go...*

As she continued to run and the beast continued to give chase, an unusual voice pierced her hectic mind—squirmed into her ear like an obsession. It presented itself like a thought of her own, only it wasn't that. It wasn't her voice. Someone else's.

It said, *"Keep going."*

An absolutely pointless bit of advice, she thought. She had no choice *but* to keep going, to continue hurdling through the lake's dark intestines even as her muscles reached their limit, aching to the point of trembling, and as her mind reached its limit likewise, succumbing to the dizzying waves of hunger. She had no choice, and yet she wasn't sure how much longer she could keep this up.

"This way!"

Another voice in the dark. Less in her mind this time, more beside her, on her right. Eerily, as she fled a few steps farther, she arrived at a sharp turnoff—one she'd have missed completely had she not been made aware of it. She pushed in its direction, feet threatening to slide out from under her. At her back, the thing's movements were ever-present, charging through the tunnel like a fat crab through a narrow vent. Drew followed this new path more alert, eyes darting over the sap-filled roots on the walls with desperate attentiveness, seeking her next move, her next direction.

"Climb."

Sure enough, the tunnel sloped upward, until she was faced with an unexpected half-wall—or rather, a rising shelf in the rock, jutting up at waist level. She loathed it even as she immediately proceeded to scale it, pushing herself up on quivering arms. She lifted one leg, planted her foot for leverage, and pushed herself onto the ledge with what seemed to be the very last of her strength. She stood up, and promptly stumbled sideways against the wall there, barely able to keep standing. Behind her, the *other* was drawing near, and quickly. She glanced in its direction, over the slight drop of the raised ledge where she now stood, and saw the faintest hint of its shape in the darkness—a messy silhouette of stiff-moving limbs in the shadows, clambering and pulling itself closer.

"Keep going," another voice repeated in her ear, different than the last, to which Drew audibly panted, "Right..."

She pushed off the wall and continued ahead. She could hardly sprint. The most she could manage was a slow and clumsy jog. But she was *going*. She was still going. Behind her, the thing bellowed its own frustration as it must have arrived at the awkward rise—or drop, from Drew's new vantage point.

"Here," another voice announced, on Drew's left.

Two more paces brought her to another branching passage. Another she'd have missed if not for the voices. She obeyed them and veered that way. As she stayed the course ahead, the noises of the *other* fell behind, gradually, until finally she couldn't hear its sounds at all—only the lonely hush of the warm cavern air. Air that probably shouldn't have been so warm, but now she understood why it was.

Because there's something living down here, Drew thought, *and it's poisoned the very ground that harbors it.*

The tunnel she followed curved around and around, until just as she was certain she should loop back to the place she started it snaked in the other direction. It switched back and forth like that for some time with no additional forks or connected paths. Linear. Ongoing. Drew also noticed the farther she followed, the cooler the cave became. And darker. The pockets of glowing fluid within the roots became sparser, until soon it was dark enough that Drew was forced to rely on touch as much as her vision to navigate, one hand on the wall as she cautiously followed its twisting length. The roots she touched, grazing them with her fingertips, stirred grotesquely in response. Her breaths were shallow and thin and *loud* in the new silence.

And then her feet splashed into shallow water.

She hesitated. She took a few more steps, and with each and every one the water climbed. Up to her knees, her thighs. Not only that, but the ceiling overhead sloped. She reached for it, grazed it with her fingertips. She waded deeper into the water, up to her waist, and the ceiling fell steadily toward it.

Nowhere to go but forward, she thought. *Nowhere to go but in.*

She turned back and listened carefully. Still no signs of being followed. She faced the water again, a quiet dread ballooning inside her.

How long can you hold your breath?

What if the voices had meant to deceive her? This

occurred to her like any other anxious concern, always anticipating the worst. Except these were the voices of those trapped down below—their bones entwined in the roots that had doomed them. These were the voices she had heard before, on the surface, calling for her help. Thinking on this, it stood to reason, Drew thought, that the water before her could only lead to one place. A place she'd already discovered and seen with her own eyes. The *'bear's den.'* This was it, she thought with a strange certainty.

The way out.

She stepped deeper into the water. Colder than the lake water. Another couple steps and she was up to her breasts. She shivered. She took a moment to breathe, anticipating the blind swim ahead, however long it might last. Then, with a willful stilling of her mind, forcing all thoughts aside, she took a deep lungful of air and plunged herself in.

She kicked her feet, paddling with one hand ahead as she used the other to press off the tunnel's ceiling where her body wished to rise against. Deeper and deeper, all was black and aimless. Aimless except for the ceiling she followed. However, even as the amber light had vanished, the roots themselves did not. They were here, too, beneath the water. She touched them along the ceiling, felt them wriggle against the palm of her hand. And as the ceiling began to rise once more, rising toward the hopeful surface, those roots took on new life.

Still kicking delicately with her feet to propel her, Drew startled to a sudden rush of movement where her hand touched the ceiling next—a rapid slithering of tendrils over her fingers, around her wrist. She fought against them, yanked her hand out from their grasp. She choked out some of her air, a flurry of bubbles escaping her mouth. She stopped kicking in her distraction, legs sinking beneath her, and more roots rose up from the water's depths to catch her feet in their looping knots.

Shit!

She kicked, bucked. Her chest ached. On fire. She reached ahead and paddled with both hands against the wet dark, and suddenly it seemed as though the roots were on all sides, releasing themselves from the rock like a closing net. Their bristly feelers tapped against her legs, her arms. She breaststroked toward what she thought was the surface and bumped the back of her skull against the ceiling. A cutting, scratching throb.

Goddammit...

They fell upon her back, wriggled between her shoulder blades, reaching their way up toward the nape of her neck. She clawed at the water, pulled herself higher still. She felt them exploring blindly like worms rising to the rain, like a series of frayed threads trying to form a noose around her throat. She coughed another plume of bubbles. She reached ahead with one hand, paddling the water, and with her other hand she grasped the roots taking hold around her neck and she pulled them away, tore them down like breaking a necklace. There were still roots clinging to her feet, lacing around her ankles, just enough to keep her in place, to keep her from rising toward the surface. In a blind panic, she folded herself up, reached for her feet, and pulled the damned things away with irritating ease. Her lungs felt fit to burst now. She straightened in the water, pulled herself upward once more, guided one hand toward the ceiling to prevent a concussion. Their stringy little feelers were everywhere. She found the ceiling, kicked her feet wildly for forward momentum, and gradually followed the tunnel's slope toward the surface. Her lungs screamed for relief, for another breath. Soon. *Now.* The tunnel's ceiling steepened until it wasn't a ceiling any longer, but the wall of a vertical passage, straight up, and she pulled both hands through the water to climb it, one after the other, until finally, suddenly, her next stroke broke free and swiped cool air above. Cool air... and something else. Something that swiped back. Another hand. It grabbed Drew by the wrist. She grabbed it back. With a strong, helping grip, she was hauled up from the water, over the ledge of the hole where she was released, scrambling and gasping and rolling herself onto the floor of the dark cave.

The bear's den.

Her first instinct might have been to pull herself upright, to question the stranger in the dark who had helped her, but all she could do was breathe. She coughed, wheezed, spat some water she'd swallowed. She lay on her back for a minute, breathing deeply.

The cave was utterly silent.

Before she'd caught all her breath, she asked, "Hello?" No answer. No movement. Not even the sigh of another's breath in the dark. She sat up finally, blinking her eyes, and said again, "Hello?"

Still nothing.

She shivered a little, but whether it was with realization or the damp cold, she wasn't sure. She'd grabbed *someone's* hand. Someone waiting for her here. Or perhaps...

"Thank you," she said, as it dawned on her. To no one in particular. *"...thank you..."*

She couldn't make any real sense of it, but she wouldn't wonder about it too much. Not now. There were more important things to consider. Such as getting Isaac the hell out of this place.

She wobbled to her feet. She leaned against the wall of the cave for a moment to gather her bearings. Despite her swim, her forearm was still sticky with root sap.

Gross.

Finally, she moved along the cave's perimeter until she happened upon the narrow passage out. She followed that on dragging feet. She was so utterly *exhausted.* She couldn't fathom facing them again—assuming she could even carry herself back to camp. She worried it was too late. Blaine had likely already turned them against her somehow—made her out to be some unstable, unpredictable threat. Dangerous.

If only they knew what they were really up against.

A fragrant breeze hummed through the cave's passage, clinging to her damp face. Pleasantly familiar. Then she saw the faintest light. The pitch black gave way to the nightly woods. The cave's entrance. Her exit. She staggered out into the dirt, under the breezy branches of the forest, and had to stop herself from bursting into tears of relief.

You're not out yet. Not even close.

Disoriented, she made her way to the worn path, where the outhouse waited visibly at its end. In the other direction, the lake. The cabin. The others who would be even more surprised to see her now than the last time.

She started back. The trees rasped and scraped in the

wind. The dark storm brimmed with thunder and menacing clouds overhead, and yet still no rain. Not even a sprinkle. The dirt under her feet was bone dry. But she could *smell* it. The storm and its moisture. A clean, electric scent. She glanced warily at the branches above as thunder rolled low across the sky.

Something swooped from the shadows overhead—a darting ball of fluttering feathers. She flinched back, raised a defensive hand before her, and then gasped as another shadow came immediately after the first. This one *landed* on her. A dark little bird on her wrist. Its eyes twinkled. Its little claws softly tapped against her arm, pulling up from the tacky residue on her skin...

You've gotta be kidding me.

The sap in the roots. The same sap secreting through the trees here, up above. They were drawn to it, she thought. The birds. Perhaps the insects as well. The exercises Blaine encouraged them to do—Sherry's little tree-hugging excursion—connecting with nature, the forest, the *Mother*. Somehow, the Mother chose them. Through the roots... *through the trees...*

"Get the fuck off me," Drew snapped, and whipped her hand, so that the bird took flight back into the branches.

She wiped her arm against her wet clothes—for all the good it would do—and hurried onward, ignoring the sounds of nightly *critters* following through the branches above and the underbrush at her back.

She arrived sooner than she expected. The cabin's shape revealed itself through the trees. She moved close, clung to its shadow, and made her way toward the front, where she eyed the lake ahead. Across the lake, many lanterns were still lit outside a handful of cabins. The others were still awake, probably restless from all the *excitement.*

So far as she could tell, there was nobody near. She hurried to the front door and pushed inside easily, then closed it securely behind her. She surveyed the empty quarters. Isaac's unmade bed. *Her* unmade bed. Her bag was gone from the floor. Taken and disposed of, most likely, before telling Isaac she'd left home without him...

Did he believe it? she wondered, and felt a worrisome pang.

She moved swiftly to Isaac's bed, where his bag lay on the ground like always. She crouched, pulled it open by the zipper, dug around inside until her hand happened upon the cool metal of the handgun. She pulled it out, gleaming softly in the cabin's gloom.

Now what?

She would find Isaac. With the gun as their security, she'd escort him back to Blaine's, where they'd take Kent's truck if possible. Maybe put a bullet in Blaine's thick skull, if he tried to stop them first.

The cabin door opened. Drew sprang to her feet. She clapped both hands to the pistol, pointed it at the door as a silhouette stepped inside, and watched as they turned rigid at the sight of her, head rearing back in surprise.

"Woah," the man said, raising both hands to show he meant no harm. Then, "Wait... Drew?"

It was Robert, she realized. Even so, she kept the gun trained and ready to shoot.

"Close the door," she told him.

Robert remained as he was. Frozen with shock. "How are you... how did you..."

"Close the fucking door, I said."

Jerky with nerves, he finally did as she told him, shutting the door and sealing them back into stuffy, dark silence.

"I need you to listen to me," she said.

"Okay, but... do you gotta point that at me like that?"

Drew considered. She wasn't sure she could trust him. She wasn't sure if she could trust *any of them,* really.

"What happened to you?" he said. "We all saw you go into the lake... into the light... and then..."

She hardly knew where to begin. "It's not like you think. Blaine's lying to you. All of you. There's something down there, under the lake. It's not a spirit like he says. It's not..." She paused. What *was* it, exactly? Even down there like she was, she never got a good, clear look at the thing. "It's something else. And Blaine, he knows. He's not who he says he is, either. I don't even know if he's..."

What she wanted to say was *human.* But considering the community had probably been led to believe she was insane, she wasn't sure how that would go over at the moment. Better to start with what she *knew,* she thought.

"I'm not crazy," she blurted preemptively. "He held me captive in his basement. That's where I've been the last... I don't know, however long it's been. That stuff he feeds everyone before sending them into the lake? It's some kind of drug. It paralyzes you, and..." She found herself becoming lost in the preposterousness of it all, knowing just how it must sound to Robert's ears. "He's killing you. That's what he's doing. He's sending people out into that lake to die. To feed... whatever that *thing* is down there..."

"Hold on a second," Robert said. Even in the gloom, his features hidden from view, it was clear he was grappling with Drew's words. "You're saying there's a... what, a monster, or..."

"I don't know what it is. It's nothing we know about. And that's not all Blaine's been doing. He's a murderer. Both him and Kent, together. This is going to sound crazy, too, but I found my ex's things in Blaine's cabin. My ex must have tried to follow me here and somehow... I don't know, exactly, but he was down there, in Blaine's basement. And several other bodies that must have been there before we ever arrived." Drew racked her brain for a second, trying to remember the names she'd read in Olivia's journal. "Cameron? I think one of the other bodies must have been his."

"Cameron?" Robert spoke thinly, obviously reeling. "You asked me about him before..."

"Where's my brother?" Drew asked. When at first Robert didn't respond, like he couldn't hear her for all his own thoughts, she repeated, "Robert, where is Isaac?"

Robert shook his head. "Isaac... he's fine. Or he's safe for now. He's at the main lodge... with Blaine..."

"He's with Blaine?" Drew's stomach twisted up painfully.

"I came to get his bag. He asked for it."

Drew eyed the gun in her hands, which she'd hardly noticed she'd lowered toward the floor. Isaac must have known he was in trouble, she thought. It was the gun he wanted.

"I need to get him out of here," she said. "You should *all* get out of here, Robert. You have no idea what you're dealing with."

"I don't think I'd have an easy time convincing the others," he said. "They think you're out of your mind, after what happened to Kent."

"I was protecting myself. That was self-defense."

"I believe you."

This was more relieving to hear than she expected. She wasn't entirely alone. She had some help, whatever good it might do them.

"Is he dead?" she asked. "Kent?"

"No, not dead. But he's not doing super well, either. He's also with Isaac, both of them bedridden." Robert sighed. "It's possible Kent still has his keys on him. If I can get myself alone with them—if I can get Blaine to leave, I mean—I could probably take the keys to Kent's truck. I could bring Isaac back here, and then…"

"And the three of us can go," Drew finished. She still wasn't wholly certain she could trust Robert. But at the moment, he was their best bet.

"You should lay low in the meantime," Robert said. "Several of the others are still awake, and I don't think it's a good idea, them seeing you. I don't think they'll accept your story like I have."

"Have you?" Drew asked. "Really?"

"I believe you, I said." He studied her a moment. "Are you gonna keep the gun, then?"

"I'm keeping the gun," she said. "You can take his bag."

She picked the bag up off the floor and tossed it onto Isaac's bed. Robert moved from the door to the other side of the bed, and grabbed one of the backpack's straps.

"I might be a little while," he said. "Depending on how long it takes for Blaine to leave. And also... however long it'll take me to get Isaac here in his current condition."

Please don't sell me out, Drew thought.

"I'll be waiting."

22

THE UNRAVELING

Blaine was noticeably agitated. In waiting for Robert's return, he stood up from Kent's bed and paced about the lodge, frequenting the door and looking out into the storm. Over and over, compulsively.

"Looks like rain..."

Then he shut the door and paced some more, around and around until he eventually returned to their beds to check on them both. Kent was still breathing, from what Isaac could gather.

"And what about you, Isaac?" Blaine said, bending over him and studying him point blank, peering into his eyes. Isaac made an effort to appear foggier than he was—loosening his gaze, looking through Blaine rather than *at* him, hoping he might trick him into thinking he wasn't cognizant yet. "It will wear off soon. Sooner than this, usually. You must be quite the lightweight."

Shock, my ass, Isaac thought.

Blaine knew. He knew everything. It was all a farce, just

as Drew had predicted. Isaac's heart ached at the thought of her. She'd tried to warn him and he hadn't listened. She'd tried to save him, and got herself sunk for the trouble.

It was a great relief to them both when Robert returned. Blaine bolted upright as the door opened. Robert entered with Isaac's bag slung over one shoulder. He moved past Blaine, avoiding him, and dumped Isaac's bag on the floor next to his bed.

"Have you spoken to any of the others?" Blaine asked Robert. "Since everything's happened?"

Robert hesitated. "No, not really. I've been here, helping out."

Blaine nodded understandingly. "Sure. Sure..." In the low light, he stroked his goatee between his index and thumb, contemplating something. Worrying about something. "I don't know the last time there was so much unrest around the commune. I only hope..." He trailed off, and didn't finish the thought.

"I can stay here for the night," Robert offered. "And keep an eye on these two, in case they need anything. If that would help, I mean."

Blaine appeared more than grateful. "That would be fantastic, Robert. Thank you. I appreciate that." He looked over his shoulder at Isaac, then to Kent, then back to Isaac, and then finally to Robert again, and said, "Let me know if anything changes. They should be fine. Kent is stable now, it seems. And Isaac... I imagine he'll be right as rain in no time."

Robert nodded. "Will do."

"Thank you again, Robert. Truly. I have much to think about tonight. Perhaps I'll swing by some of the others' cabins before heading back just to check in." He sighed heavily. "What a mess, what a mess…"

"Try and get some sleep," Robert told him. "We'll all need you sharp tomorrow, right?"

"Right," Blaine said, laughing a little. "Right, right… You get some sleep yourself, if you can."

"Will do," Robert repeated.

Blaine lingered, his attention lingering specifically on Isaac—the biggest of his concerns, without a doubt. Would Isaac have a change of heart, for instance? What additional trouble might that cause?

Finally Blaine stepped out. As soon as he shut the door, lightning strobed through the cabin windows and Isaac caught a full glimpse of Robert's fear. He moved to the window and watched for a short while, waiting for Blaine to be good and gone. Then he returned to Isaac's side. He got down on his knees, leaned against the edge of Isaac's bed. He hesitated, glancing nervously toward Kent behind him, whose wounded airway rasped with sleeping breath.

"How mobile are you?" he whispered to Isaac, extra low as if Kent might be listening.

"Not very," he admitted, although he'd regained more speech mobility since last they spoke. "Why?"

Once more, Robert peered over his shoulder. Then in an even lower voice, barely audible, he said, "Your sister is alive."

Isaac's stomach flared with anxiety and relief simultaneously. "How do you know?"

"She nearly blew my head off with that gun of yours," he said, and managed to smile. "She's waiting for us right now, back at your cabin. I promised her I'd get you there.

I'm sure she can fill you in on everything, but as of right now—"

That was as much as Robert was able to say before Kent appeared over his shoulder, teeth bared like a territorial dog, and surprised him with a chokehold. Isaac twitched—all the involuntary movement his body could muster. Kent pulled Robert upright, feet shuffling, Robert gagging and spluttering as he pried at Kent's muscular arm. Then Isaac's bed gave a tremendous shake as Robert forced his foot against its edge and sent them both sprawling onto the floor, out of sight. Isaac willed his body to move. He could do it, he knew he could. He tried to press his elbows into his mattress, to push himself into an upright sitting position, but his arms were sore beyond belief. He'd never felt so tired, so sluggish in his entire life. He listened to their grunts and gasps, legs sweeping the floor, kicking the feet of his bed, jolting him in place. Robert wheezed, choked, sucking air. Kent's ragged voice panted freely, with an audible strain under his breath.

Until slowly, dreadfully, the sounds of their struggle became less and less.

She couldn't sit still. She felt like an anxious dog, fearing the storm outside, its persistent thunder. Lots of thunder. Still no rain. She peered from the cabin window, across the glimmering lake toward those lit lanterns on the other side—signs that the community was still very much awake. Robert was right about them. They wouldn't believe her story, even if they couldn't explain her reappearance themselves. She stuck a knife in Kent's throat, which made her too dangerous to give the benefit of the doubt.

She sat on Isaac's bed and forced herself to be still. She studied the gun she held, turned it over in her hands, and idly wondered if she should have given it to Robert just in case. She still couldn't entirely trust him. For all she knew, he was informing Blaine of her return at this very moment. If that happened, she'd put a bullet into each of them without hesitation. She was beyond that at this point. Hesitation. She wasn't going back into Blaine's basement. Nor was she going back into the lake.

She thought again of that *thing*—so terrible that her mind was already shielding her from its memory, her time in the tunnels a dizzying blur of adrenaline. A dream. A nightmare.

Julianne was still down there.

I couldn't save her...

Lightning flashed, rousing Drew from her rumination. Through the window, it cast an oblong rectangle of light across the cabin floor, nearly reaching her feet, and within its light there appeared the shadowy shape of someone standing inside it. Drew looked up with a gasp. Someone at the window. Someone looking in. A dark silhouette. A second flash of lightning followed, just as the first's thunder traveled overhead, and Drew made out the figure's face. Its identity. Then, in the lightning's quick departure, it was gone. The window was empty. No one.

With a shudder threatening to rattle her skeleton to pieces, Drew jumped to her feet. She gripped the handgun fearfully in both hands. For a moment she simply stared at the now empty window, not believing her eyes. She'd seen plenty less believable things tonight, but...

It was Robert she'd seen standing in the window.

With a heavy heart, Drew opened the cabin door and peeked outside, finding no one. No one at all. She peered across the lake once again, toward the main lodge by the dock, where the door was closed and no one wandered to or fro.

"Shit," she said under her breath.

The skirmish on the floor quieted. One of their two voices fell silent. Deathly silent. Whoever remained, they lay breathing on the floor for some time. Tired and *rasping*.

Meanwhile, Isaac lay in a heap of useless nerves, his chest pounding, limbs yearning to carry him far from imminent danger but doing no such thing. He found himself able to move his arms at last, but could barely slide them, moving at a snail's pace. He inched his right arm until his hand found the edge of his cot, and his shaky fingers grasped the mattress and strained to pull himself away.

A hand slapped the other edge of his bed. Then another. Kent hoisted himself into view, onto his feet. He swayed with exhaustion. He gingerly placed a hand to his throat, where blood had seeped through the bandages. His shoulders heaved with each ragged breath. He looked upon Isaac, his gaze cold, eerily empty. Enough to stir some more life into Isaac's limbs. He grasped the side of the mattress a little tighter, pulled a little harder, and managed to drag himself slightly across its surface, felt the weight of his body sinking over the edge, slipping, until finally he dropped to the floor in a paralyzed heap, onto his back.

Kent laughed—a haunting sound. Wounded. From the ground, Isaac peered across the underside of the cot and met Robert's dead, half-lidded gaze, his mouth parted, tongue protruding between his lips. Kent kicked Robert's corpse as he started around the end of the bed, and came to stand before Isaac on the other side. There he loomed, shoulders stiff, fists balled.

"This has gotten... out of hand," he croaked.

Barely able to lift his head, Isaac could only watch as Kent straddled him—could only wheeze as Kent placed each of his hands around his throat and began throttling him. Slowly, Isaac lifted his own arms off the floor. He reached for Kent's, plopped each of his hands onto Kent's veiny wrists without the strength to truly grasp them.

His blood pounded in his skull. *Boom, boom, boom.* The dark cabin darkened further, as Isaac's heavy lids drifted shut.

Like falling asleep.

Lightning cracked the sky like a hammer, sent its brilliant sparks daggering through the clouds overhead as Drew jogged along the lake shore, running on fumes. She kept the gun halfway stuffed into the pocket of her shorts so as not to cause immediate panic should someone see her from afar. There were bodies out and about. She saw them across the way, shadows moving around the lanterns in the distance, too restless to sleep, killing time until morning, perhaps.

Ominous thunder rolled from one black horizon to the next.

"Drew?"

She didn't stop moving—her legs didn't stop scissoring along the shore—but she flicked her attention toward the voice and saw Sherry, standing in the open doorway of the cabin there, carrying a stack of clean blankets which Drew guessed she was preparing to take to the lodge for Isaac and Kent. At the sight of Drew, however, Sherry appeared ready to drop everything and flee. Drew paid her no mind. She turned ahead, kept going. Even without any stamina left to keep going, somehow she did. There was no alternative. No giving up. No taking a break. No time to consider.

Hold on, Isaac.

It wasn't too long before she was coming up on the main lodge ahead. Six or seven minutes total, perhaps. Behind it, the forest shivered, trees writhing in the wind. She pulled the gun from her pocket as she neared the door. She didn't know what she might discover on the other side—was rather dreading finding out—but again, there was no time to hesitate.

She pointed the gun into the cabin's darkness on her way in. At first she saw nothing. Two empty beds on her right. Then she saw someone's feet sticking out from between them, on the floor. Bare feet, as still as a sleeper's. She moved deeper inside, despite her mind's endless warnings not to. Past the second bed was *another* pair of bare feet. Then a pair of legs. Then a third body sitting atop the other. *Strangling* the other.

Two steps. Three steps. Four steps. Drew put the muzzle to the back of Kent's head and pulled the trigger. A loud, punching *pop*. The gunshot jolted her wrist a bit. It zapped the life right out of Kent. He flopped sideways off her brother's paralyzed body and thumped to the floor in a dead mound, the bullet lost somewhere in the confines of his skull —or at least Drew couldn't see any kind of exit wound from his slack, lifeless face.

Isaac coughed violently from the floor. Drew dropped beside him. She set the gun down for a moment as she took her brother's face into her hands. He wheezed, and already she could see the marks of Kent's hands upon his throat.

"Isaac? Can you hear me?" Very weakly, he nodded. "Good. Good... Can you move at all?"

"Barely," he said. His voice was small. Damaged. He coughed some more.

"Do you think you can stand?"

Isaac struggled to even lift his head. Drew's heart sank. He did move his arms a bit, very slowly, and she watched with amazement as he tried to prop himself up on a single elbow, his other arm having a harder time of it. He hadn't received nearly the same amount of sap she'd received in Blaine's cabin, she knew. He would recover faster. He was *already* recovering, in fact. How much longer, though, she wondered?

"Robert's dead," Isaac said in a tired whisper, and lay back down as he couldn't hold himself up any longer.

"I know." Drew glanced in his direction—the first pair of

feet she'd seen on the floor when she entered—and was thankful she couldn't see him now. She wouldn't tell Isaac that she'd known he was dead before she even got here.

Do you believe in ghosts?

Another morbid, intrusive thought.

"I'm sorry," Isaac groaned. "I'm sorry I didn't listen before..."

"We don't have time for that right now..." She crawled over him, to the corpse beside him. She turned Kent over onto his back, rolling him in the pool of his own blood. She went through each of his pockets. In the first she found a pack of cigarettes. In the second she found a set of keys. She pulled them out, held them in the palm of her hand: a ring containing six keys, one of them clearly belonging to his truck. Her spirits lifted somewhat. She hovered over her brother again. "I'm gonna get us out of here. But I need you to try and stand. Even if you can't, I need you to try. I'll help."

She thought maybe they could speed things up a little. Get Isaac's blood flowing. Sober him up, so to speak. She took one of his hands, and his fingers squeezed her hand in return, a stronger grip than she'd expected. That was good. Next she very gently pulled him into an upright sitting position, to which Isaac did his best to meet her halfway. His forearm visibly flexed, pulling himself up as much as she helped. That was good, too. Great, even.

"There we go," she said. "How are your legs?"

Isaac held his head up well enough, though his neck was tilted slightly, as if he was ready to doze off any second. He wagged his feet back and forth, rotating his ankles. His knees, however, appeared reluctant to bend.

"I don't know," he said. "It feels like I just ran three marathons..."

Drew had been fed enough sap that it knocked her on her ass for an entire day, which she'd mostly slept through. How long could a single lick of the stuff last? He was regaining *some* mobility, at least.

Lightning flashed once again. Drew turned to see it, illuminating the windows on either side of the cabin door—which she'd left open behind her—and was shocked to see a spying face peeking through. Upon noticing them, the figure drew back. Drew sprang to her feet. She hurried to the door and slammed it shut. Then she went to the lefthand window and peered out into the stormy night, where a handful of people were already gathered outside. Further down the shore, a couple more figures were coming. Was one of them Blaine? She couldn't tell. She ducked back out of sight, then froze.

"Fuck," she said.

"What's going on?" Isaac groaned, sitting forward.

I don't know how to get us out of here, she thought. *I don't know what to do.*

Thunder softly growled. Drew returned to the window and took another peek, glimpsing the several forms outside, standing about with their arms folded idly like people waiting to get into a concert venue. A couple of them were carrying oil lanterns for light. One of them was holding what looked like a fire poker. And another held...

Seriously? Drew thought. *You brought an axe?*

What exactly had Blaine told these people?

"What's going on?" Isaac asked again.

"We're trapped." Drew chewed her lip, watching them gather.

Did they know she had a gun? If they did, they wouldn't have gathered so close, she thought.

There came a knock on the cabin door. Three knocks, hard and loud.

"Drew? Are you in there?"

Of course Blaine already knew she was inside. Sherry had seen her. And some other hapless twit had *just* spied her through the doorway a moment ago. It was a stupid question, to say the least.

He wants to talk, she thought. *He wants to talk to the person whom he knows has seen* everything.

She was curious how he planned to handle her in front of all the others. Was he simply banking on making her look crazy? She did appear that way, she knew. Attacking Kent, after they'd all been told she left. Diving into the lake after her brother. But her story was the truth. Blaine's was the lie. And her story wasn't entirely without evidence.

"May we come in?" Blaine asked on the other side of the door.

Drew moved away from the window. She stood before the door herself, and considered firing a few rounds straight through its soft wood, perhaps directly into Blaine's soft body on the other side. What would happen then? She didn't have enough bullets to finish them all off. As she stood there, with the gun held securely in both hands, she vaguely marveled at her ability to even consider such things.

I just killed a man. And I feel almost nothing.

Maybe she was a little crazy after all.

"Drew? Are you listening? Can we come in—"

"No, you can't fucking come in," she said, speaking loudly so they all might hear her.

"We don't want anyone to get hurt," Blaine said.

Drew paced back and forth, heart beating out of her chest, her blistered feet stinging vividly with each step. She needed to think. How best to convince them? How to tell the truth and make it palatable? Was it possible? She paced to the door again, and briefly wondered if any of them had a gun, by chance—if she was equally in danger of being shot where she stood. Somehow she didn't think so. Keeping guns around a place like this was too dangerous for Blaine, should any of his followers become wise.

Beside the door, she yelled, "I want to open the door so everyone can hear me. I have a gun. If anyone so much as tries to come in, or approach me, I'll use it. I won't hesitate." To this, she was met with silence. Unintelligible murmurs. Perhaps taking bets on whether or not she really had a gun? "I want all of you to get away from the fucking door, is what I'm saying!"

With her back against the wall, Drew watched as Isaac meanwhile continued trying to move himself between the beds, sitting forward, straightening his back, then sitting forward again, his legs mostly useless on the floor before him. Slowly but surely.

"Okay," Blaine said, and his voice was a little more muffled now, a bit farther away than he'd been before.

Didn't he know letting her speak was a mistake? Was he

that overconfident? Was he so sure his followers would dismiss everything she might say?

Or maybe he's just that unafraid. Unafraid of burning this whole place to the ground if that's what it comes to...

With the gun ready, Drew twisted the doorknob, then pulled it open an inch. Two inches. She stopped at three, enough that she could shout through the gap and be heard by those gathered outside, over the sound of the wind and thunder and everything else. As soon as she finished with the door, bracing herself beside it, Blaine began to speak again—trying to get ahead of the narrative.

"Is Robert in there with you?" he asked.

Drew glanced at those sun-tanned feet lying pointed at forty-five-degree angles opposite each other, motionless.

"Robert's dead," she said, and before the wild murmuring of the others could drown her out, she added, "It was Kent!" The murmuring was so instantaneous, however, she wasn't sure whether or not they absorbed that last part, so she said it again, even louder. "Kent killed Robert! I had nothing to do with it!"

The others' voices continued whispering, like cicadas buzzing in the summer heat.

"And I'm guessing Kent is dead as well, then?" Blaine asked.

"Kent killed Robert," she repeated one last time. "And he was trying to kill my brother when I got here."

More whispers. More sensational mutterings.

Blaine said, "Sure. Sure. And how is dear Isaac feeling now?"

Drew opened her mouth to speak, and was surprised

when her brother called out first, *"I'm just great!"* Even more surprising, Isaac was now up, leaning against the foot of his bed on his own two trembling feet. Drew had been so preoccupied with the gap in the door she hadn't noticed. He called out again, loud enough that his tired voice broke shrilly with the effort, *"She's telling the truth! Kent killed Robert... and he tried to kill me!"*

Drew's whole body thrummed with nervousness, but a great surge of gratitude swept through her at Isaac's words, at his newfound strength.

"I highly doubt that," Blaine said in a quieter tone, for the others' sake. Attempting to keep them doubtful. Then he said, "And how did Kent manage this miraculous feat, with his injuries?" Then, once more to the others, "You all saw him. Stabbed in the throat by this *maniac...*"

Drew could hardly stand it anymore. Whether it was a mistake or not, she didn't care at this point. She pulled the door open fully and stepped into everyone's view, smack dab in the middle of the cabin's entry, gun raised slightly but not pointed in anyone's direction. Still, as she did this, the whole group visibly tensed. They stepped back, shocked to find that she *did indeed* wield a gun. They shifted nervously in unison. Blaine stood centered between them all, the closest and most available to plug. He watched Drew with utter venom in his eyes, practically dripping with it.

"Please listen to me," she said, ignoring Blaine and doing her best to speak earnestly for the others. Even so, she could feel the wildness in her own eyes—the desperation worn plainly for all to see. She couldn't control it. Couldn't mask it. "This is going to sound—"

"Your gun doesn't scare me," Blaine interrupted, raising his hand to Drew as if his palm was a force to be reckoned with. "This is my family, and I'm not afraid to take a bullet for anyone here."

You're the only one I'd pull the trigger for, anyway, Drew thought. *You and your atrocious goatee.*

Ignoring Blaine's obvious attempt at provoking a different kind of argument, she said, "I never left. I've been in Blaine's basement for the past... however long it's been..."

"Lies." Blaine looked over each of his shoulders at the skeptical faces who stood behind him. "Do not trust the outsider."

"I wasn't the only one down there." She briefly considered mentioning Quentin—another outsider whose part in this story would only serve to muddy it. Instead she said, "Cameron was down there, too. And some others I don't even know..."

The wary faces changed—the shadows of their mouths and eyes smoothing with a different breed of doubt. They began whispering again, even lower than before. She saw his name touch each of their disbelieving lips: *Cameron? How does she know about Cameron?*

"He never left, either," she told them. "You can look for yourselves. In fact, I implore you to do so. Send someone to search Blaine's basement. We'll wait right here in the meantime. Fifteen, twenty minutes tops. And then we'll see who—"

"We're not interested in the ravings of a murderer," Blaine said.

Judging by the looks on quite a few of his followers' faces, it was clear he didn't speak for everyone. Even Caroline, whose eyes were on *Blaine* and not Drew, appeared gravely confused.

"I'm telling the truth," Drew said. "Blaine's not who you think he is. This *place*... isn't what you think it is..." There was so much more she could say about that, but to do so would risk saying too much. Denial was a powerful thing, and much often easier than the alternative. Especially when confronted with the seemingly impossible.

"We saw you swim into the light," someone said. A man stepped forward, nameless but vaguely familiar to Drew, in that she'd seen him around before. As he stepped forward, his eyes darted nervously between Drew and Blaine beside him, the small but distinct fear of disapproval. "How did you come back?"

"She didn't go *anywhere*," Blaine said. "We were clearly mistaken. She must have swam to the other side of the lake... after getting disoriented in the light and leaving her brother to nearly drown in the process..."

"That's not what happened," Drew said. She hesitated. It was hard enough for *her* to swallow the truth, and she'd actually *been there*. "I saw... I've seen..."

"She is a reckless soul," Blaine said. "She endangers those around her with her rash, self-destructive actions. I allowed her into our community to please one of our own, and I regret that decision entirely. I take full responsibility—"

"Bullshit," Drew said. "You invited us here because our mother was too afraid to take the next step in your..." She paused. She had a choice. There was absolute honesty: telling an unbelievable truth. And there was strategic honesty: a

303

simplification of the truth that would be much easier to stomach. Drew had never considered herself a diplomat—she was actually feeling quite stung by the accuracy of Blaine's assessment in regards to her self-sabotaging tendencies—but realized this was an imperative time to be one. "...in your suicide cult."

Call it what it is, she thought. What she'd been calling it all along. It was a shocking word for most: suicide. Uncomfortable as hell, definitely. But these people knew exactly what it meant. In one way or another, it was what they'd come here for, even if they could never acknowledge that reality. To submit themselves to the ultimate unknown, with no hope of returning once the journey was made...

"The truth is, there is no spirit of the lake."

"Do not listen to a word she says." Blaine's voice was slow and brooding, like a man resisting the very charms of the devil.

"There is no spirit of the lake," she repeated. Then, sticking with the theme of simplification, she said, "The only thing waiting out there are the bodies who swam out before you." She looked at Blaine directly then. They could have lit a match between their gazes. "Tell them about the sap. The stuff you let them taste before sending them to their doom. Tell them what it's really for. Why my brother can hardly stand up right now."

"Tree sap," Blaine said. "Nothing more than a harmless tradition."

Reading the others' expressions, and their body language, Drew knew she'd screw herself over trying to convince them of what she'd seen down there. But what else was there to say? Still they stood behind Blaine, figuratively and literally, too unsure to make a move of their own. Drew was certain there was some psychological phenomenon in effect—the comfort and safety of letting a leader call the shots, tell them what to think and how to behave.

She startled as Isaac arrived beside her, planting himself clumsily against the doorframe from the effort it took to shuffle there. A simmering gasp rose from the group outside, as he promptly lifted his chin and presented his throat to the gleam of lightning that flashed in the distance, displaying the bruises there.

"My sister's saved my life twice now," he said, rasping. Then he pointed with a heavy hand to Blaine. "He's the murderer here, not her."

Blaine shook his head with a joyless smile. Drew studied his flock—from the bubbly Sherry to the territorial Caroline and every strange face in between—and was frustrated to see only more confusion. No conviction.

"Look in his basement," she pleaded. "I'm telling you... everything I've said... you'll know it's true once you see for yourselves—"

"Enough," Blaine said. Then once more, louder, angrier, *"Enough!"* Still shaking his head, he licked his lips, pressed them tightly, his evident frustration coming to a boil. In the warm glow of the lanterns the others carried, his face was clearly burning, as red as the goatee on his chin, as the hair pulled back around his head into its loose bun. "This is a place of community! It is *sacred!* We're here to find *harmony,* to connect with ourselves and each other and the earth... Why does it not surprise me that an outsider does not understand us? And of course she can't just be satisfied with *not understanding,* no, she can't accept that, so she's made it her mission to call everything we do here into question. A suicide cult? Now she calls *me* a murderer? When she's the one with blood on her hands?"

Drew couldn't help but look at her hands as he said this. He was quite right about that. There *was* blood on them. Probably Kent's blood. Then her attention drifted from Blaine's words to the gun she held. A dangerous tool. A tool that gave her power. Without it, she'd be swarmed already, wrangled into Blaine's possession. Somehow she wasn't getting through to any of them, even if they *did* seem perturbed by some of her claims. The problem was that they'd spent enough time with each other, with Blaine, that their bond was strong enough to dismiss reason.

Drew could understand that. From the corner of her eye, she looked toward the weak and haggard boy beside her—the primary reason she was here in the first place, was *still* here, and for whom she would not be leaving alone to save herself. She couldn't turn these people against Blaine any more than they might turn her against Isaac. Which, under the circumstances, left her very little choice...

"She wants to undo what we've accomplished here simply because she's not—"

Blaine was interrupted by another crack of thunder. Only this thunder didn't come from the skies. It came from the deadly tool in Drew's hands, its barrel quivering violently. She pulled the trigger again, and then a third and final time, and miraculously each bullet found its way home—two in

Blaine's chest, one in the gut. Each gunshot sent the crowd flinching, gasping.

After the third pull of the trigger, however, something came down from the side of the doorway where Drew stood —someone she hadn't seen standing in wait all the while. The fire poker swept against her wrist with sharp, bone-cracking speed. She cried out. The gun fell from her grip. She bent forward as if to chase it, and was tackled by the same man, pushed onto the ground just as Blaine collapsed to his knees before her. The others' voices rose up in a cacophony of panic and horror.

Isaac screamed hoarsely from behind: *"Get off her!"*

Several bodies rushed them. A stampede of bare feet. A nameless hand snatched up the gun she'd dropped. Beyond them, Blaine held the final bullet wound in his stomach, before falling forward flat on his face in the dirt. His followers swarmed him, rolled him onto his back.

"Blaine?"

"Oh my God, Blaine..."

The man on top of Drew held her there, as Isaac shuffled up behind them both and tried to wrestle him off. In another moment, Isaac screamed out as the others grabbed hold of him, forced him down onto the ground, out of sight. With her face pressed to the dirt, Drew jerked and shimmied to no avail.

"You got her?"

"I've got her," the fire poker man replied.

A woman slapped Blaine's face gently, but he was unre-sponsive. Drew thought she heard someone murmur as much. And then, more loudly, someone announced with great anguish, *"Oh my God, he's dead…"*

They turned their attention on Drew, their faces twisted with despair and hatred, as well as a lingering confusion about everything that had happened tonight. Their denial was working overtime.

"What do we do?" someone asked. Sounded like Sherry.

"We have to get help. We have to report this."

There were audible groans. For a moment, Drew was hopeful—that she would be handed over to the authorities, where she might plead her case and let *them* do the investigating, if these miserable, halfwitted sheep wouldn't.

Cattle, she thought. *Blaine called them cattle…*

But as she lay stiff and sore against the ground, with a man's full weight upon her back—not for the first time this weekend—she glimpsed something strange.

Lightning flashed, and for a moment she wasn't certain she'd truly seen it. Perhaps a trick of the storm's light. Then thunder soon followed. And it happened again. Through the restless crowd, through their meandering legs and feet before her, she watched Blaine's corpse upon the dirt, the odd angle of his face looking to heaven… and watched as his body jerked in place. A twitch of the arm. A hiccup in his chest. A jump of his shoulders, as if someone had just defibrillated him.

Then he began to squirm. From head to toe. Finally Drew wasn't the only one who noticed. The others fell silent, caught in momentary disbelief. Someone said, hopefully, *"He's still alive…"*

And then all hell broke loose.

23

THE PRETENDER

Blaine came apart at the seams.

Writhing in place, his body let loose terrible, wet cracking noises, until suddenly his neck bent at a right angle and something tore clean through the flesh there, nearly decapitating him in the process.

The others broke into screams. The crowd dispersed, staggering away. The man on top of Drew let up, forgetting her entirely. She pushed herself upright just as Blaine's left arm burst from his shoulder in a spray of sparkling crimson, elongating on a new, sinewy length of corded flesh underneath. Except it wasn't flesh. Not the human variety, anyway.

The screams popped off at random, everyone getting their turn as they gasped and shuffled farther and farther from the scene. Keeping her eyes on the grotesque transformation, Drew managed to feel her way for Isaac on the ground beside her. She pulled him up onto his feet by the arm, steadying him against herself.

The Blaine-thing thrashed with its long arm, as the rest of his body continued to judder, and a strange nest of feelers slithered out from his half-opened throat. Those feelers scraped across the dirt, creeping toward Drew and Isaac near the cabin. The closer they came, the more Drew was able to make out their alien features—the way their shoots branched with smaller ones off the sides, the way those smaller feelers ended in what appeared to be tiny, round buds.

"What is that?"

"Is that... is this..."

The others were already losing their minds, by the sounds of it. Drew pulled Isaac back as those feelers crept closer. She pulled them right up against the cabin, bumping roughly into it before sliding toward the entrance, toward the door still standing wide open beside them. The Blaine-thing's long, ropy arm swung over its body in an arc. It planted Blaine's hand upon the dirt there, where it proceeded to turn him over, off his back and onto his front. His legs regained themselves, and he pushed himself up into a kneeling position. His loosened head bobbled against his shoulder like an awful rubber prosthetic. Those weedy tendrils slithered out endlessly, as if his entire body were a mere shell to contain them.

A wave of frightened shouts lifted as the Blaine-thing snapped its elongated arm toward the nearest body in proximity. It happened to be Sherry. Poor, naive, ill-fated Sherry. Blaine's human hand found her in the fringes of the crowd, seized her by the throat, and lifted her screaming and kicking into the air. Then, like his arm had already done, his fingers around Sherry's throat exploded. Smaller tendrils gushed out from the burst knuckles like roots, which visibly wormed their way around the back of Sherry's head, until they looped back around to her face and across her cheeks like black veins, and finally into her screaming mouth. Drew was petrified, as were so many others. Sherry's screams became stifled. She hung in its grasp, legs firing like pistons until they began to merely tremble. Then she turned utterly still, arms at her sides, legs swinging like a doll's.

A guttural, warrior cry rose up from the rest. A man—Drew believed his name was Marcus—charged the monstrosity with his oil lantern lifted behind himself, which he slung against Blaine's back. The lantern broke. Its fire leapt out from the glass and clung to Blaine in a splash of blazing heat. The beast retaliated in the blink of an eye. With Sherry's body still entwined in its grasp, it flung her overhead like a human flail and struck Marcus onto the ground beneath her corpse.

Holy mother of—

Drew flinched to the sound of gunshots. Whoever had snatched up Isaac's gun fired it now—one, two, three, four, five shots rang out. Blain's torso absorbed each bullet with hardly a shrug. It swung Sherry again, this time toward the shooter. Drew felt the breeze as Sherry's dirt-stained feet blurred past, and then heard the choked scream of the gunman as her body swept him like a club. From Blaine's throat, the coil of tendrils—*branches,* Drew thought suddenly, *they're fucking branches*—crept closer still, spidering over the dirt toward them, toward the cabin.

"Come on," Drew said, struggling to move even as she said it.

She pulled Isaac through the cabin doorway, where she immediately bumped into the waiting bodies of several others who had already managed to shrink inside from the chaos. Drew paid them no mind. Those creeping, gore-covered branches were nearing the door's threshold. She slammed the door as they lashed out, caught them in the doorframe, where she heard the same little squeals she'd heard before, down in the tunnels.

"Help me!" she cried.

Behind her, the nameless faces stepped forward and placed their weight against the door alongside her, crushing the weedy tendrils enough to grate them into slivers within the doorjamb. The door shut, but there was no lock.

"What the hell is that thing?" a woman asked.

Drew looked over her shoulder. There were six of them inside. Herself, Isaac, three more women, and one other man —the man who brought the axe. He carried it now in both hands, ready to swing, whatever good it would do. Outside, those who hadn't turned and fled already could still be heard screaming. Drew jolted as something heavy smacked the door. A thrown body? Blaine's body, trying to get in? Fear-fully, they each stepped back. Isaac was standing on his own now. Drew stayed close by his side.

"It just... came out of him," another women said.

"No," Drew said. "It is him."

Under the noise of mayhem, there came another shat-tering of glass—another lantern broken on the thing's body —and the windows on either side of the door briefly bloomed with a fiery glow. The door thumped again, then groaned as something pressed against it. Wood on wood. Because the thing inside Blaine...

Like mother, like son, Drew thought, reminded of the creaking, stomping monstrosity in the tunnels.

The door shook in its frame. More screams outside. Although Blaine's human form was quite literally unraveling, it was still him, she thought. And what he wanted wasn't out there, it was *in here*. Her and Isaac. The troublemaking outsiders.

They each gasped as the door ripped from its hinges with one fearsome yank from the beast on the other side. Lightning clawed the storm and illuminated the *thing* there, filling up the doorway like a nightmarish bramble of human limbs, thorn-covered branches, and licking flame. It was enveloped now. It reached in. Drew recoiled as a group of tendrils swung for her, then cried out as another found her leg, her ankle, and pulled her feet right out from under her. She hit the floor on her tailbone, before it dragged her hastily across the dusty floorboards and into the doorway. Isaac threw himself onto the floor where he just barely managed to grab Drew by the hands. Those tendrils dragged her further.

Then, to Drew's astonishment, the others came to her rescue. Two of the women joined Isaac on the floor, and grabbed Drew's wrists, her forearms. The tendrils around her ankle pulled, pulled, pulled. The others pulled back. Drew winced, her shoulders aching—an agonizing game of tug-o-war. The other man hurried into the doorway, the axe raised. He was promptly struck by another cluster of tendrils. He stumbled back, fell hard onto the floor, his nose bloody. The branches tugged harder, until Drew's shoulders were screaming for release, until her mouth was doing the same.

"Let go, let go, lemme go!"

Before her arms could be torn from their sockets, the women let go. Isaac reluctantly let go. Outside, the Blaine-thing scrambled backward like a dog with a rope in its jaws, dragging her outside with it, onto the dirt beneath its burning bulk.

From the half-detached head still dangling off Blaine's shoulder, he impossibly spoke, *Wretched! Vile! Vermin!*

From seemingly out of nowhere, another lantern was thrown. It burst against Blaine's side, flashing the night with another wave of heat. He audibly squealed, a different set of vocal cords altogether, wherever those sounds emanated. Drew tried to pick herself up, her ankle still snared. She nearly got standing before the tendrils reeled her back in, dropping her onto her ass once again.

Someone ran past. The man from the cabin. He circled behind Blaine, where Drew only caught a glimpse of the axe's sharp head lift above the glow of the fire, then fall out of sight. From the Blaine-thing, another shrill cry pierced the night, rising above the crackling roar of fire and the clapping thunder overhead. The tendrils on Drew's leg seemed to loosen. She jerked her foot through the loop of their branches, and clambered away on hands and knees. Isaac was there. His strength must have come back to him in a rush, as he was now the one helping her up, keeping her steady.

A low, melancholy groan behind them. Together, she and Isaac retreated against the cabin once more, and watched as the now engulfed creature struggled to keep itself upright. Its ropes of branches and roots trembled in the firelight. Burnt, weak, stiffening. The man with the axe stepped back, gleaming with sweat, squinting against the light, the heat. The thing struggled to hold itself up, before finally it collapsed onto the shore. Drew wondered, had it not been so focused on killing her and the others, if it might have saved itself in the lake.

"Are you okay?" she asked Isaac.

His lips parted slightly, and his unblinking eyes remained fixed on the impossible thing burning to the ground. He nodded, wordlessly, and Drew thought to herself, *he's seen ugliness at last.* Then he tore his gaze away, and regarded her with the same disbelief.

"Are *you* okay?"

"Sure," she said. "I think I'm okay."

The others hadn't fled far. As the Blaine-thing burned like a bonfire on the shore, it drew them back little by little, reappearing in the edges of its firelight. They flickered with it, the firelight, like fluttering moths. They were in shock, Drew thought. She couldn't blame them.

Then, as the Blaine-thing crumbled in on itself, Drew noticed a few of the others' attention had moved elsewhere, craning their necks toward the lake. She took Isaac's hand and led him around the bonfire, until they could see the water and what the others were now noticing.

The light was alive out there. The amber glow had risen again to the water's surface—what Drew now had the unpleasant honor of knowing was actually a lure, like the nectar of a flytrap. It spread open, stretching across the lake's dark surface. The steam on the water was belated, forming wispily after the fact, trying to catch up. If there was ever a more appropriate time to warn the others of what truly lurked out there...

Before Drew could utter a word, however—to the others, to Isaac—the ground beneath their feet heaved, and sent them each sprawling.

24
THE MOTHER

The entire forest seemed to shift in one violent shake. Like flipping a pancake in a frying pan, Drew and Isaac spilled onto the ground, barely catching themselves as the shore tried to pitch them forward into the water. An enormous vibration rolled through the valley, louder than thunder.

Then the lake collapsed in on itself.

A terrifying spectacle. The usually tranquil water crashed upward as the ground dropped inward. Drew's stomach dropped with it. The lake water fell pattering and splashing into its new, steepened bowl, leaving behind a warm mist in the night air. As the water sloshed with ocean-like waves, the ground continued to vibrate, and the lake water slowly continued to sink, shrinking further from them, the shore growing larger in between, revealing the edges of its new crater.

The tunnels, Drew thought. *That's where the water's gone.*

Slowly but surely the quaking eased. The shrinking lake

water settled in place, vanishing no more, looking more like a large pond down the cracking slopes of the shore, a third of its original size. The ground stilled at last. The amber light still glowed out there.

The others stirred, picking themselves back up. Drew took Isaac's hand again. They helped each other to their feet.

"What is that?" someone called.

Drew didn't want to look. She didn't want to stick around any longer than they already had. But she *did*. She looked. She was helpless not to. In the shrunken lake's center, from the wrinkled, glowing amber light, something moved. It pulled itself up from the glowing membrane like a sleeper emerging from its bedsheets. Alive and hungering. Only Drew knew what it was—what was coming.

"Isaac," she said, her own voice sounding strange to her ears. "We need to go. Now."

As the thing crawled out from the lake—a silhouette against the cracked shore—Drew pulled Isaac along, skirting the bonfire. The smoldering corpse of its *child*.

Not good, she thought. *Not good at all.*

The worst was yet to come. The others had no idea.

Drew and Isaac moved past the fire. Isaac stumbled, tripping over himself as he craned his neck to see the lake. More ugliness. Even uglier than what preceded it.

"Hurry," she told him, physically tearing his gaze away from the soon-to-be nightmare show. "We're getting out of here, Isaac. We're leaving..."

She repeated this under her breath like a mantra. Like a wish that only might come true if she wished it enough.

"What is that?" Isaac asked, struggling to keep up.

Panting, pulling, Drew answered, "That's Mother."

The anguished bellow of a giant carried on the storm's breeze. Drew looked back and she saw her. Creeping over the crest of the lake's crater, into the firelight. Towering. Alien. A sentient nest of roots and branches. Shifting and strange. Several smaller shadows stood nearby—the lingering moths —small and vulnerable under the Mother's shadow, as she gazed upon her dead child.

Run, you idiots, Drew thought.

Kent's keys jostled in her pockets. Thunder rumbled in the distance. Lightning flashed off and on, off and on—a cherub playing with heaven's light switch. Behind them, the others' screams rose up once more. Drew didn't care, but Isaac's grip pulled taut as he slowed yet again, clearly turning to see them. Drew urged him onward.

"Don't look back, Isaac," she said.

Don't look back. Don't look back.

Shouting. More screams. Worse, a rising shriek which suddenly terminated. Drew didn't need to look to know what that meant. They hurried along, following the lake's old shoreline, now receded. Down the slope beside them, the crumbling lake bottom was revealed, and the dark trenches of exposed tunnels which were now partially filled with water. Drew thought of their own mother then, trapped and left to drown...

There's nothing you could do. Nothing you could do...

She tensed as footsteps came up behind them. A man sprinted by. And shortly after someone else arrived behind them, panting, struggling not to whimper as they fled the *thing* in pursuit. She was heading for them now, Drew realized. The Mother, gaining incredibly fast. Her form remained halfway concealed beneath the darkness of the storm, but her size could not be mistaken. Elephantine, in all but shape. She was a chaotic thing. So many branches and moving parts. Against the odds, Drew quickened her pace and urged Isaac to do the same.

Ahead, Blaine's cabin was drawing nearer all the while. Every step. Isaac remained somewhat sluggish, which was both a blessing and a curse as Drew could hardly push herself to move any faster, anyway. The whimpering woman ran parallel to them. Three in motion. She might have moved faster if not for checking over her shoulder every other bound.

The Mother's feet pounded in chase, coming closer, imminent, and it was all Drew could do not to peer back herself. She could hear the rustling of her moving parts, the chafing of her wooden flesh, the creaking of her old limbs. The woman beside them chanced yet another glance, nearly tripping over her own feet in the process, and she let out a terrible scream. In an instant she was plucked away. There one moment, gone the next. Her scream was stifled amidst a grisly crunch and a series of gnashing branches, followed by the deep, inhuman chittering of the Mother's satisfaction.

We're not gonna make it to Kent's truck.

They were nearly to Blaine's cabin, however.

"In there," she gasped.

The front door was already open, just a sliver, along with the face of a man on the other side peeking through. Drew's stomach churned nervously, anticipating that he would shut the door in their faces. Surprisingly—thankfully—the door opened instead, and the man stood back for them to come through. They staggered across its threshold. He slammed the door shut, twisted the lousy deadbolt, and stepped back alongside Drew and her brother, all but collapsing to the floor in exhaustion.

"Thank you," Drew told him.

The man—who had raced past them only a minute ago —simply said "Uh huh," as he stared at the door in anticipation.

Blaine's cabin was softly lit with yet another lantern sitting on his modest table. Another weapon, Drew thought. If not for the others who had already bombed Blaine with their own lanterns, she might not have had the idea.

She grabbed it from the table, handle swinging in her fist. Through the windows, the Mother's shape appeared outside. Her feet struck the ground like clubs, pounding her way to the door. Twisted limbs and stray branches scratched against the window glass. Drew, Isaac, and the man each took another step back.

Behind them, Blaine's basement door stood open. Could they find refuge down there, she wondered? Taking Isaac's hand, Drew led him there. She extended the lantern before her, into the basement doorway, and was disappointed to see the murky, reflective surface of water just below the third step down—where the lake had flooded the tunnels.

No dice.

They each gasped—the man cursed under his breath—as the cabin groaned under an incredible weight. The Mother pressed herself against its exterior, extended herself against the cabin's roof, standing tall, checking for another way in. It wasn't as if the deadbolt could really stand the brute force of her body, Drew thought.

"What do we do?" Isaac asked.

Standing at the basement door, Drew turned to see the window beside it, which opened out to the woods at the rear of the cabin. She contemplated their odds.

Smarter to sneak out the back? Or safer to hold up inside for as long as we—

Her thought was interrupted by the crumbling hole which opened in the cabin's roof. A scream *eeked* from Drew's grimacing mouth as she held the lantern out before them, toward the monstrous paw reaching through the ceiling. The Mother's hand—gnarled, knobby claws groping in the dark—was revealed in the lamplight, covered in flowering pink and white blossoms. The hole in the ceiling continued to grow as she clawed her way in deeper. Wooden splinters and black-asphalt roofing shingles rained to the floor.

The man reared back from her blind swiping, then turned to them and said, "Open the window!"

The cabin groaned, begging for the creature to let up. A long length of board came loose and rattled noisily to the ground as Drew found the lock on the window. She flipped it, then strained to drag the thing open along its dust-filled track. Jerking, sliding inch by inch. Isaac helped, pulling the window as she pushed. Behind them, the roof caved in with a great, crumbling downpour, and suddenly the Mother's wild branches were spilling inside.

"Come on!" Isaac screamed.

Drew wasn't sure whether she imagined it or not, but the sweet smell of springtime blossoms wafted beneath her nose at the Mother's arrival. Mildly intoxicating. She hadn't smelled anything like that down in the tunnels.

"Got it!" Isaac shouted as he dragged the window fully open on his end.

Drew urged him through first. Isaac straddled the windowsill, one foot out at a time, then dropped into the weedy woods on the other side. Once he was out, Drew followed suit. Her hamstring screamed as she lifted her knee against the windowsill. Then another scream gave her pause. A real one. She turned toward the sound—a reflexive gesture —and felt the wet, warm spray of blood upon her own face. The man beside her stood on tiptoe, then lifted off his feet entirely by the thick, squirming tree branch impaling his chest.

Drew *threw herself* at the window then, scrambling across its ledge in a cartoonish flurry of arms and legs. Isaac was there to catch her as she toppled over the other side. He helped her to her feet. Drew shoved him ahead, her clumsy legs propelling them both onward.

"Go!" she said. "Get to the truck!"

They charged through the edge of the woods. Drew listened to the window behind them shatter as the creature forced herself against it, like a cat reaching through the wrong end of a mouse hole.

Lightning flashed. Kent's truck appeared like a ghost under the trees ahead, at the edge of the clearing. Drew stuck her hand into her pocket, tore the keys free in her fist. Isaac ran straight for the passenger door as Drew hurried around its other side. She fumbled the keys in her hand, took hold of the obvious one with its chunky end, the manufacturer insignia stamped into the plastic. She unlocked her door, pulled it open, jumped inside, reached across the seats, and pulled the lock up on Isaac's door. He climbed in, slammed his door shut.

Along the edge of the woods they'd just fled through, Drew glimpsed the shadow-drenched back of Blaine's cabin blowing open like a shed in a tornado—boards flying, along with a shadowy bulk that resembled something like a great, uprooted tree. She plunged the key into the truck's ignition and gave it a twist. The engine roared to life on the first try. Never having driven a truck before, she panicked momentarily as she reached for a nonexistent shifter beside her legs.

No, dummy, not there.

The shifter was on the righthand side of the steering wheel. At least it was an automatic.

She put the truck in Reverse. She floored the gas. The truck growled backward out of the trees. She spun the wheel hand over hand, throwing them in a wide arc. Something heavy rattled and thumped in the back—whatever Kent had loose back there.

Then Isaac said, "Oh shit. Drew—"

Something struck them. The rear end of the truck spun, tires sliding across bumpy dirt. Drew bounced her shoulder off the door, neck whiplashing. As the truck came to a squealing halt, the windshield promptly cracked, spiderwebbing. Over its cloudy surface the Mother's immense shadow fell. Drew floored the gas again. The truck lurched backward yet again.

"Drew?" Isaac said shrilly. *"Drew?"*

She wasn't paying much attention. Mostly her attention

was on the *thing* before them, tracking them, following after them.

They reversed straight into the trees they'd just pulled out from, a blunt impact, rocking them both in place with a jarring *whump*. The Mother's shadow moved across the windshield again. In a flash of lightning, each of her spindly branches and shuddering blossoms appeared starkly silhouetted on the broken glass. She loomed over them. The crunched windshield bowed inward against her investigative paw. The creature pressed the glass along the top, enough to reach over its edge, grasping it firmly in her claws, and tear the whole thing loose. Drew and Isaac both screamed.

A large, tree branch of a hand grated its way into the truck. Both Drew and Isaac reached for their doors, but before Drew could pop hers open she felt the rough, pinching fingers around her back, around her waist and stomach, and it *gripped* her like a Barbie in its fist. It lifted her out of her seat. Isaac screamed after her as the Mother turned Drew in place, easing her through the open window as if it meant to be careful.

As if it meant to keep her alive.

Suspended off the ground, lifted into the stormy night, Drew truly laid eyes on the thing for the first time. Up close. Personal. She looked upon the Mother's face... and was momentarily arrested by what she saw.

First, that the creature *had* a face. A human face. Like a mask carved from the trunk of some ancient tree, with a flowing lion's mane of branches and roots on all sides. The face was truly wooden, however. Stiff. Unmoving. As seemingly purposeless as Drew's ongoing struggle to be free of it.

The Mother clutched her tighter in her grip, threatening, and finally Drew turned still. Why the creature didn't kill her outright, she couldn't guess.

Perhaps because it knew.

You're the one from before. You're the one who caused all of this. You're the one who killed my child.

Of course Drew hadn't really killed Blaine. She'd started the process, certainly, but it was the fire and the axe that had finished the job...

The Mother pulled her in closer, as if to study her, and suddenly a wreathe of eyes opened around the face's perimeter. Green, glowing eyes. The ones she'd seen before, in the darkness. She counted nine. Nine eyes, arranged neatly around its wooden face, blinking, rolling independently in their soft, gummy sockets, taking her all in at once. Their soft green glow cast eerie shadows across the face's wooden features, so that it almost appeared as many different faces, shifting from one to the next. Hypnotic. Surreal. Another wave of sweet fragrance hit Drew, tickling her nostrils with pleasant scents—rose petals, jasmine, lavender, as well as the grassy, citrusy scent of vetiver. She couldn't take her eyes away. Even as lightning struck overhead and illuminated the creature, its many flowering blossoms trembling in the corners of her eyes, Drew could only stare at the hardened expression of its mask.

The Mother's eyes rotated in deliberate patterns, shadows pooling across the mask in strange formations. One moment, it was a woman's face Drew saw. Delicate, soft, lovely. The next, the shadows swept into something else, revealing wide, masculine jaws, deep-set eyes, and a powerful brow. It could have been anyone's face at any given moment. And as was human nature, Drew saw in these ever-shifting features identities she recognized.

She saw Julianne, her mother, serene as a sleeper.

She saw her father, Paul, with his wide cheekbones, and the gaunt valleys of shadow underneath.

She may have seen Isaac, briefly and vaguely between the two, somehow serene and stern as either of them at once.

She saw her own visage looking back at her, like a terrible mirror—a face she often failed to recognize, even with all the time in the world to become familiar...

The claws around Drew's waist squeezed harder still. Claws as thick as her own wrists. Her ribs ached under the pressure. And still she couldn't take her eyes off the thing, even as it promised to crush the life from her at any moment...

And then she heard the roar of an engine, the sound of dirt spitting up behind its tires, and suddenly none of what she saw mattered at all.

Isaac plowed Kent's pickup directly into the bulk of the Mother's knotted body. Those squeezing, root-like fingers released Drew on impact. The Mother bent over the hood of the truck as its engine revved and carried her across the hard dirt. Drew landed painfully on top of the truck's cab—a solid punch to the small of her back—and then tumbled over it, landing with a jarring rattle right into the truck bed. Two seconds later, they collided into the face of Blaine's cabin. Drew pitched forward, drove her shoulder into the back of the cab. Something else in the bed slid toward her, squealing and bouncing with the weight of a bowling ball against her folded up legs. A loose cinderblock. Drew gasped with pain. Then, as everything came to a stop, she realized she was sitting on top of something. Another loose item in the back of Kent's truck...

For a moment, the engine continued to growl and rev as Isaac floored the accelerator. Drew lifted her weary head. Peering through the rear window, she saw Isaac behind the wheel, and beyond him the Mother, pinned between Blaine's cabin and the truck's metal grille. Drew squirmed in place, hurting all over. She glanced down to see what uncomfortable thing she was sitting on. Red plastic gleamed. A pause to comprehend.

The Mother groaned. The sound was somehow both the saddest and most chilling noise in Drew's recent memory.

Her gaze lingered only briefly on the plastic gas can beneath her, but it seemed a long time before her gears locked into place and suddenly she knew what had to be done.

There were two gas cans, actually. Drew picked up the first she was sitting on. She got standing, knees shaking, and lifted the gas can into her arms. At least half full. She heaved it up onto the truck's cab, where she quickly—and clumsily —scrambled up on top as well, onto her hands and knees. Once more she pushed herself up, standing tall as she could, and lifted the gas can. She twisted off the cap, dropped it carelessly to her feet, and with the can held firmly in both hands, she doused the Mother with its contents.

Don't look at me like that, Drew thought, as the wooden mask stared lifelessly toward her.

The pungent, nostril-burning scent of gasoline washed out the Mother's perfume. Her ring of green eyes blinked repeatedly, wincing. She pressed against the truck with her many thick branches, like a squashed spider, as Isaac continued to drive the truck against her endlessly, tires spinning, whining, kicking up a cloud of dust around them. Drew shook the can several times, several splashes of fuel over the monster's writhing form. When the can shook empty, she tossed it aside. She bent, opened her mouth to shout for her brother, and saw he was way ahead of her.

Isaac slipped out from the driver's seat with something in his own hand. A lighter, procured from Kent's glove box. He'd remembered. He flicked the lighter open, sparked a beautiful tail of flame, and tossed it into the kindling that was the Mother's body.

She ignited like a bomb. A scorching heat bathed Drew as the fire *whooshed* to life before her, nearly sending her staggering back off the truck cab. Quickly, carefully, she crouched and slid herself over the cab's edge and dropped down to the ground on both feet, barely catching herself. Isaac grabbed her, steadied her, then pulled them both away from the rising, licking flames.

The Mother squealed with many voices. Shrill animal cries. A deep, troll-like undertone. She flailed her branches, pressed them against the truck which Isaac was no longer accelerating, but to no avail. In her desperate bid to escape, she managed to lift the truck up off its front wheels, but still failed to climb out from under it. A great nest of roots wriggled and creeped from the truck's undercarriage.

Drew watched all of this mindlessly. For a time, she forgot her aching bones and tendons and everything else. She and Isaac simply stood watching the creature burn.

It wasn't long before it stopped its thrashing, before its many voices quieted, and were replaced with the crackling pop of its slow and steady destruction. It wasn't long before its many limbs grew still and charred, curling in on themselves. The storm raged on. The sky was a roiling black thing above their heads, and even as Drew *felt* it in the air, its electricity, its *promise*, the air remained impossibly dry. This had to qualify as the ugliest day of her life, she thought, and yet...

"Now what," Isaac said suddenly.

Drew could hardly peel her eyes away from the fire. It would burn for quite some time. She studied the truck parked on top of the thing, burning just as well. Inoperable now.

She murmured, "I guess we have a long walk ahead of us."

25
THE SIBLINGS

They didn't start walking immediately, of course. Tired, and wishing to rest her feet, Drew took a seat upon the ground where the shoreline *used* to be and looked out over the shrunken, sunken lake, where the once-glowing membrane was still visible, floating darkly like an abandoned parachute—no longer glowing in the least bit.

Because it's dead, she thought. *Like the rest of it.*

Isaac sat beside her with an exhausted groan.

Drew figured they'd grab some things before starting their journey home, like better clothes and shoes—even if they had to borrow some from the dead. She wouldn't be able to hike back down the mountain from whence they came with her bare and blistered feet, that was for sure. And she doubted she'd be able to find her own, wherever she'd flung them in her heroic race to save Isaac earlier.

"They're still over there," he said, and pointed across the lake.

For a moment Drew was confused, wondering how her

brother knew she was thinking about her shoes. Then she followed his gaze and saw what he pointed to: a few survivors, stragglers, moving about the shore on the other side near the main cabin, near Blaine's crispy remains which appeared only as a black smudge at this distance under the gloom of the storm.

Where would the others go now, she wondered? Surely they wouldn't consider staying here. No, more than likely they would return to the nearest town as well. Perhaps return to whatever their old lives had been. Or find another community to join, to discover themselves all over again—or lose themselves, Drew thought.

"Where the hell did it come from?" Isaac muttered under his breath. He looked over his shoulder, at the fire still going, consuming not only the beast under the truck but the entire truck now. Drew didn't bother speculating. After a brief pause, Isaac followed up with, "No one's gonna believe us when we report this."

"Probably not," she said.

Not until they see it for themselves, anyway.

Isaac stood up suddenly, springing to his feet with a dreadful urgency.

"Do you see that?" he asked. He pointed again, this time *toward* the lake. His pointing finger was trembling. "Is that..."

Drew peered toward the spot he indicated. When she saw it, her guts turned cold. Like a dog at the races, Isaac bolted down the silty slope of the exposed lake bottom toward the water below, where something clearly floated at the water's edge.

It was a naked body, floating face down. Drew stared vacantly, her thoughts escaping her momentarily. Until the first emerged in a floundering of denial.

That could be anyone. That could be...

The body was clearly, utterly nude. With long dark hair. With all its flesh still intact, however withered or deflated that flesh might be at this point in time, after spending a full day within the creature's lair. It had washed up when the tunnels flooded, of course. But as clearly as the body was naked, it was equally clear that it was—

As Isaac reached the water down below, Drew sprang to her feet likewise. Not to chase after him, but... quite the opposite.

I don't want to see this. I don't think I can take it...

Isaac carelessly splashed into the lake water, up to his thighs, and Drew watched with horror as he took hold of the corpse, turning it over, dragging it in his arms toward solid ground. She watched as he laid the body against the mud, and stood over it very still. His expression was indiscernible from here, observing what was obviously their mother's remains. Then the pale oval of his face lifted, peering toward her.

I can't.

She turned away, before he might beckon her to come. She closed her eyes.

It was almost ridiculous, she knew. After everything she'd already seen, and she couldn't handle this? Somehow, she knew she couldn't. She was already at her limit. Her threshold. It was the straw that would break her. She took a deep breath, hot with shame and other feelings she couldn't navigate right now. She saw the flash of lightning against her eyelids, bright and startling.

When she opened her eyes again, she found herself peering toward Blaine's cabin, toward the *thing* pinned by the pickup truck, and her eyes filled with flames. They'd caught to the cabin now, climbing toward the roof, where a thick current of smoke rose into the dark sky. And around the fire, she saw something else.

I don't want to see.

But she saw. She blinked a couple times, hard, just to make sure. But they remained. Shadows at the edges of the firelight. A great number of figures stood around the corpse of the Mother. Faceless, featureless figures. They were fuzzy enough that Drew blinked a third time, in case the flames caused her to see things which weren't there. Specters. Spec*tators,* watching as their captor released its own ghost to the night, where theirs might soon follow...

Upon the third blink, suddenly Drew noticed one shadow in particular. Clearer than all the rest. It turned, and a woman's visage was revealed in the light of the flames. She looked at Drew. Even at a distance, her expression was unambiguous. A *knowing* smile, soft and familiar. A look which reminded Drew of brighter days, full of sunshine and ocean waves...

"Drew?"

She nearly gave up her ghost as well, as Isaac appeared beside her. He regarded her hesitantly, a gentleness about him, as he saw he'd startled her.

"Sorry," he said.

"It's okay." Drew looked ahead, toward the fire again,

and was only halfway surprised to find the figures had gone. All of them. She swallowed down her fear, and said, "Was it her?"

"Yeah."

Drew nodded. "I don't want to see her. I'm sorry, I just—"

"It's okay."

Isaac looked toward the fire as well, admiring its growth. Then he looked at her again, and she saw him studying her from the corner of her eye. Finally she turned to see him, and he held her gaze intently.

"What?" she asked.

"Nothing." He smiled faintly—*incredibly* faintly, which was still miraculous given what had just transpired, and after what he'd just pulled from the water down below. "I'm ready to go home when you are."

Music to Drew's ears.

"Okay," she said. She sighed, as she began collecting her bearings. "First we should grab your bag and fill it with water and some food, whatever we can find..."

"Drew..."

"I don't know how far down the mountain we'll have to walk before we reach town, so we should probably—"

"Drew."

"Huh?"

She turned as Isaac threw his arms around her unexpectedly. He squeezed her, tight enough to reveal once again how sore she'd become from all the strenuous *surviving* she'd done tonight.

"Thank you," he said. His voice was thick in her ear. Just

the sound of it spurred a lump in her own throat. "For always being there. For not leaving me, even when you should've... even when I've been such a dick..."

"I'm not going anywhere." She wrapped her beanpole of a brother in her arms. "Ever."

Isaac's arms loosened around her, but Drew didn't let him go. She held him even tighter. She closed her eyes, and she saw their whole lives together, remembered it suddenly like the beautiful train wreck that it was, holding each other like they were kids again, holding on for dear life before *dear life* could tear them up by their fragile roots and crush them in its grip. It went on, she knew. *Life.* And so would they...

As she squeezed her brother, Drew felt the first drop on her eyelid. She felt the second drop on her bicep. She opened her eyes and saw the dirt slowly spotting with droplets, the storm finally spilling its promise. For just a moment, just a breath, she thought worriedly, *what now?*

And then the moment passed. And the rain continued to fall.

She released Isaac, each of their faces wet with more than just rain, and said, "Let's go home, then."

A SPECIAL THANKS

Dear brave, adventurous reader,

I must say thank you. Without readers like you, authors like me wouldn't be allowed a paddle in this violent, ever-changing sea—otherwise known as the publishing world.

I was just a scrawny eighteen-year-old when I wrote my first novel, *The Writhing*. A bit nervous and unsure of myself, I held onto it for TEN YEARS, writing a couple more novels in the meantime which I was equally unsure about. It took me a decade to realize my stories weren't doing anyone any good just sitting on my laptop, and in 2019 I decided it was finally time to take the plunge. All I can say now is *thank you*. I only write this disturbing filth with the utmost love and sincerity. To be granted your curiosity means more than you can ever know. You are truly the best.

If you have a moment, let me know your thoughts by leaving a review. It's a simple gesture that means the world to us indie authors and helps other curious readers such as yourself find books like mine. I'd greatly appreciate it.

Thanks again! There's plenty more horror to come!